First came us

A Novel

RACHEL CULLEN

*To my Parents, who have been married
for fifty years, and know what it takes*

Prologue
Austin, TX – October 2000
Jack

For a brief second before I open my eyes, I forget where I am. Am I in my bed on the Upper West Side? The new queen-sized bed that Ellie and I bought together a few months ago when she moved into my apartment? But something isn't quite right; it's not dark enough to be my apartment (Ellie can only sleep with black-out shades, and I've grown quite accustomed to them as well.)

As I start to wake up, both of my temples begin throbbing like miniature jackhammers are inside my skull, and I grope the night table searching for a bottle of water to get rid of the horrible sensation in my mouth – sandpaper laced with tequila.

I glance at the hotel alarm clock and re-orient myself in the lackluster Sheraton as I finally locate a bottle of water and am pleasantly surprised to see that it's only seven-thirty. We aren't supposed to meet for golf until ten o'clock, which gives me plenty of time to go back to sleep and get rid of some of this hangover. I'm not sure why we're even playing golf, but Richie said that's what everyone does at a bachelor's party, so he wanted to do it too.

Richie also wanted to check off many other items on the traditional bachelor's party list last night, which left us dragging him out of a strip club and practically getting in a fight with a University of Texas linebacker when Richie tried to kiss his girlfriend. Thankfully, he passed out and we brought him back to the hotel before he could do any more damage.

Suddenly, an image from last night pops into my head and it's so vivid it almost seems real. It's from the same bar where Richie tried to kiss that girl. We were all talking to cute UT girls, because it was fun and harmless. More importantly, it felt like we were reliving our college days when we went to school here. In the dream I was talking to this really hot girl and then we were kissing in the bathroom at the bar, and she must have really gotten to me because I am picturing us here in this bed having sex. The whole dream is coming in and out, but unlike most of my dreams, the parts I do remember are really intense.

At that moment, I hear the water from the shower stop running. It must have been on when I got up, but it was white noise and I didn't even realize it in my haze – now in its absence, I am painfully aware.

"Hello?" I call out, secretly hoping that no one answers, or better yet, that one of the guys crashed here last night.

"Hey, you're up," a voice calls back. She pokes her head into the room and she is even more beautiful than in my *dream*. Her long dark hair is tied up on top of her head with some sort of clip and her face is scrubbed clean of all of the makeup she had on last night, revealing a stunning olive complexion and what I can only hope is the youthful glow of a college senior or perhaps graduate student.

"How are you feeling?" she asks, walking into the room with only a tiny towel wrapped around her body, barely covering her ass. I try to look in the other direction, because my body already has other ideas, even though my brain knows how wrong this is.

"I've felt better," I mumble, trying desperately to piece together the events from last night, while she searches for her clothes.

She locates her black tank top on the coffee table and without any notice she drops her towel to the floor before pulling the shirt over her head; leaving her completely naked less than six feet from me.

My head may be foggy and pounding, but my lower half seems to be in perfect working order. Seeing her spectacular body brings flashbacks from last night of us together in this bed. I've never cheated on anyone before. I can't believe that now that I'm in a serious relationship, I've actually slept with someone else – Ellie is going to kill me if she ever finds out!

"I've got to get to class," the girl says, as she pulls on her jean shorts without any underwear (I'm guessing she just couldn't find them, although it's possible she didn't have any last night – I don't remember.)

"Okay, this was fun," I say feebly, wishing I could make myself say something nicer and not be the douchebag guy who's too hung-over to properly say goodbye or ask for her number or even remember her name.

"It was super fun," she says. "And don't worry, I remember that you're not single. You told me about twenty times last night. Stop looking so worried; you don't even *live* here," she laughs, picking up her purse from the sterile hotel desk.

That should make me feel better, but it makes me feel ten times worse. Apparently in my blackout drunken stupor, I repeatedly told this college girl that I had a girlfriend? Wow, what a dick move. Although, she still slept with me, so I guess she isn't totally blameless, I rationalize, trying to make myself feel better.

6

"By the way, I'm Nikki, in case you don't remember" she says, introducing herself, and laughing as she walks toward the door. Her long, dark, wet hair is the last thing I see as she softly closes the door behind her, and disappears into the industrially carpeted hallway.

I roll over, attempting to find a more comfortable position on the bed, but as I do, I come face to face with Nikki's red lace thong. My head is starting to throb again, and the guilt is beginning to wash over me as I realize the enormity of my transgression. I have no memory of giving Nikki my name, but as I fall back to sleep, I do feel the slightest bit better knowing that she doesn't seem like the kind of girl who's going to want to track me down.

Chapter One
Westport, CT – September 2019
Ellie

"I'm really sorry, Ellie, I just can't make it in today. I promise I'll be there tomorrow," Maureen says, her voice echoing throughout my car on speakerphone.

"Don't worry about it. I can cover your classes today," I say, taking a deep breath and trying to control the resentment in my voice. As a yoga teacher, there is an expectation that I am calm and zen-like and nothing rattles me; but in reality, I think it just leads to people taking advantage of me.

"You're the best! It won't happen again," Maureen says, as she hangs up the phone.

I would love to believe her, but this is the third time this month that she has cancelled on me at the last minute. I would fire her, but the regulars seem to love her. Maureen's classes always fill up first *and* she has mastered both the barre class and the booty shaping class. Darcy and Roman still insist they only want to do yoga, which means hiring more people to expand the studio. Maureen is happy to learn anything and she's good at it; if only she'd show up!

I take a long, slow sip of creamy coffee from my thermos and contemplate the changes this development brings to my day.

It's barely past eight o'clock and already everything feels like a disaster.

I stare out of the window across the street at the beautiful storefront, with the purple and gray sign that says "Body & Soul" and remind myself that there are worse places I could be spending my day, even though I was only supposed to be here for an hour. I take one last sip of coffee and then put my thermos back in the cup holder. I'll have to switch to a mug of green tea once I get inside. Similar to the expectation of being tranquil and composed; yoga teachers are also expected to drink tea. It's not that I dislike green or herbal teas, but there's no way I would get through my day without coffee. I'm pretty sure people would go crazy if they found out that I have the occasional cheeseburger, but there's only so much I can do.

Darcy is sitting at the front desk when I open the door. She looks up from the meticulous gray oak desk and smiles when she sees me. "Good Morning, Ellie," she beams.

"How was your class?" I ask her as I walk over to the large closet to drop my bags.

"It was good, we had fourteen," she says.

"That's great! The seven o'clock has been full every day this month," I remark.

"Ellie, it's been full almost every day for the past two years," Darcy laughs. "There's a wait-list for most of our classes, you shouldn't worry so much," she says, leaning back in the ergonomic desk chair to reveal four inches of unbearably toned abs.

Darcy is one of the few people who see me when I'm unnerved and decidedly un-zen-like. Although I may be the founder and owner of this studio, Darcy is the true Yogi in my opinion. I met her in a Yoga class in Greenwich right before I started my studio and I never could have made it happen without her.

Darcy lives and breathes yoga. She has helped me build "Body & Soul" over the last five years and sometimes I still see it as the new business, struggling to get people in the door; whereas Darcy is such an optimist, she thought we were the best on day one, so she has no trouble believing the praise and great reviews we are getting now.

"Any chance you want to stay and teach at nine?" I ask hopefully.

"Sorry, I can't. I have class," Darcy says. I know she is referring to her *other* class when she says this – she is studying to be an herbalist, and unfortunately this is taking an increasing amount of her time. I assume that she plans to do this part-time and still teach yoga. I can't imagine Darcy's life without yoga, but mostly, I can't imagine trying to run this studio without her, so I try not to think about it, and we rarely discuss it.

"Anyway, I thought Maureen was teaching the next class," Darcy says.

"She was supposed to. She cancelled," I share.

Just as Darcy opens her mouth, I stop her. "Don't say anything, I know," I tell her.

"Who's signed up for the class?" I ask Darcy, trying to change the subject.

Darcy swivels the screen of the computer around to face me and I nod as I look over the list of names. I recognize all but two of the fourteen names. Most of the ladies are Maureen's regulars – hopefully they won't be too disappointed to see me (although I try to remind myself that they all came here for me long before they met Maureen).

I'm thrilled to see Dorothy on the list. At eighty, she is my oldest student, and she might also be my favorite! I haven't seen her in class in the last couple of weeks and I was starting to worry, but now I'll get to see her today and check on her myself.

***

There are a chorus of "Thanks Ellie!" and "Great class today!" and "I'm going to feel that tomorrow!" as everyone rolls up their mats and makes their way to the front room to put on shoes and gather purses. I often find it ironic that most of these women have elaborate alarm systems in their homes, yet they come in here and leave their Birkin bags on the benches in the unmonitored front room, with an unlocked door, during class. I should probably do something about security before something happens (God forbid). But then the rustic oak benches and alpaca throw pillows in my beautiful studio will be replaced with metal lockers and it will look like Soul Cycle – no fucking way.

"I feel ten years younger," Dorothy says, coming over and resting her hand on my shoulder.

"You looked great today," I tell her, reaching over to squeeze her hand. I feel her enlarged arthritic knuckles, reminiscent of my grandmother's, and am amazed at how relatively nimble she seemed in class today, given what I know of her aches and pains.

"Pretty soon, I'm going to start buying my yoga clothes at Lulu-whatever it's called and then I'll blend right in with all the other girls," Dorothy chuckles.

"You wouldn't want to blend in," I say to her. "Besides, I like your outfits better than everyone else's anyway."

Dorothy glances down at her black gauzy pants and long-sleeved maroon top and then looks at me. "You're very sweet, Ellie," she says. Then she looks around the studio, as if just realizing and adds, "I'm sorry to have kept you, I didn't realize

11

I was the last one here. I'll just grab my things and get out of your hair."

"Dorothy, don't worry about it. I'm here for most of the day anyway. I have another class at eleven and then at one and three," I tell her, attempting to sound cheerful.

"Oh my. Won't you be tired teaching all of those classes?" Dorothy asks.

"Thankfully I don't have to do all of the work, I just have to teach them. It's the students that will be tired," I joke, trying to get her to smile.

"Maybe if I taught four yoga classes a day, I would look like you," Dorothy jests.

"Actually, only two of them are yoga. Two of the classes today are the new fitness classes we are offering," I tell her.

"Oh? What are they called? Would I like them?" Dorothy asks.

I wish I hadn't said anything, because now I feel my cheeks burn slightly as I tell Dorothy, "The new classes are called 'Booty Bootcamp.' It's a silly name. It's an hour of cardio and weights and some other exercises," I try to explain.

"Maybe I'll try that next week," Dorothy says, with a straight face.

"Sure, if you really want to," I say, trying to picture Dorothy in class with the loud hip-hop music and all the ladies' yelling and grunting.

"Sweetie, you should see your face! I can barely handle yoga. I'm just teasing you," Dorothy says, a smile spreading across her face, amplifying the wrinkles around her mouth.

"You got me!" I say to Dorothy, laughing as I bend down to roll up her yoga mat for her. "Are you good for a ride home?" I ask her, as I do after every class.

"I'm all set," Dorothy says. "Thanks for a great class Ellie, I hope to see you next week," and she leans over and gives me a peck on the cheek and then makes her way to the front room to slip on her Birkenstocks and she's gone.

As much as I feel I've gotten to know Dorothy over the past four years that she's been coming here, I realize that I still don't know that much about her. She seems quite independent, but I don't know if she drives herself to class, or gets a ride – she just appears and then she's gone. She made a comment once that her husband passed away several years ago, but other than that, she never talks about herself or her family, and when I do ask if she needs a ride or needs any help, all she says is, "I'm all set."

Before I can spend any more time wondering about Dorothy, my phone buzzes with a call from the middle school. I hold my breath before I answer the call, because there has never been a time when school has called in the middle of the day with good news.

"Hello?" I say, tentatively, hoping school dialed the wrong number – that's actually happened before.

"Hi Mrs. Miller, don't worry, nothing is wrong," I let out an audible breath after hearing this. Clearly they know their audience. "Max is here in the office and he forgot his violin at home. Sixth graders are allowed to call home once in the first two weeks of school, after that it will impact their grades, but we give a little bit of leeway to the new students. You can bring his violin anytime in the next hour before his orchestra class," the school secretary informs me.

"Okay, thank you," I tell her. I'm about to tell her that I'm not sure that I'll be able to bring in the violin when I hear a dial tone – I guess that means our conversation is over.

Crap! I don't think I can make it across Westport to the house, over to the middle school and back here in time for class at eleven. It's a long shot, but I decide to give Jack a call.

"Hi honey," Jack says, when he answers the phone.

"Are you still home?" I ask, cutting right to the chase.

"I am. Why?" he asks.

"Max forgot his violin at home and the school called - someone needs to bring it to him, but I don't think I can get home and get it to him in time. Any chance you could drop it off?" I ask optimistically.

"Sorry, I can't do it. I have a lecture at noon, I'm about to walk out the door," he says.

"But it's only forty-five minutes to New Haven. It's ten past ten. Can't you just drop it off on your way?" I plead.

"Sorry Ellie, traffic could be bad, and I need to go to my office first and my class is on the other side of campus. You know I can't be late for class," Jack says.

"And I can be late for *my* class?" I challenge.

"I never said that. Don't bring Max the violin – he forgot it, he has to live with the consequences. I've got to go, I'll see you tonight, love you," Jack says, as he hangs up.

"You too," I say absentmindedly.

I'm sure Jack is right, but I feel terrible picturing Max in his second week of orchestra sitting alone in the corner of the room without his instrument. I'm pretty sure the middle school doesn't put sixth graders in the corner and make them wear dunce caps, but I can't get the image out of my mind.

It's ten-fifteen right now. Without traffic, it's nine minutes to get home, then eleven minutes to school, and thirteen minutes to get back here – that even gives me a few extra minutes to actually find the violin in his room and run in and out of school. If I leave right now, I can be back a few minutes before eleven to let everyone into the studio before class!

I run out to the car, quickly locking the door behind me, hoping that Max appreciates what a great mom I am, and also silently cursing both Maureen and Jack.

***

"How was your day?" Jack asks, as he wanders into the living room that night. I heard him come in a little while ago, but he must have used the time to get himself some dinner, because he's holding a beer and a half-eaten bowl of leftover risotto.

"If I told you that I gave everyone in my eleven o'clock their class for free and a credit for another free class, would that tell you anything?" I ask him.

"Oh shit, what happened?" he asks, taking another mouthful of risotto.

"I over-estimated my ability to navigate Westport traffic," I say.

"The violin, huh?" Jack asks, taking a swig of his beer and sinking down onto the velvet couch.

"Don't say *I told you so*, I don't want to hear it," I tell him.

"I didn't say anything," Jack says, holding his hands up in mock surrender, which is difficult to do with his hands full.

"I think I'm going to go to bed," I tell him.

"It's not even ten," Jack points out.

"I know. But I'm exhausted; I can barely keep my eyes open. I don't know why I'm so tired," I say. "Max and Isabelle are asleep, but Sydney is obviously still up," I inform him. "Actually, I think she mentioned she needed help on her calculus homework, so you might want to check on her," I tell him.

"Alright, I'll go up and see her in a few minutes. I've got papers to grade, so I'll be up late anyway," Jack adds.

"I'll see you in the morning," I say to Jack, blowing him a kiss as I turn to go upstairs, something that only old married couples must do I realize. For a moment, I imagine telling him to grade his papers in the morning and leading him upstairs for a spontaneous quickie, but it's fleeting and exhaustion and reality take over, and I say good night again and go to bed as planned.

Chapter Two
Sydney

It doesn't seem quite fair that I wear bigger jeans than my mom. It also doesn't seem right that she is forty-three and struts around in tiny extra small Lycra outfits, and I am sixteen and trying to squeeze into last year's size eight jeans, because I refuse to admit (or tell her) that I might need a size ten. I don't think she even knows that clothes come in double digits.

I glance in the mirror again to assess my outfit and see if the jeans are passable or if I have to change. The orange and white off-the shoulder shirt looks decent and the skinny jeans are a bit too tight, but as long as I don't sit down they don't look too bad – and I can always unbutton them during class when no one's looking. Thankfully my waist-length chestnut hair never lets me down. I give it a toss and watch it cascade across my back and fall perfectly into place (I get my hair from my dad – mom also never has a hair out of place, but of course her hair is blonde). Finally, I do a once-over of my makeup. I'm not allowed to wear much to school, but unlike most of my friends, I don't need a lot. I've still never had a single pimple – a source of contention with many of my friends who use a ton of creams and special washes every night and then have to load up on concealer every day. Mom always says I'm a "natural beauty," but she has to say that, since she's my mom. She knows I'm not nearly as pretty as she is – I think it's just a nice way of saying plain. I get closer to the mirror to try and make a closer assessment, although I can't imagine it will be different than what I see any other morning.

My inspection is interrupted when I hear my mom's voice from the bottom of the stairs, "Sydney, hurry up or you're going to be late for school!" For such a small woman, she has a surprisingly loud voice.

"I'll be down in a minute," I yell back, taking one last look in the mirror, and grabbing my far-too-heavy backpack off my bedroom floor.

"You look nice!" My mom says, as I shuffle down the stairs. As expected, she is wearing miniscule black capri leggings and a matching tight black tank top.

"Thanks," I mumble.

She walks over to me and has to stand on her tiptoes to give me a kiss on the cheek, her five-foot-three frame is no match for me at five-seven.

"Do you think that shirt would look cuter tucked in?" she asks, hopefully.

"Nope," I say, hoping this will end the conversation.

"Okay," she says, taking the hint. "What do you want for breakfast? You need to grab something quickly, or we're going to be late," she reminds me.

"I'll just grab something at school," I tell her.

"What are you going to get at school?" she asks, as if we haven't had this conversation many times before.

"I'll take a granola bar," I say, heading toward the snack cabinet.

"Are you sure?" she questions.

"Yes, Mom, it's fine. Let's just go, or I'm going to be late," I reply.

As she backs out of the driveway, I say, "Wouldn't it be great if I could drive myself to school so you didn't have to get up this early to drive me?"

"That would be nice," my mom says. "But where are you going to get a car?" she asks.

"Seriously?" I say.

"Yes, seriously. Do you think we are just going to buy you a car?" she asks.

"Everyone has a car!" I explain, rehashing the fight we have been having for months.

"It must be nice to have that kind of money," my mom says snidely.

"You and Dad have a lot of money," I challenge.

"Not money like the rest of your friends," she says. "And even if we did, I don't think that you should have your own car at the age of sixteen!"

"I would drive Max and Izzy everywhere if I had a car. You hate driving us around – it would be so helpful for everyone if I had a car," I plead.

"I don't want to talk about this now. Have a good day at school," she says as she pulls up in front of the high school.

"Ugh," I say, slamming the door as I get out.

"I'll pick you up after soccer," she calls out.

"Jenna is driving me home!" I call back, referring to one of my many friends who has her own car; and with that I storm away.

***

"Why do you even need to go home?" Jenna asks, as we are walking through the parking lot after practice.

"You want me to go out like this?" I ask, using my free hand to indicate my sweat-stained gray tank top, green soccer shorts and Adidas soccer sandals.

"Of course not," she laughs. "I barely want to let you in my car like that," she jokes.

"Bitch," I say, playfully swatting her arm. "You're no prize either," I tell her. Although now that I look at her, Jenna's ivory skin has a subtle glow, but other than that, there is no evidence of sweat or dirt anywhere on her. Meanwhile, I look like I've been rolling in the mud.

"I mean you can shower and change at my house, and then we can go out," she explains.

"That would be great, but I didn't bring anything to change into," I say.

"Just borrow something," she says.

Luckily we have reached her car, so we have to separate to our respective sides, giving me a moment to contemplate my answer.

"Where should I put these?" I ask Jenna, pointing to my soccer bag with my cleats and shin guards.

"Just throw them wherever," she says, climbing into the driver's seat.

I open the back door and gingerly place the bag on the floor, trying to make sure I don't get any dirt on the tan leather seats.

"Hurry up, Syd, what are you doing?" Jenna asks, rotating her petite frame to watch me.

"Nothing," I reply, shutting the back door, and climbing into the passenger seat. I know Jenna may not care if I get dirt anywhere, but I would still feel bad, especially since it's a new Porsche Cayenne. I barely like sitting in her car because I'm scared I'm going to spill or scratch something, and Jenna just tosses her stuff around like it's a used Kia.

"So, we'll go to my place and you'll borrow something," she says definitively.

"I don't know. Maybe it's easier if I go home and I'll meet you at the party?" I suggest.

"But then I'm going to have to pick you up!" she complains.

I should just tell her that none of her clothes will fit me, but that's mortifying. I'm sure she's trying to be nice by offering, but does she really think that I will fit in her clothes? She's not tiny like my mom, but she's probably a size six, and she's certainly not curvy like I am, so I can't imagine she'll have anything I can wear. I suppose I could always wear my clothes from school? Or at least my jeans from today, those aren't so bad…

"K, let me text my mom and let her know," I tell Jenna. I'm still not convinced about the clothes, but getting ready at her house means I get to use her makeup, which is way better than mine and her parents won't regulate how much I put on.

Sydney: hi mom. practice is over. i'm going to get ready at Jenna's. be home by midnight.

Mom: Hi sweetie! How was your day?

21

Sydney: fine

Mom: How was your calculus test?

Sydney: fine

Mom: You've been gone all day. Are you sure you want to get ready at Jenna's?

Sydney: yup

Mom: What will you do about dinner?

Sydney: we'll eat at her house. see you tonight

Mom: Okay. Have fun tonight. And be safe! Remember you can always call us if you need a ride home.

Sydney: i know

Mom: I love you

Sydney: bye

"What did she say?" Jenna inquires. "That's a lot of texting just to tell her you're not coming home," she comments.

"Oh nothing," I respond. "She says it's fine," I tell her, tucking my phone back into my bag.

When we get to Jenna's house, it appears that no one is home, but truthfully, it's so big that it would be difficult to hear or see someone even if they were in the house.

"I'll use the guest bathroom to shower," she tells me, "you can use mine. There are plenty of extra towels in the closet, so grab whatever you need," she instructs.

"I don't want to steal your bathroom," I object. I don't really care where I shower, but I'm confused as to why she made these assignments. Also, I know there are at least three guest bathrooms, so wouldn't it be easier if I used one of those?

"Don't worry about it," Jenna says. Before I know what's happening she strips off her clothes from practice and tosses them in a heap on the floor, and is standing naked in the middle of the room, scrolling through Instagram on her phone. I try to find somewhere else to look, but it's nearly impossible with her flawless body less than five feet away.

I'm not remotely attracted to her, or to any girls, I just wonder what it would feel like to have her body as my own; to stand naked in front of another person (or even the mirror) and feel completely comfortable. Where I have a small round lump of flesh underneath my bellybutton, Jenna's is completely flat. Where my thighs touch slightly when I stand with my legs too close together, Jenna has at least two inches of space, not to mention that each thigh has a certain amount of muscle tone I have never been able to achieve, no matter how much soccer I play and how many laps I run. And where my boobs take up almost half of the area from my collarbone to my navel, her nipples point to the sky and she fills out her 32B perfectly.

Jenna puts down her phone and grabs a black silky robe from behind her bedroom door, as if she just realized she was naked. Unfazed, she says to me, "I think everything you need should be in the bathroom. I'll do my hair in the guest room and then come back in here so we can get dressed and do our makeup together."

"Got it," I tell her, still crossing my fingers that she has something in her closet that stretches a lot.

***

"Are you sure about this?" I ask Jenna, while reviewing my appearance in the full-length mirror.

23

"You look hot!" she declares, quickly glancing my way, and then looking back into her professional makeup mirror to continue applying mascara.

My hair and makeup are already complete, so I continue to study my reflection. I'm wearing a black V-neck velvet shirt that reveals about two-inches of cleavage (I've seen Jenna wear this shirt before and it looks sort of boring, but I have to admit, I do look pretty good in it). Miraculously we found a distressed jean skirt in her closet that fits me and it's just short enough to show the muscular part of my leg and not the bad parts. Jenna and I are both size eights, so I wasn't worried about shoes, and she lent me the cutest black Ferragamo booties to finish off the outfit.

"It's not a bit too much for Mary's party?" I question.

"Nope. Because we aren't going to Mary's party," she says, with a devilish grin.

"What? Why not?" I ask her.

"Do you really want to go sit in Mary's basement and watch Katie pretend to be drunk after one beer and Madison throw up again?" Jenna questions.

"I guess not," I reply. It doesn't sound quite as appealing when she puts it that way, but I had been looking forward to going out tonight, especially now that I almost like my outfit.

"So what are we going to do?" I ask, trying not to sound dumb.

"One of my brother's friends is having a party. He said we could come, as long as we don't say we're in high school," she says excitedly.

"You mean at Yale?" I ask, on high alert.

24

"No, it isn't a friend he goes to school with now, it's one of his friends from high school," she clarifies. "He goes to Fairfield."

"Oh, okay," I reply, still unsure how I feel about going to a college party, but tremendously relieved it isn't on a campus where my dad is on the faculty.

"Come on, it will be great! I'm so over high school parties," Jenna says, checking herself out in the mirror one more time and pursing her lips in approval.

"Yeah, uh, me too," I agree. Although I'm not sure I actually do agree with her. We are only one month into our junior year; of course Katie is a little annoying and Madison needs to learn not to take four shots in the first twenty minutes of the party, but these are our friends and I feel like we are finally starting to figure out high school – how am I going to pretend to be in college?

"Tonight is going to be the best night, I can feel it," Jenna says, linking arms with me as we abandon her warzone of a room and head down the hall.

"Totally!" I reply, even though all I feel is nauseous.

Chapter Three
Jack

Saturday morning is my favorite time of the week. I loved it when the kids were younger, but not the same way I do now. Then it was a mad rush from one early morning sporting event to the next. Ellie and I would exchange the children, portable chairs and water bottles at pre-arranged times and meeting points and rarely see each other until late in the afternoon when we would collapse on the couch and swap stories of wins, losses and unfair referees.

Izzy is only in third grade, so we aren't quite empty nesters; but her games are now in the afternoon and she sleeps until almost nine on Saturday and then finds her way to the nearest screen without assistance.

When I get up at seven o'clock on Saturday, the house is so quiet you could hear a pin drop. As a full-fledged teenager, Sydney sleeps until at least eleven on the weekends now, unless we wake her earlier; and Max is getting closer every day. Even if he isn't asleep, he's barricaded in his room (I'm certainly not going to disturb a twelve-year-old boy with his door shut). And then there is my darling Ellie. She teaches a six o'clock class on Sunday, so Saturday is her only day off and she could sleep almost as late as Sydney if she didn't set her alarm for nine-thirty. So that just leaves me.

I tell myself that one of these mornings I will go for a run, but then I get downstairs and the attraction of the coffee pot, The

Wall Street Journal, and my leather recliner are simply too strong.

"Did you hear Sydney come in last night?" Ellie asks, interrupting a riveting article on the flattening yield curve.

"I didn't even hear *you* come in," I comment, trying to make a joke. "What are you doing up so early?" I ask.

"It's almost nine," Ellie says, making her way to the coffee pot. "Is there any left?" she asks.

"There should be a little left. I can make more," I assure her.

"I think Syd came in after midnight. I tried to wait up, but I was so tired I fell asleep on the couch pretty early," she says.

"If you were already asleep, how do you know what time she came in?" I ask her, not sure why I doubt her.

"I swear I woke up at twelve-thirty and the hall lights were still on; and then when I woke up again at two and came to bed they were off. So I think she came in somewhere between those times," Ellie says.

"You're almost like Nancy Drew," I say playfully. "But so much cuter," I add.

"Jack, I'm serious," she says, but she's smiling. This version of Ellie on Saturday mornings is also why it's my favorite part of the week. She's relaxed and in her pajamas and she isn't rushing around in six different directions. Maybe it's unfair, but this Ellie reminds me of Ellie from when we first met. It's only for an hour or two and then the kids will all swarm the kitchen and slowly she will tense up and it's like I can see her transform into a Westport Mom again right before my eyes. But for a few short hours on Saturday mornings, it's coffee, the paper, and Ellie at twenty-four.

"I think I'm going to head up to bed," Ellie says, startling me as she appears in the doorway of my office. She's always been small and light on her feet, but with the addition of yoga, she becomes more like a cat everyday. She thinks it's funny, but she scares the hell out of me on a regular basis.

"I'm finishing up in here, I'll be up in a few minutes," I tell her.

"Okay," she says, turning to leave.

"Wait up for me?" I call after her hopefully. She's been asleep early every night this week; I'm not one to keep count, but at this rate it will be over two weeks without sex.

"I'll try. You better hurry," she calls back down the stairs.

It's nine-thirty on Sunday night and I have hours of work left to do. I glance at my editor's notes on my manuscript and the outline for my ten o'clock Monday morning lecture and decide that those will still be there in an hour, or in the morning, but Ellie probably won't last another five minutes.

"You're still up," I say with relief, when I walk into our bedroom and find Ellie in bed with a book; she is dwarfed by the enormous king size bed and overstuffed duvet and all I can see is her head and her little flannel covered arms sticking out.

"Yes, but not for long," she says, and then yawns as if to prove her point.

"Any chance I could convince you otherwise?" I whisper, sliding into my side of the bed, and kissing her neck.

"Hmmm," she says, reaching over to put her book on the nightstand and turn off the lights. "I'll try, but no promises," she jokes.

"Wait, did you talk to Sydney today? You said you were going to talk to her?" Ellie asks, practically springing up in bed.

"Shhhh, not now," I say, kissing her softly.

"But…" she tries to object.

"Shhhh, it's all okay, I sorted it out, I promise. No kids right now. Pretend we don't even have kids," I say, trying to recapture the mood.

"Okay, she says," hesitant, but seemingly willing to play along and relax as I pull her nightgown over her head.

"It's just the two of us, just for a few minutes," I tell her.

"Okay," she says, it sounds like she is about to say something else, but then she reaches for my boxers and I forget all about it.

***

I know I'm going to pay for not getting that work done last night, but I still find myself whistling as I walk across campus this morning.

"Hey Professor Miller," a student calls out excitedly and waves.

"Hey there," I reply, momentarily forgetting his name.

"Hi Professor Miller," the girl alongside him echoes.

"Hi Chloe," I reply, pleased with myself for remembering her name.

I could probably blow those kids' minds if I told them that I was in this good of a mood because I was thinking about having sex with my wife last night and I was totally unprepared for my lecture this morning and would likely just wing it. I know that as an undergrad at UT Austin, I never thought about my professors as being actual people or having real lives; and I'm sure Yale students aren't any different.

"How was your weekend Ginny," I ask my assistant, as I enter the offices in the economics department – my home away from home. There's an overwhelming amount of dark wood in the office, as if someone said "money equals dark wood and green carpeting," but that's what we're stuck with. Thankfully, they repainted a few years ago and the walls are now ice blue, almost white, which lightens up the otherwise gloomy interior.

"It was good, too short as always, but can't complain," Ginny says. Ginny says pretty much the same thing every Monday morning; I would be quite alarmed if she said anything different. Ginny has been my assistant ever since I became a tenured professor ten years ago; something that happened much sooner than anticipated due to the success of my research. Ginny is in her early sixties and has worked at the University for forty years. At first glance she appears to be a mild-mannered almost-grandmotherly type, but I learned long ago that she is tough as nails and is not to be messed with.

"There was a girl in here waiting for you this morning, she was here for over an hour, but then she said she had to leave," Ginny informs me.

"Did you tell her that my office hours are this afternoon at three?" I ask.

"I told her," Ginny replies.

"Do you know who she was? Or what class she was from?" I ask her.

"She didn't tell me her name, but I don't think she was a student," Ginny says, matter-o-factly.

"She's not a student?" I question. "Then who was she?"

"I told you, she didn't really tell me anything. She said she wanted to speak with you, but then she said she had to leave," Ginny recaps. "She'll probably come back if it's important," Ginny adds.

"Sure," I say, no longer listening to her; focusing solely on writing a lecture on spatial fragmentation in the US economy in the twenty-five minutes I have until class time – something that ordinarily would take me three to four hours.

Chapter Four
Ellie

A chorus of "Namaste" quietly echoes around the studio, and with that I am done for the day; at least I am done teaching yoga, my day is far from over.

"Thanks Ellie," calls out one student.

"Great class," says another.

All the ladies gradually roll up their mats as they quietly whisper to their friends about lunch plans or whatever it is they have scheduled after this.

"How are you?" Jillian gushes, coming up to my spot in the front of the room to say hello. Jillian was one of the first friends I made when we moved to Westport ten years ago. Sydney was six at the time and Max had just turned two. She had two kids the exact same ages and we met at a Storytime event at the Westport Library and hit it off immediately. I didn't learn until a few months later that Jillian was a fixture in Westport society. She always seemed down to earth at the library and playgroups, but when I told Jack about her, he acted like I had befriended a massive celebrity – which in some ways I had.

Jillian was one of my biggest supporters when I decided to change paths and open this studio five years ago. I like to believe it's my hard work and great classes that have made it a success, but Jillian's influence with the women in this town definitely helped get me started in the right direction. For the first six months she came to at least five classes a week and wherever Jillian goes, everyone follows.

"I'm great!" I tell her, "How are you? I love your outfit by the way," I add.

"Thanks, I just got it this morning, grabbed it at Athleta before I came in," she says, looking down to admire her black floral tights and coordinating sports bra.

"Are you sure you're okay?" she asks me, squinting her eyes and trying to raise her eyebrows as high as the Botox will allow. And I'm not judging her for the Botox; I use the same dermatologist for mine (although I go a little less frequently).

"I'm totally fine," I try to assure her. "Hold on one second, let me just say goodbye to everyone."

I check in the front room and say goodbye to the last few stragglers and then come back into the studio to find Jillian back on her mat in happy baby pose. "Sorry, just thought I'd get a little more stretching done, if I'm still here," she tells me.

"No need to apologize," I say to her. "Why did you think something was wrong with me?" I ask her.

Jillian has moved into a full straddle pose, with her face shoved into her mat, but she turns her head to the side so I can hear her speak. "You just seemed a little off today," she says.

"Was the class bad?" I ask, suddenly concerned. I had some of my fussiest students here today and one new woman; today wouldn't be the right day to be off my game.

"No, it was a great class," she assures me. "I just felt like there was something bothering you. No one else would have noticed anything, I promise," she says confidently.

"Too many things on my mind, you know how it is," I tell her. "I promise, I'm fine," I assure her.

"Okay, if you're sure," Jillian says, unfolding herself from the floor and rolling up her hot pink yoga mat. "I've got to run, I'm meeting Lara for lunch at the club. Do you want to join us?" she asks.

"I can't, but thanks for asking," I reply. Even if I weren't busy today, Lara is one of Jillian's fancy friends that has never liked me. Jillian swears up and down that it isn't true, but I know better. Lara made her mind up the first day she met me. Jillian told her that I used to be a social worker and my husband was a professor and Lara practically spit out her buttery Chardonnay – she wasn't friends with people who needed to work for a living, especially in such menial jobs. But the final straw was when I opened the yoga studio; then I officially became "the help."

"Alright, I'll see you tonight," Jillian says.

"What do you mean?" I ask, confused.

"At the girls' soccer game," she says.

"Oh right, of course," I reply, although I actually had forgotten.

"You *do* have a lot on your mind," Jillian laughs, pulling me in for a hug.

I try not to wince when she squeezes me; I didn't think about it all morning, but both my breasts ache again as she pulls me into her chest. I wonder again if I pulled a muscle or maybe this is what menopause feels like? I can't remember the last time my boobs were this sore.

It's not until Jillian is gone and I'm enjoying the peace and quiet, while I wait for Maureen to relieve me and takeover for

34

the afternoon, that I glance at the online sign up sheets for the morning classes and notice that Dorothy had signed up for the nine a.m. class, but she wasn't here this morning. I have the email address that she reluctantly uses to register for classes, but she has told me many times, that she never checks it. I know it's none of my business, but I wish I had a way to check in on her. I like to think that she has several children and grandchildren right here in Westport who check on her all the time. Maybe she's not here today because she's having lunch with her daughter? That certainly is a better picture than anything else I'm envisioning.

A tear trickles down my cheek as I begin to seriously consider that something has happened to Dorothy. Good Lord – what is wrong with me?! She is only eighty, and she just missed one yoga class! Why am I so crazy and emotional about this? Maybe Jillian was right, I do need to pull it together. Thankfully, Maureen walks in the door just in time to save me from my pity party.

"I'm here! And I'm even early!" she announces, as she breezes into the front room. Her blonde hair is in shiny waves, cascading down her back, as if she has just come from a blow-out; seems like a waste to get your hair done right before teaching two mixed barre classes and a hot yoga class tonight, but that's Maureen.

"Perfect!" I reply. "I'm going to grab my stuff and get going," I tell her.

"What are you doing today?" Maureen asks excitedly, as only a twenty-five year old can.

"I'm going to the grocery store and CVS, then I need to do about five loads of laundry and make dinner. Oh and I'm driving carpool for Max and Izzy today," I tell her.

"Oh," she replies, trying to digest this information. Single and mid-twenties looks pretty different than married, early-forties with three kids – she must think I have the worst life ever. "Um, have fun!" Maureen says, cheerfully, but I'm quite sure she thinks having a root canal would be more fun than the rest of my day.

***

Just moments ago, I applauded myself for how efficiently I made my way through Trader Joe's, getting everything on my list without getting sucked into the multitude of appealing, unhealthy snack options that I usually buy and then eat before the kids even get home from school. But now I am wandering the aisles of CVS and I can't even remember why I came in here. I know there was something I needed, but I forgot to add it to the list and my mind is completely blank.

I pass oral care and grab a few toothbrushes, because we can always use more of those, and I do the same with deodorant – maybe if I buy new deodorant for Max he'll actually use it. I come to a somewhat dramatic stop in the massive feminine care aisle, as the light bulb finally goes off and I remember that Sydney told me she needed tampons. She actually texted me with her request, but in our relationship that is what seems to pass for communication.

As I grab the box of Tampax Pocket Pearl, specifically as instructed, it hits me that I haven't had my period in quite a while. I've never been like clockwork, and I've noticed since turning forty that it's usually almost five weeks apart, but that's probably just another joy of getting older – the beginning of menopause. I've never been one of those women who writes down the date of my period in my calendar, so standing here now in the middle of CVS I am racking my brain trying to think about how long it has been and I simply cannot remember. Wait, I had it when we were on vacation in August; phew, that wasn't that long ago.

"Do you need any help?" asks a CVS employee.

"No, I'm fine," I reply. Although, I've been staring at the tampon display for at least five minutes, so I can see why she is concerned.

And then I do the math – it's been six and a half weeks since vacation. I feel my knees start to buckle and I have to hold on to the shelf to steady myself. I reach down with my free hand and push on my breast and the soreness is shockingly familiar - as is my inability to stay awake past nine, and my recent forgetfulness. "Fuck!" I utter, way too loudly.

"Are you sure you're okay?" The CVS employee asks again.

"Yes, sorry, I'm fine," I reply. I didn't mean for that to come out so loud, but seriously, why is she still standing there?! And hasn't she ever seen a forty-three year old woman have a breakdown in the feminine hygiene aisle before? I can't be the first one.

I march past her toward the end of the aisle and hurriedly grab two boxes of Clearblue digital pregnancy tests; maybe it's odd to have a preferred brand, but this is the only brand I've ever used, so it seems strange to switch now. Although until now, every time I ever bought a test, I was giddy and praying for a positive result. I've never wanted to fail a test more than I do today.

Chapter Five
Sydney

It's so cliché, but everything looks a little brighter this morning; even my mom's annoying questions on the drive to school seemed slightly less annoying. I know that it's crazy to feel like this after one kiss, but it seemed like so much more than that. And more importantly, it wasn't a kiss with just any guy – it was a kiss with a hot college guy! I should have trusted Jenna all along – going to that party was the best thing I've ever done!

The sound of the bell interrupts my daydream and reminds me to copy down the chemistry assignment from the Smart Board. Thank God we have lunch after this, so I can find Jenna and we can talk about Friday night. She wasn't answering her texts all weekend, and she was too drunk on Friday night to carry on much of a conversation.

"Is everything okay?" I say to Jenna, when I find her at her locker.

"Yeah, I'm fine. Sorry about everything. My mom took away my phone for the whole weekend after what happened on Friday night," she says, staring at the floor.

"Oh. Was she awake when you got home?" I ask, although I assume she must have been or Jenna wouldn't have gotten in trouble.

"Yeah, she was up. She was pretty pissed that I was so drunk, but she was proud of me for having you drive the car home, so she only took away my phone and the car for the weekend – so we're back to normal now," Jenna says, flipping her hair and trying to laugh it off.

I cannot even imagine what my mom would do if she caught me like that! I can guarantee it would probably involve military school, not two days without my phone and my non-existent car. Luckily, no one was awake when I got home forty-five minutes after my curfew. I would have been on time, but I had trouble getting Jenna to leave the party and then I had to drive her home and take an Uber to my house. I convinced my dad that I was on time, but dropped my phone outside and had to go back out to look for it and that's why the lights were on and off – I'm not sure he believed me, but he didn't have proof otherwise.

"I haven't heard from Brandon yet, do you think he'll text me? Would it be really lame if I texted him?" I ask Jenna, as she slams her locker and we begin our walk toward the cafeteria.

"Who's Brandon?" she's asks.

"You know. The guy from the party on Friday," I remind her.

"What guy?" she says, sounding completely perplexed.

"The guy that I was talking to all night and then hooked up with," I tell her, bummed that she doesn't seem to remember anything I told her on the ride home.

"Holy shit! You hooked up with someone at the party?" Jenna says, stopping in her tracks to look at me.

"Well, we kissed," I confess, knowing that she won't be quite as excited by this news, "but it was really good," I assure her.

"It wasn't one of Drew's friends, was it?" she asks, slightly panicked, the concern visible on her face that this could get back to her brother.

"No. He said he came with a friend, but didn't really know anyone there," I assure her. "And I think he's older than Drew."

"Tell me all about it!" She gushes, as we resume our walk, her fears eased.

Although I already told her the entire story, in detail, on the car ride home Friday night, I'm happy to tell her again! I've been dying to talk about Brandon and I didn't want to tell any of my other friends yet, since we ditched them to go to this party in the first place. Since I haven't heard from him yet, I don't want to make a big deal about it.

"He's really cute," I begin, feeling the smile spread across my face as I think about him.

"What does he look like? Tell me everything!" Jenna demands.

"He has brown hair. And I think he has brown eyes – it was dark at the party, so I'm not sure. He kind of looks like Harry Styles," I say earnestly. Jenna gives me a look that says she doubts my comparison.

"I swear he does!" I tell her. "Only he's a little bit taller, and he says he plays soccer. He seemed like he had a great body," I say.

"Wait, he plays soccer for Fairfield?" Jenna asks.

"That's what he said," I reply.

"And you haven't looked him up yet?" Jenna asks, dumbfounded.

"I didn't think about it," I admit, embarrassed.

Jenna grabs her phone from her back jeans pocket and is on the Fairfield soccer page in seconds. "Holy crap! There he is!" She exclaims.

"I told you he was cute," I say to her.

"He is seriously hot!" Jenna says. She continues to read from her phone, "Brandon Thomas is a junior from Wilmington, Vermont. He is six foot one and weighs one hundred and eighty five pounds. He plays right midfield for the Stags. This is the guy you kissed?" Jenna probes, as if she can't quite believe it.

"That's him," I say, staring at the tiny headshot, and getting giddy all over again.

"Not to be a bitch or anything, and you definitely looked amazing on Friday night, but what did you say to him? This guy is a lot older than you, and could probably have any girl at Fairfield," Jenna says.

I flash back to Friday night, when Jenna told me that I was definitely the prettiest girl at the party and he was lucky to even be talking to me – I guess that was drunk Jenna talking.

I debate for a second whether or not I should tell her the truth, but then decide there's no point in lying (at least not to her). "I told him that I was a freshman at Yale," I admit, with a mixture of embarrassment and pride.

"No way!" Jenna says, playfully punching me on the arm. "Do you think he bought it?" she asks.

"I do know a lot about the school," I remind her. "Between my dad and Ainsley - and it's not like he was quizzing me, we only talked about it a little bit," I tell her.

"I forgot your cousin goes there too," Jenna says, as we finally make our way into the cafeteria and get into the long lunch line.

"Yeah, between the two of them, I feel like I could lead campus tours," I joke. "Ainsley is actually away for the semester doing her junior year abroad," I inform Jenna.

"I'm totally going to do that. I'm going to Paris or maybe Milan," she says. "Where's Ainsley?"

"She's in Dublin, at Trinity College. All she does is party," I say confidently.

"So, do you think I should text Brandon?" I ask Jenna, changing the subject back to what I actually want to talk about.

"I don't know. It was probably more like a one-night thing, right?" she asks. "Even if you were actually a freshman at Yale, he's a junior at Fairfield; I don't think that sounds like something he's going to chase after one drunk hook-up," she says.

At that point we both grab our trays with what passes for Caesar salad and our Diet Cokes and walk toward a table in the back of the cafeteria. The table is full of our squad from the soccer team and a few of their boyfriends, so Jenna and I each slide into open chairs at opposite ends of the table. She's probably right about Brandon. He obviously seems too good for me, and I know he's too old for me; but it felt like something when we were together on Friday night. No one has ever looked at me or talked to me the way that he did. All the boys at school worship the same three girls that they've worshipped since the first week of ninth grade; they adore the tiny, cute blonde girls (of course Jenna is one of those girls). And I will always just be the best friend – the sidekick. I know it was only a few hours, but Brandon didn't see me that way.

"Sydney, hey Sydney, you okay?" Mary asks, disturbing my daydream.

"I'm fine," I reply, a little harshly.

"You're staring off into space. I said your name like three times and you didn't even respond," Mary accuses.

"Oh sorry," I apologize.

"And your phone's been lighting up," she says.

As if on cue, my phone vibrates again and dances on top of my tray as it does. It's probably just Jenna texting me from across the table, but I pick it up to see what she has to say. I gasp out loud when I see who it's from.

"Whoa, what's it say?" Mary asks, clearly intrigued by my reaction.

"Oh, nothing," I reply, hoping to downplay it. "It's just something dumb from my mom," I tell her.

"That's the worst!" Mary says, sympathetically.

Only this isn't anything from my mom, it's from Brandon! OMG, I'm trying to act calm while I read this, but it's basically impossible.

Brandon: Hey there.

Brandon: Friday was fun. Want to meet up again this weekend?

Brandon: LMK

I feel like I should talk to Jenna before I text him back, but honestly, she was a little bitchy about the whole thing anyway. I don't need her to tell me that I shouldn't go out with him; or worse, to tell me that he's not really into me. Before I lose my nerve, I write back.

Sydney: Hey

Sydney: Yes – def this weekend

I send the message and then instantly worry about what I wrote. Should I have waited longer to respond? Should I have written something else? I guess it doesn't matter because I see the dots showing that he's typing back.

Brandon: want to come here? Or want me to come to new haven?

Sydney: I'll come to Fairfield – if that's okay

Brandon: Friday night?

Sydney: sounds good

Brandon: I'll think of something to do and text you on Friday

Sydney: okay – see you Friday

Brandon: see you Friday

Oh my God! I can't believe I have a date with Brandon on Friday night. Like an actual, real date.

"That was your mom?" Mary says, looking at me suspiciously.

"Yeah," I say, hiding my phone face down in my lap.

"You seem pretty happy to be texting with your mom," Mary says, looking at me like I'm the biggest loser ever.

"Sometimes she's funny," I respond, not caring what Mary thinks at the moment because I can't contain the enormous grin on my face. "I have to get to class, see you later," I tell her, grabbing my phone and my tray and rushing from the cafeteria so I can re-read and analyze my conversation with Brandon at least twenty times before my next class.

Chapter Six
Jack

No matter what time I get up in the morning, I can't get out the door before eight-fifteen. On Tuesdays and Thursdays, I want everyone to pretend like I'm not here so I can get to the gym, come home, shower, grab breakfast and get in the car to get to campus by eight-thirty. Then I would have enough time to go through email before office hours and have the rest of the morning and early afternoon to work on my book before class at two.

But that never happens. Instead, Ellie or the kids grab me the second I walk in the door from the gym and I get sucked into making breakfast or packing lunches or scouring the house for missing homework assignments; and then it's thirty or forty minutes before I can get in the shower. *And* the traffic is also worse when I leave later, so I never get to my office until right before (or after) nine and I'm greeting the line of students that's waiting to discuss problem sets and squabble about grades.

As predicted, I look at my watch to see that it's already seven fifty, and I'm still in the kitchen in my squash clothes. I abandon the sandwich I'm making for Izzy and tell her that her mother will finish making her lunch for her when she comes back downstairs.

I pass Ellie on my way upstairs and give her the message, "I started Izzy's lunch, but you need to finish it. I really don't want to be late today," I tell her, as I rush by her on my way to take a shower.

"You didn't forget, did you?" Ellie shouts up to me.

"Didn't forget what?" I call down, feeling annoyed.

"We have parent-teacher conferences this morning," Ellie shouts back. "You promised that you would come with me."

Shit. Shit. Shit. I do remember saying that, but it was weeks ago; I'm sure she told me exactly what day and time it was and I said it was fine, but couldn't she have reminded me about it this weekend, or last night?

"What time is it again?" I yell back.

"Izzy's conference is at nine and then we have to drive over to the middle school for Max's conference at ten," she yells up the stairs.

"Okay," I call back down, somewhat helplessly. I grab my phone to send Ginny an email; I know she isn't going to be happy, but there isn't much I can do about it.

To: Ginny Adams
From: Jack Miller

Subject: Office Hours – Reschedule

Dear Ginny,

I need to reschedule my office hours for today. Please send out an email to the students letting them know I will not be there this morning. I will hold office hours today immediately after my lecture from 5-6pm. Sorry for the inconvenience.
I will hopefully be in the office between eleven and noon.

Regards,
Jack

I know she'll be annoyed with me, but it's better to piss off Ginny and my students than to make Ellie mad – especially when I apparently told her I would go to the conferences weeks ago.

***

"I hope everything is okay," Ginny says, as I walk into the office at eleven-thirty. Her words convey concern, but her tone is a little too snarky for the worry to be believable.

"Everything is fine, thank you for asking. Something came up at school, but it's all okay," I tell her as I walk into my office and close the door behind me. The morning has certainly not gotten off to the start I was anticipating and as much as I appreciate all the work Ginny does for me, I'm not in the mood to listen to her complain about the issues she had rescheduling my office hours.

A quick glance out the window onto the quad brightens my mood as I see students walking, laughing, running, lying in the grass and simply enjoying this beautiful early October day surrounded by the stunning Gothic buildings of Old Campus. I take a breath and remember that I am lucky to be here; to call this esteemed institution my home and to be surrounded by smart, eager students and have a chance to shape their minds. Not to mention the opportunity to work on my research, write books and sometimes go on CNBC or Bloomberg as the guest economic advisor – I really don't have anything to complain about.

I try to tell myself this, as I look at my inbox, with seventy-five new emails that have come in since I checked this morning – and two new emails from Ellie since I saw her an hour ago. I'm sure they both have something to do with Max; his conference was not what we were expecting. Apparently he is struggling in almost every subject except for Mandarin (go figure) and the teacher said he doesn't even seem to care. I told Ellie that we would discuss it tonight, but she bit my head off, and then she was in tears as we were leaving the school. I probably should have stayed to figure out what was wrong, but there's really only so much I can handle; and I was already three hours late to work!

Not taking the hint, Ginny buzzes the intercom on my phone: "Hi Ginny, what is it?" I say, tight-lipped.

"I wanted to tell you that the same girl showed up today for your office hours," she says.

"Which girl?" I ask, confused and irritated.

"Remember? I told you there was a girl who came by the office last week and waited for you for over an hour. I gave her the times of your office hours for this week, so she came back today," Ginny says.

"Didn't she get the email that my office hours were rescheduled for tonight?" I ask, getting really annoyed.

"She's not a student, so she didn't get the email," she says.

"She doesn't go to school here at all?" I ask, confused.

"I don't believe so. But she says she needs to speak with you," Ginny says.

"But she won't leave her name or any information?" I ask.

"No. She waited for the whole hour even though I said you weren't going to be here, and then she said she would try again," Ginny tells me.

"Okay. Thanks for letting me know," I reply.

"She's a *very* pretty girl," Ginny adds.

"I don't see what that has to do with anything," I add quickly. "I'm sure she is just interested in applying to Yale, or maybe she has a question on my research," I say, but I don't feel as confident as I sound.

"Okay. I'll let you know if she comes back," Ginny says.

"Thanks," I say, hanging up the intercom. For reasons I can't quite explain, I'm now even more upset than I was when I first came into the office.

***

The rest of the day passed in a blur of writing, lecturing, office hours and unexpected traffic due to an accident on I-95 on the way home. When I pull into the driveway, it feels far later than the actual time of seven forty-five.

"Hello?" I call out as I enter the mudroom and close the door to the garage.

"Hi," Ellie replies, I can tell she is around the corner in the kitchen based on her voice, but I can't tell her mood from her greeting. It's definitely not an effusive "hello" but she doesn't seem as upset or aggravated as she was this morning.

"How was the rest of your day?" I ask, trying to get back on normal footing.

"It was fine," she says, somewhat curtly, but not inquiring about mine.

"Mine was pretty hectic," I offer. "Terrible accident on the way home. It took me almost an hour," I tell her, trying to make conversation.

"You could take the train," she says, not looking up from her position at the sink where she's scrubbing the Dutch oven.

"Did you already eat?" I ask, changing the subject.

"I ate with the kids," she says.

I'm trying to figure out if she's in a bad mood because of something I've done, or if I'm supposed to ask her if she wants to talk about it, or if it's the end of a long day and this is just how it is. I'd like to think after eighteen years of marriage that I could figure this out, but sometimes I can't.

"I'll just grab some cereal," I say, walking over to the cabinet to get a bowl.

"You don't want the lasagna?" Ellie says sounding particularly irritated.

"I would love lasagna. I didn't realize there was dinner left," I stammer.

"I didn't say there wasn't any dinner for *you*, I just said *I* ate with the kids," Ellie says, raising her voice.

"Oh, okay. Thanks. You know I love your lasagna," I tell her, exchanging my bowl for a plate and making my way to the fridge to get the lasagna.

I don't know how I screwed up so badly, but clearly I've done something wrong. I run through the day in my head, and even the last few days; but other than forgetting about the conferences (which I attended anyway), I can't think of anything. I know this is a totally shitty thing to think, and I'm definitely not allowed to say it, but maybe it's just "that time of the month." I'm going to tread lightly and assume she'll be in a better mood tomorrow, or at least in a few days.

Chapter Seven
Ellie

The test has been shoved in the back of my closet for three days. It's still wrapped up in the plastic CVS bag and stuffed behind my heavy winter sweaters. I can't remember the last time anyone else went in my closet, but I hid this better than I hide the Christmas presents. I know I have to take it, but I can't bring myself to do it. I almost talked myself into doing it yesterday, but then I thought I felt a cramp, so I decided to wait and see if my period was going to start – spoiler alert, it didn't.

The kids are all at school and Jack is at work; the house is almost too quiet. I have an urge to turn on music to fill the void, but then I reconsider – I should appreciate the silence, it happens so rarely. There are plenty of things I should be doing with my time right now before I have to be at the studio, but I can't put it off any longer; I have to take the damn test so I know for sure what it says.

I trudge up the stairs, passing over the sixth stair to avoid the creaky step that Jack says he will fix, but hasn't managed to repair in the last five years. I take my time as I walk down the gray-carpeted hallway to our bedroom, my pace is reminiscent of how Izzy moves when we tell her she needs to hurry and get ready for school. Sydney's door is closed, the perpetual state for the past two years. I know she would prefer that no one ever invade her personal space, but she allows me in to collect her laundry and she's more than happy to let the cleaning lady inside. Max's door is wide open to reveal his attempt at tidying his room and making his bed. He pulled his navy and white comforter up to the top of the bed, concealing multiple pillows, piles of clothes and Lord knows what else. Sticking out from under the bed I can see his baseball mitt and at least three different shoes. The final result isn't very good, but at least he's trying. Izzy's room is the best of the bunch. Her bedroom is still decorated in the pink and white butterfly theme that she chose when she moved from a crib to a twin bed six years ago, but luckily it's pretty basic and she hasn't asked to upgrade it yet. All of her stuffed animals are lined up neatly on her bed, her books are lined up on her bookshelves, and her toys are put away in the baskets that line the periphery of her room – it's funny how three kids can have such different personalities.

I've done an excellent job stalling, but I do eventually make it to the master bedroom, and as I approach the closet, my heart starts racing. I'm probably just being too sensitive – there's no way I can be pregnant. I rummage through the back of my closet to try and find the tests, and for a moment I think they have disappeared, but then I hear the plastic bag crinkle.

I tear off the plastic outer wrapper, open the cardboard box only to take out the next heavily plastic wrapped item. Then I struggle to tear the package that contains the test and at this point the thought occurs to me - why are pregnancy tests packaged so securely – are there a lot of people trying to tamper with them? Or is this just another way to fuck with women?

I skip the packet of instructions, because I can't imagine anything has changed since the last time I took a test, but then just as I am starting to pee on the stick, I forget exactly how long I am supposed to hold the stick "in the stream," and I wonder if I've ruined the test after all. I put the cap on the test and place it on a tissue on the Carrera marble counter that we finally put in last year, and then I leave the bathroom to wait – I can't possibly sit there and watch it for an agonizing three minutes.

Sitting on the blue and white floral duvet that covers our king size bed, I try to give myself a little perspective as I wait. First of all, I'm forty-three years old, I have friends who are my age and starting to go through menopause, it's pretty unlikely that I would get pregnant at this age. Second, it took us several months of "trying to get pregnant" when I was twenty-seven and we were trying to have Sydney, so how could I possibly be pregnant now after one night with a broken condom? Third, I have a sixteen-year old daughter! I can't be pregnant *and* have a daughter who's almost out of high school; that would just be ridiculous! I check my watch and see that it has been six minutes, which is plenty of time for the little crystal ball in there to tell me the future. I take a few deep breaths before I unfurl myself from the ball I've been in and head into the bathroom.

Like a small child not wanting to ruin the surprise, I close my eyes as soon as I get inside and inch over to the counter. I know I've gotten myself worked up over nothing the past few days, now that I've thought about it, I can see how preposterous it is, and when I open my eyes, I know that I will see the words "NOT PREGNANT" staring back at me in that little window and life can return to normal.

But when I open my eyes, there is only one word in the little window. My cheeks are wet before I even realize I'm crying. This isn't supposed to happen this way. Of course there is no visible change from a few moments ago, but I still place my hand on my belly, and sob even harder.

Chapter Eight
Sydney

Every day this week seems longer than the next as I wait for Friday to arrive. Even with two soccer games and a ten-page paper due this week, it still dragged on since the only thing I can think about is seeing Brandon again.

Now that Friday afternoon is finally here, I realize that I've been obsessing about what I will say to him and what I will wear and what will happen if he asks me to go back to his room, but I haven't thought about what I'm going to say to my parents! I should have told Jenna right away, but she seemed so dismissive originally that I didn't want her to ruin it. But now I need to tell her, or tell someone, because I need an alibi for where I'm going tonight.

"Jenna, wait up," I call out, as the bell for last period rings and nineteen students all race to the door at once to escape for the weekend.

"Hey, what's up?" Jenna asks.

"What are you doing tonight?" I ask her.

"Emma and Kate and Naya are coming over," she says, sounding annoyed. "I texted you on Wednesday to tell you about it and you didn't even reply," she fumes.

"Right, I'm so sorry," I say, trying to sound contrite.

"So are you coming?" Jenna asks, staring at me with her hand on her hip, her sharp hipbone jutting out as if it is also upset with me.

"That's what I wanted to talk to you about," I say, still unsure of the best way to tell her about my date with Brandon and how to ask her to cover for me. "I'm actually going out with Brandon tonight, and I was hoping I could tell my parents I would be at your house so they don't ask any questions."

"Who's Brandon?" Jenna asks, looking legitimately confused.

"The guy I met last Friday at Fairfield?" I remind her, even though it comes out as more of a question.

"No way!" Jenna screams, loud enough for everyone around us packing up at their lockers to turn and stare. "Why didn't you tell me?" Jenna demands, but she sounds excited, not angry.

"I don't know," I admit, suddenly feeling foolish for keeping it from her. I don't really have a *best* friend, I haven't had anyone that fit that description since Ava Marzak in the second grade, but Jenna is probably my closest friend out of the girls I hang out with. Because of soccer, I spend the most time with her, and she's definitely the least bitchy of the group, so maybe I should have told her right away; but that's the problem with Jenna, and with all of my friends, I'm never sure exactly how they are going to react or what they are going to do. Sometimes they keep their promises and keep secrets, and other times, they are catty, backstabbing liars. Whenever I really stop to think about it, I wonder if it's really worth it to be part of the popular crowd; but this far along in high school I don't think I could switch crowds even if I wanted to. So I'm learning to keep my mouth closed if there's something I care about, spend more time by myself, and bide my time for the next two years until I'm done with this place and can escape to college.

"He's so hot, I can't believe you're going out with him," she says, playfully slapping me on the arm. It's hard to tell from her tone if she can't believe that I'm going with him because he's really hot and too good for me, or just that the whole situation is so unbelievable. Either way, I should probably be pretty offended, but I'll let it go as I remind myself this is why I didn't tell her earlier.

I crack a smile, and lean against the locker next to hers, trying to act like it doesn't bother me, and then proceed with my request. "I'm meeting him at eight, but I don't know how late I'll be back, so I want to tell my parents I'm going to be at your house…"

"Oh my God! It's finally going to happen!" Jenna says gleefully, cutting me off mid-sentence.

I wish I could say I didn't know what she meant, but I know exactly what she's talking about. "This is our first real date, it is *so* not going to happen tonight," I tell her.

"He's a junior in college. I promise you, it's going to happen," she says confidently. "I can't wait til you get it over with and finally know what it's like," Jenna says, discussing my virginity as if it's like jumping off the high dive at the town pool. Jenna was the first to go, losing hers at the end of freshman year, but somewhere over the last year and a half everyone else in our group has also had sex, leaving me the token virgin.

"So, can I tell my parents I'm at your house? It won't matter, but just in case something happens, will you cover for me?" I ask, trying to change the subject.

"On one condition," Jenna says, grinning at me.

"What?" I ask, unsure what to expect.

"You have to tell me everything! Actually, you should come straight to my house after your date and then you can tell all of us right away!" she squeals. "Unless you end up sleeping over in his dorm! Then just call me in the morning," she says, trying to wink at me and then cracking up at herself.

"There is no way I am sleeping over in his dorm room," I reply. "And I bet nothing else is even going to happen," I say to her, but I definitely don't feel as confident as I sound. I'm not planning on waiting until I'm married or anything, but I did want to wait until it was with a boyfriend and not just a hook-up. Mary has been dating Todd for three years and like me, she seems to think that it's a big deal, but Jenna and my other friends act like it's just what you do at a party when you're bored – doesn't mean anything – no strings attached – "sex is just whatever" (that's literally what Jenna always says).

"Text me tonight when you are on your way and I'll unlock the door so my parents don't hear, not that they would care," she adds.

"Okay, I will," I say, resigned that this is my only option. "We better go, or we'll be late for practice," I remind her. Only another few hours to trudge through before tonight becomes a reality – after talking to Jenna, I am even more nervous than I was before, although I didn't think that was possible.

***

Surveying myself one final time in the mirror, I determine that it's not going to get any better and this is the best it's going to get. I've watched Jenna look at her reflection (she checks herself out as often as possible) and it's clear she's quite happy with what she sees staring back at her, but I don't think I'll ever be that girl. I catch my mom staring at herself too; sometimes she checks out her perfectly toned ass, always on the hunt for cellulite, but more recently she's focusing on the imaginary wrinkles on her forehead. I'm sure she'll start to get Botox and fillers soon like all of her friends, but she barely looks thirty-five, let alone over forty. I would never give her the satisfaction of telling her that, but she is by far the youngest looking and hottest of all the moms around.

I survey my outfit one more time – black skinny jeans (with plenty of stretch, so they are actually comfortable and *somewhat* flattering), a crimson lace camisole that is suggestive without being too slutty and black three-inch ankle boots. Thankfully my hair didn't decide that tonight was the night to stop being the one thing I can rely on, and it hangs in a shimmering wave down my back – my trusty companion. I tried not to go overboard with the eye makeup, because I heard somewhere that college girls actually wear less makeup than high school girls, and most of the girls I've seen at Yale actually wear no makeup and sweats most of the time. At the last minute I grab my denim jacket from my closet in case it gets cold, but mostly so I don't have to answer any questions from my parents about my outfit.

"I'm going over to Jenna's," I announce, as I reach the bottom of the stairs. "I'll be back tomorrow morning," I call out to the empty living room. I practically tiptoe across the room, hoping to make a clean escape. I already asked my dad about going to Jenna's when I got home and he said I could have the car overnight as long as I'm home by nine, so there's no reason I have to say any formal goodbyes.

"Have a good time!" my mom says, popping her head in from the kitchen.

"Thanks," I say, reaching for the door.

"Who's going to be there?" she asks casually.

"Just a few girls," I tell her.

"Sydney," she says. All she says is my name, but there is so much loaded into that one word.

"Jenna, Emma, Kate and Naya," I tell her, trying not to let my frustration show.

"That should be fun," she says, trying to keep the conversation going.

"Yup, it will be fun. I'll be back in the morning," I tell her.

"And you girls are staying at Jenna's the whole time?" she prods.

"Yes, Mom," I say, looking toward the front door while I roll my eyes and then plastering a smile on my face when I turn around.

"You girls are always going out, it's nice that you are staying home for a change. It's almost like when you were younger – you can stay up late and eat junk food and watch movies," she says excitedly.

"Yeah, sounds great. I gotta go. I'll be back tomorrow," I tell her, desperately trying to make it out the door to freedom.

"Drive safely! Text me when you get there," she calls out, as I'm about to close the door.

"What?" I ask, completely surprised by this request. "You want me to text you in five minutes when I get to Jenna's?"

"It's more like ten minutes; and it's Friday night *and* you are borrowing our car, so yes, I think it is reasonable that you text me when you get there. Do you have a problem with that?" my mom counters.

"Nope. I'll let you know when I'm there," I tell her through a tight smile, and I slam the door behind me.

Shit, now I'm going to have to pull over in ten minutes and tell her that I'm at Jenna's. If either of my parents had a newer car,

I could just use the voice activated text and do it while I'm driving, but both of our cars are too old to have that technology. I have friends who text and drive, but it just doesn't seem worth it, and I'd probably be the one to get pulled over doing it, and *that* definitely doesn't seem worth it. Besides, I'm not meeting Brandon for another hour, so I have plenty of time to get to Fairfield.

***

I didn't end up having quite as much extra time as I thought, because there is absolutely nowhere to park on a college campus! I never have to worry about it in New Haven because we have Yale parking permits, but everywhere I tried to park is zoned for one type of parking or another – after thirty minutes of searching, I found something that I desperately hope is a legal parking spot and then had to text Brandon and explain why I'm running late.

Sydney: On my way. Couldn't find parking. Think I'm walking the right way ☺

Brandon: np – where ru?

Sydney: just past science center? Think I see it now

Brandon: Yes campus center is next building. I see you…

I tuck my phone in my back pocket and give myself a minute to look around and take a deep breath before this actually happens. This is all I've thought about all week, but now that Brandon is walking toward me, I can't believe I am really here and going through with it. He is even hotter than I remember. Tonight his thick, dark brown hair is flopping onto his forehead and almost into his eyes – last week it was tucked into a baseball hat. His hair is longer than most of the guys' hair at school, but it is yet another thing that I like about him. He's wearing faded jeans and a quarter-zip hunter green sweater that matches the green in his eyes perfectly. To finish off his look, he has on clunky hiking boots, but they're perfect – rugged and outdoorsy and so sexy.

"Hey," Brandon says, when we meet up on the path. He leans in and gives me a kiss on the cheek and I can smell his cologne or body spray or whatever it is and he smells just as good as he did last week.

"Hey," I echo back, returning his kiss, and trying to act like I do things like this all the time.

"Sorry about the parking. I should have thought about that," he apologizes.

"It's okay," I say, thinking it's adorable that he is apologizing. I can't imagine a single boy in school who would apologize for anything!

"There's a show at the student center at nine thirty, so I thought that could be fun, but we could do something else if you want?" he offers.

"That sounds great!" I tell him.

"Do you want to get coffee first?" he asks. "Or did you eat yet? Do you want to get something to eat?" he asks.

"Coffee would be great," I tell him.

We walk in silence for a minute toward what I assume is the Campus Center and I look around at the campus on Friday night. Although I've spent countless hours with my dad at Yale, I haven't spent much time there on a Friday night. I assume it's similar to this – students walking around in groups and pairs, yelling, laughing, on their way to parties, and a few loners with backpacks on their way to the library (maybe there are more of those outsiders at Yale).

Brandon breaks the silence as we are walking into the Campus Center and he holds the heavy door open for me. "I'm sure it's not as fancy as Yale, but we should be able to get you some coffee," he jokes, steering me toward the Einstein Brothers Coffee counter. We both order coffee with milk and sugar and find our way to an empty table in the corner. This part of the Campus Center seems to be pretty empty for eight on a Friday night; but I guess most people are off at parties or bars – maybe it's lame, but I'm so glad that we're *not* doing that.

"Have you been to the campus?" I ask him, while we're stirring our coffee.

"Just for soccer," he replies, with a grin.

"Oh right, of course," I say, feeling stupid.

"That's our easiest road trip," he laughs. "But I haven't really been to the campus. Do you like it?" he asks.

"I do. So far so good," I tell him, thinking that's a pretty simple answer.

"Freshman year can be hard. Do you like your roommate?" he asks.

I take a sip of my coffee and try to figure out how I'm going to answer this question – or how I'm going to answer any of his questions!

"I have three roommates. We're all pretty different, but I do like them," I tell him.

"You have *three* roommates? That's awful," Brandon says.

"Well, it's not so bad. We each have our own room and then we share a common room," I explain.

"Wait, that's awesome. That's not three roommates, that's like you have no roommates! If you can close the door and get rid of them, that's all that counts," he says definitively. "And you have that as a freshman? That's crazy," he says, shaking his head.

"It's pretty great," I say. Ainsley's roommate set-up *is* pretty great – although Brandon is probably right, that they would only give that to juniors and not to freshman, but I didn't think about that…

The rest of our coffee date continues with fun conversation and thankfully I am able to remember a lot more from Ainsley's freshman year and by the end, I have morphed my life with hers and somehow become a version of my pre-med cousin who also loves drawing, painting and eighties music (I wanted to let him know as many real things about me as I could). The only bizarre thing is that it seems like he just wants to be friends. We have been talking and laughing the whole time, but he hasn't tried to kiss me or touch me and he seems to really want to go to this show and not go back to his room or anything – I guess Jenna was right about me not being his type.

***

Two hours later, I'm driving down I-95 to Jenna's house with absolute certainty that Brandon is interested in me. The show turned out to be an improv show that a couple of his friends were in, and it was hilarious. I didn't get all of the jokes, because some of them were about student life or professors at Fairfield, but I laughed so hard I had tears in my eyes. Then Brandon insisted on walking me back to my car; which I was thrilled by, because even if he didn't like me, I was worried about walking by myself and about getting lost. But when we got to my car, he told me how much fun he had, and said that I'm different from all the girls he knows and then he kissed me. It wasn't the type of kiss that I've had with a few boys from school, where it's wet and sloppy and suddenly they are grinding up against you, as if the kiss has made them so horny they can't control themselves. Brandon's kiss was soft and deliberate at the same time (I know that sounds weird) and his lips were soft, but not at all wet, and it was like he held me, but didn't push against me, and didn't expect anything else – in other words, it was perfect. Then he said he wanted to see me again, *and* told me I'm beautiful…

In a moment of stupidity, I told him we could meet at Yale next time, but I'll figure out how to fix that. Right now, I need to decide what I'm going to tell Jenna when I get to her house – I know she isn't going to believe I spent four hours alone with a college guy and we kissed once. She would definitely have slept with him, or at the very least, given him a blowjob. I know its only one date, but Brandon isn't like that, I can just tell, he's different – he's special. Jenna definitely won't understand; and honestly, I don't even want to try to explain it to her because she won't get it.

***

"Tell us everything!" Jenna demands, when I walk into her house forty-five minutes later. The girls are all wearing pajamas and sitting around the kitchen table; everyone has a beer bottle and shot glass in front of them, and there is a bottle of Smirnoff in the middle of the enormous farmhouse table.

"We're playing 'I Never' and you're just in time!" Naya shouts, patting a spot on the bench next to her.

"Aren't your parents going to be back soon?" I ask Jenna, dropping my stuff by the door, and taking my seat at the table.

"They decided to stay over in the City tonight," she says bluntly. "Don't change the subject," she directs. Now I can tell that she is starting to slur her words and I'm guessing they didn't just start playing the game, or at least they were playing some other game before this. "So what happened with the hot soccer guy?" she asks.

"Wait!" Jenna screams, interrupting herself. "I've never had sex," she laughs, taking her turn at the game, and then taking a huge pull from the beer bottle in front of her to let us all know that of course this is something she *has* done.

All of my friends go around the table and follow her lead by drinking their beers, which is not a surprise, since we all know that everyone has done it by this point. I don't think Jenna really expected me to lose my virginity tonight, but she's drunk and she thought it would be a funny way to ask, and to confirm my status yet again. But then I surprise both of us, by picking up my beer and chugging the entire bottle.

Jenna screams and runs over to hug me, and I can barely hear through everyone's cheering and chants of "finally" and "it's about time!" I've learned enough from all of their endless sex stories that I will be able to answer any questions and now I can keep the real Brandon to myself.

Chapter Nine
Jack

"Did you girls have fun last night?" I ask Sydney as she enters the kitchen. I heard her come home this morning around eight, even earlier than promised, but she went straight to her room, and four hours later is the first time she's emerged.

"Yeah, it was great," she says casually, making her way to the fridge and opening both of the French doors of the brand new stainless steel appliance that we finally broke down and bought after repairing our vintage Whirpool for years. "Is there *anything* to eat for lunch?" she asks, staring at the excessively packed fridge.

"I was just going to make something for your brother and sister, what would you like?" Ellie asks, chiming in.

"Anything," she mumbles, as she sits down at the table next to me. I close my laptop in the hopes of having a conversation, but the moment her butt touches the chair, her phone is out, her eyes are glued to the screen and her thumbs are typing furiously – it's a miracle that she and her friends don't all have carpal tunnel or some other ailment yet.

"Do you want me to make tuna salad?" Ellie asks, putting an assortment of cold cuts, vegetables, cheeses, and other containers on the counter.

"Ew, that's gross," she replies, not taking her eyes off her phone.

"I thought you liked tuna?" Ellie asks, opening the deli container of tuna and then quickly closing it after smelling it, as if she also thinks it's gross, which is not going to help her argument with Sydney.

"Maybe I used to like tuna when I was little, but not anymore," Sydney says with disgust.

"We could order Chinese?" I offer, trying to be helpful, since I know Sydney loves Chinese food.

"Oh yes, I would love Chinese," Sydney says, actually looking up from her phone to smile at me.

"But we have all this food," Ellie protests, gesturing to the display in front of her.

"Right, of course," I say, trying to backtrack. "Sorry Syd, maybe we'll get Chinese for dinner?"

"No, I really want Chinese now. You suggested it and it sounds so good," she whines.

"Isn't Chinese food a little heavy for lunch?" Ellie says, trying a different tactic.

"People do eat things other than salads, you know," Sydney mutters under her breath, but it's too quiet for Ellie to hear her. I try to catch her eye to give her a look, but her mane of glossy brown hair is covering her face and she won't give me the satisfaction of making eye contact.

At that exact moment, Izzy runs into the kitchen, closely followed by Max. They have been playing in the backyard together since we returned from Max's football practice earlier this morning. They are both covered in dirt and Izzy's hair is full of leaves, but it is such a rarity that they will do anything together anymore without fighting, that I'm certainly not going to mention the state of their hygiene and I hope Ellie won't either.

"I'm starving!" Max declares. "What are we having for lunch?"

"Dad said we could have Chinese, but Mom won't let us," Sydney answers.

"I want Chinese!" Izzy squeals, jumping up and down, the dry, crunchy leaves falling out of her hair as she jumps.

"Why can't we get Chinese?" Max asks Ellie. "I'm soooo hungry, and I don't want another sandwich, that's what I have *every* day."

"Please Mommy!" Izzy begs.

"Fine, you can all do what you want. You're in charge." Ellie says, glaring at me, as she throws the plastic-wrapped bag of American cheese down on the counter and storms out of the room.

"Looks like we get Chinese food," Sydney says, still texting away furiously on her phone.

"I'll get the menu," Max says, pulling out the old, stained menu from the cabinet in the kitchen. Even though our favorite Chinese place moved to Grubhub years ago, and now we only need the app to order as much greasy Kung Pao chicken as we want, the kids still insist on using the obsolete menu to make their selections.

"Wait guys, don't order anything yet, let me go talk to Mom," I tell them.

As I leave the kitchen, I hear Izzy shout, "I'm getting the sesame noodles."

I find Ellie sitting in the living room (the formal room that we keep ready for visitors and actually utilize about three times a year). She is on the ivory couch, her legs tucked up underneath her, staring out the window into the backyard where the trees are just starting to change into the brilliant reds, oranges and yellows of autumn.

"You okay?" I ask her.

"Yeah, I'm fine," she says, unconvincingly.

"Sorry about the food. I'll tell them we aren't going to order Chinese food and we'll just eat what we have here, okay?" I say, trying to pacify her.

"What? Oh, whatever, I don't care," she says, still staring out the window.

"Are you sure?" I ask, taking a seat on the matching ivory ottoman and sitting down across from her.

"If we don't order, then I'm the bad guy, and Sydney will just be mad at me; and if we do order, you're the good guy for letting them order it," she says, without emotion.

"That's not true," I try to argue, but I know she's right.

"Honestly, I don't care about the food. Just go ahead and order it. I think I'm going to go upstairs and take a nap," she says, slowly pulling herself up from the sofa to a standing position.

"Are you *sure* you're okay?" I ask, since her behavior doesn't lead me to believe that she is.

Ellie looks at me and opens her mouth as if she's going to say something and closes it again. When she opens it again, she says, "I'm really tired, maybe I'm coming down with something," and she walks upstairs like a zombie, leaving me sitting in the immaculate room, surrounded by knick knacks, picture frames and crystal vases, wondering what the hell is going on.

***

Even with the traffic, the drive to campus this Monday morning is a welcome escape. It's a beautiful October day. It will certainly warm up later, but right now it is the ideal autumn temperature and my mood has lifted immensely since departing from the tension that hung over our house all weekend. The air is crisp, the last trace of summer's humidity finally gone, and the sky is a stunning shade of peacock blue. It's days like today that I couldn't imagine teaching anywhere other than Yale. As I walk across the quad, I notice a photographer shooting pictures of one of the buildings and the group of students huddled together on the lawn and I silently applaud them, because they could not have found a better day to take pictures for the brochures and websites – nothing could look like a more beautiful day at Yale than today.

I'm actually whistling (not something I usually do), when I enter the economics department. Although I didn't intend to be here quite this early, I'm pleased to be here before Ginny and most of my colleagues, so I can skip the pleasantries of weekend catch-ups, close my door and get to work.

I'm so focused on getting into my office without running into anyone, that I barely notice the student sitting on the floor in front of my door.

"Can I help you?" I ask her. She doesn't look at all familiar to me, but I do have some students who sit in the back of my lectures and never speak in class, so it's possible she is in one of my classes, or was in class a previous semester. She looks relatively young, so she must be an undergrad, probably a freshman; but I've learned over the years, never to assume with the girls – I have grad students who look fifteen, and freshman who look twenty-three.

"Are you Professor Miller?" she asks, still seated on the floor, blocking my door.

"I am," I reply.

"Do you have a few minutes to talk?" she asks.

"Actually, I have specific hours designated to meet with students. I have some work I need to attend to right now, but if you can come back tomorrow at eleven, I would be happy to meet with you," I tell her, hoping she will get the message and remove herself from the floor without any further instruction.

"I'm not a student here," she says, staring directly up at me.

I want to tell her that it's irrelevant, because I have work to do; but something about the way she sticks out her chin and maintains eye contact, as if daring me to look away, makes me think otherwise. "Why don't we go into my office?" I suggest, resigning myself to the loss of time.

"Thank you," she says, pulling herself up in one graceful motion. At her full height she is only a couple inches shorter than I am, and quite striking with long dark hair, olive skin and bright blue eyes.

I unlock the door to my office and she follows me inside. I hesitate with my hand on the door handle and decide to leave it open – nothing good can come from being alone with a young girl in a closed office these days, the risks are simply too high. She must have noticed my hesitation, because she glances at the solid oak door and says, "it's okay. You can close it."

"That's fine, let's leave it open. What can I help you with?" I ask her, trying to move this along so I can get to work.

"You may want it closed," she says, easily rising from her seat, closing the door and then returning to face me in the burgundy leather guest chair across from my desk.

Her action is so surprising that I find myself momentarily unable to speak. Students constantly surround me, but they all defer to me, especially the undergrads, and certainly when they are here in my office. It isn't meant to be this way, but I've been told that my office is particularly intimidating with the bookshelves lined with the books I've contributed to and then the hundreds of books of economic theory which I've mastered, as well as the photos on the wall of me with CEO's and top academics. However, this strange girl seems to be the one calling the shots and I don't even know who she is or why she's here.

"I don't think I caught your name," I say bluntly, letting my impatience show through.

"That's because I didn't tell you my name," she says, crossing her slim legs.

Just as I'm about to tell her to leave because I don't have time for her nonsense, I notice that her leg is shaking, and she is using her hand to attempt to steady the vibration. I can't be sure, but it seems her audacity may be a cover for nerves.

"Would you like some water?" I ask, trying a different tactic, as well as attempting to have patience.

"Yes, please," she replies.

I reach behind my desk to the small refrigerator and procure two small bottles of Evian and put them on the desk for us.

"Thank you," she says, opening the bottle and drinking almost half of it in one swallow.

"My name is Hailey," the girl says.

"What can I do for you, Hailey?" I ask, trying to ease her nerves and get this sorted so I can open up my emails and get started with my day.

Hailey takes a deep breath and looks at with me with her bright blue eyes and says three life-changing words.

"You're my dad."

***

The drive home is a cruel joke. Only ten hours ago, I sat in this same car, driving the opposite direction and I took some pleasure in the beautiful autumn day, but I was worried about my "problems" at home. Now the sky is filled with the beginning of a spectacular sunset – oranges and pinks fill the sky, and I can't even begin to enjoy them. I wish I could go back to this morning when I thought a few tense moments over the weekend meant problems – ha! If only I knew that those would be my last uncomplicated moments, I would have savored them more. Now I have to go home and figure out how to tell Ellie about the love child from my past!

I keep going over and over the conversation with Hailey – but it's really pretty simple. I cheated on Ellie once in our whole relationship. I was so drunk during Richie's bachelor party that I barely remember even having sex, but I remember enough to know that it happened. When I came back from Austin, the guilt was so bad it ate at me for months, but it gradually went away, and eventually I almost forgot about it – until today.

Apparently, Nikki (that was her name) was only twenty on that fateful night and she got pregnant. Nikki's parents lived in Austin and they took over and raised Hailey so that Nikki could graduate from college and then tragically Nikki died from breast cancer when Hailey was only eleven, so her grandparents continued to raise her. To add to this poor girl's troubles, her grandmother died a few years ago and her grandfather died this past year; but as Hailey made a point of telling me, she is eighteen now, and she is fine on her own.

As life shattering as the conversation was, I'm glad I still had the paternal instincts to ask why it took her so long to find me. I don't know what would have happened if Nikki had come to me eighteen years ago, but Hailey did have a quick answer for that question. Nikki and her grandparents wouldn't tell her who I was until she turned eighteen, so she only found out a few months ago. Once her grandfather died, she deferred her admission to UT and decided to come live with her aunt in Manhattan for the year and also to meet me – and that's how we got to today.

I am barely able to process this news, and I can't imagine how I am going to tell Ellie any of this, but I know the best way to do it is going to be to tell her as soon as I get home. I should have told her nineteen years ago when I cheated, but it can't wait any longer.

***

As if she knows we need to talk, Ellie is waiting for me in the living room when I walk into the house. She is perched on the edge of the couch wearing jeans and a light yellow sweater. On the coffee table in front of her there is a plate of cheese, grapes and almonds and there is a glass of untouched bourbon with two ice cubes sitting in front of what I can only assume is my seat.

"Come, sit," Ellie instructs, but she is smiling at me, something I haven't seen much of the last week or so.

I hesitate as I slowly make my way over to the couch. I don't know what she has planned, but I know that I need to tell her right away, before I lose my nerve. A small part of me wonders if she already knows and this is some sort of trap, but she isn't like that. If she knew, she wouldn't have given me a glass of bourbon and cheese – she would have met me in the driveway and started screaming.

"How was your day?" Ellie asks.

"It was interesting," I say. "How was yours?"

"It was okay," she says, pausing, "I have something to tell you."

"I actually have something to tell you too," I say, thankful for the opening.

"Me first," she says, balling her hands into fists.

"What is it?" I ask, feeling a sense of déjà vu and wishing this day would end.

"I'm pregnant," Ellie says, her face twisting into a sad smile, before she breaks into hysterical sobs.

Chapter Ten
Ellie

"Are you serious?" Jack says, shaking his head, with complete disbelief in his tone. "A baby?" he says quietly, with tears starting to form in the corner of his eyes.

"Crazy, right?" I say, trying to gauge his reaction.

"Holy crap," Jack says, reaching out and taking my hand in his and squeezing it tightly.

"I'm still trying to get my head around it. I'm not really sure what to think," I admit.

"We talked about having a fourth…but that was a long time ago. And every time I brought it up, you said I was nuts," Jack says. He has let go of my hands and is now pressing his palms together in a way that I would never encourage my yoga students to do because it looks the opposite of relaxing.

"Because it *is* nuts! This would be completely ridiculous," I say to Jack, which is the same thing I have been telling myself since the moment I took the test. "But it could also be great," I whisper, my feelings on a minute-by-minute rollercoaster.

"You don't really mean that, do you?" Jack asks.

"I know, we're too old to have a baby," I start to say and Jack is quick to interrupt me.

"Ellie, you are the youngest forty-three year old in the world, but we have a sixteen-year old for Christ sakes! How can we possibly have a baby when we have a kid who's going to be in college in two years!" He exclaims.

I watch Jack's features start to change as he continues to mull this over. His warm brown eyes lose the sparkle they always have and I swear to God I see a few more gray hairs appear as he starts to think about putting a fourth child through college. Jack's ever-present smile is completely gone and even through his end-of the day stubble, I can see the tiny lines around his mouth become more pronounced (of course on Jack, frown lines have made him more attractive as he's gotten older, while they have made me slather on expensive night creams and start saving for collagen treatments).

"I would be sixty-five when it graduated from high school. And you would be sixty-one," he says sadly.

"I think Alec Baldwin and Mel Gibson both had babies when they were over sixty, or something like that," I tell him.

"What? How do you even know that? And is that who you really want to compare me to?" he asks.

"No, of course not. I'm just saying that forty-seven isn't *that* old to have a baby," I reply.

"Are you forgetting that I'm not a celebrity?" he challenges.

"Depends who you ask," I say, grinning at Jack

Jack looks back at me with his impish smile, and for a tiny moment I forget about the enormity of our discussion and I allow myself to laugh. In the world of economics, Jack is somewhat of a celebrity – to the very, very small group of people who care about his exact specialty. I am occasionally reminded of this when I go to a conference with him and there are a few students who ask him to sign a textbook, or ask to take selfies with him.

"Fair enough," he replies. "But unfortunately, being a celebrity in the world of economics, doesn't pay quite like being a movie star. I don't think Alec Baldwin or Mel Gibson had to think about the cost of childcare or college tuition or having enough bedrooms in their house," he says.

Jack picks up his glass of bourbon with the melted ice cubes, and then right before he brings it to his lips he says, "do you mind?"

"Of course not," I reply. "Why do you think I put it there? I probably should have brought the whole bottle. I think this situation calls for a few drinks, don't you?" I ask.

Jack takes an enormous swig from his drink before replying. "It certainly does. Quite ironic that you can't have anything, huh?" he says. "Although I guess it wouldn't really matter if you had something, right?" Jack asks, taking another sip.

"What do you mean?" I say, staring at Jack.

He looks down at the floor as if he has never seen the intricate patterns on our Oriental carpet before, and takes a deep breath before looking up to face me. "If we aren't going to keep it, then maybe you can still drink?" he suggests.

"Wait a minute," I say, pushing myself away from him on the couch. "I know we said it was crazy, but we *just* started to talk about it, I don't think we've made any kind of decision yet," I say, angrily. I know it's not fair of me to be quite this upset, since I've spent the past five days convinced that I wasn't going to keep this baby, and only in the past ten minutes talking to Jack have I thought about trying to make it work.

"I know. Right. Of course not, but I just can't think of a scenario where it makes sense," he says, shaking his head.

"I know. It doesn't make sense. I keep going over and over it in my head, and it's totally crazy – but what if it's not?" I ask.

"When did you find out? How far along are you?" Jack asks, as if he's only now remembering to ask these questions.

I feel the tears starting to form again and I rub my hands against my eyes to wipe them away. I keep remembering the other three times when we found out I was pregnant and how those discussions were so different from this one. Even as a memory, it doesn't seem fair to play favorites; but finding out about Sydney was definitely the most exciting of the three pregnancies. We were still living in our tiny apartment in the City and Jack was a new professor at NYU and I had recently gotten my Masters in Social Work and was working at a rehab clinic. I had been off the pill for four months, but we had friends who had been trying for almost a year without any luck, so we were convinced that we were going to have trouble as well. I started feeling tired and nauseous almost immediately, but I wanted to wait and take the test and then buy silly t-shirts and create an elaborate surprise for Jack when he got home from work. But I was so excited that I called Jack from Duane Reade as soon as I bought the test and he came home early from work and we sat on the bathroom floor together and watched in joy as the test showed news of our success and impending parenthood!

It is tearing me apart to think about how ecstatic that news made us and how miserable I feel right now. "I found out a few days ago," I tell him. "I should have told you sooner, but I just needed some time to process it."

"I get it," Jack replies sadly. I don't know if he really means he gets it, but I am grateful that he's choosing not to make a big deal of it.

"I think I'm about five and a half weeks. It must have happened in the Hamptons," I tell him.

"How is that possible?" Jack asks, draining his glass of bourbon.

I give him the look that says he knows exactly how that's possible, and he looks back at me sheepishly. For two intelligent adults, we have been known to play it fast and loose with birth control and we've gotten pretty lucky. Until now.

***

I think we are both relieved to have our conversation interrupted by Izzy's screams as she runs into the room yelling about something Max has done to her and she jumps into Jack's arms for refuge.

Max follows a few paces behind her and slides on the hardwood in his socks, yelling, "She's lying! Whatever she tells you is a lie!"

"I don't even want to hear it," Jack says to both of them.

"But, he said..." Izzy begins to whine, and Jack quickly cuts her off. "I said I don't want to hear it. Both of you go finish your homework and get ready for dinner," he says with authority, gently depositing Izzy's gangly body back onto the living room carpet and rising from the sofa.

"What even *is* for dinner?" Max asks, "I'm starving."

All three heads turn to look at me, since I am obviously the one who is supposed to know the answer to that question. Like most other mothers, this question haunts me each and every day, "What's for dinner?" Seemingly so simple, but feeding five people every night is a thankless task; especially five people who don't like the same things and who easily tire of eating the same seven things in my repertoire. I never thought twice about it when I was growing up, but my mom used to make a calendar each month and would hang it in the kitchen with our meal plan announcing thirty different dinners and what nights we could expect them, and then she would stick to her plan come hell or high water (one of her favorite sayings). I took it for granted, as kids do, but I have no idea how she did it – I can barely manage to figure out what I'm going to cook more than two nights in a row. Yet another thing to add to the list of questions I wish I had asked her before she passed away.

Izzy snaps me out of it by adding to her brother's inquisition, "What *are* we having? Please say it isn't chicken!" she pleads.

I glance at my watch and see that it is already six-fifteen, not an unreasonable time for my family to ask for dinner; but I had been so focused on preparing to talk to Jack, that I hadn't really given any thought to dinner. I try and envision what's currently in the fridge to see if there is anything in there that will work, and unfortunately I'm not coming up with much that is going to satisfy this group.

"Breakfast for dinner?" I suggest, throwing out an old favorite from when the kids were little. I don't think we've ever had it when all five of us were home, but sometimes you've got to work with what you have.

"Yay!" Izzy shouts, clearly thrilled with the suggestion. "Can we have chocolate chips in the pancakes? And whipped cream?" she asks hopefully, all memories of her fight with Max seemingly forgotten.

"We'll see," Jack says.

"That is *not* a real dinner," Max says, folding his arms over his chest and glaring at me.

I'm attempting not to laugh, or even crack a smile, but Max is at such an awkward stage that I can't help seeing him as a little boy when he puts on a display like this (especially when his voice cracks when he's trying to make his point). He and Izzy both share my blonde hair and he likes to think he is getting the tiniest bit of blonde hair on his upper lip, but I swear there is nothing there. Although, I did see hair under his armpits this summer at the beach and I don't even want to think about what else might be happening, but from the amount of time he is spending alone in his room, I can only imagine.

"What's not a real dinner?" Sydney asks, joining the conversation. I didn't hear her come in, but she must have gotten dropped off and come through the kitchen while we were talking.

"We're having breakfast for dinner," Max says, with disgust.

"How fun! We haven't had that in forever!" Sydney says, looking genuinely excited. "Do you need any help?" she asks.

Now I really don't know what to make of this situation. If anyone was going to complain, I assumed it would be Sydney; but now she seems excited *and* she's offered to help?! It's like the twilight zone.

Jack and I exchange glances as if to say, "Is this really our daughter? Let's proceed with caution so we don't spoil it"

"I'd love some help," I say, carefully.

"We can *all* help," Jack says, looking pointedly at Max.

"There better be a lot of sausage," Max says, realizing that he's lost the battle, but not giving up without having the last word.

"I'll get the chocolate chips!" Izzy says happily, as she runs ahead to the kitchen and Sydney, Max and Jack follow behind her.

As I gather up the untouched plate of appetizers, I listen to the joyful noises from the banter in the kitchen and my heart swells as I think about how lucky I am to have such an amazing family. We're perfect the way we are right now, so maybe Jack's right and another baby would ruin everything – or maybe it would make it even better…

Chapter Eleven
Sydney

"Do you want to come over after school today? Practice is cancelled because of the rain," Jenna says, as we're walking through the hall from history to math class.

"Huh?" I reply, trying to listen to her as I type a quick text back to Brandon between classes.

"What are you smiling about?" she says, and then she reaches out and grabs my phone out of my hand.

"Give it back!" I yell so loudly that students gathered at their lockers turn their heads to stare.

"Chill out," Jenna says, handing me my phone. "I was just kidding. I don't see what the big deal is anyway. I always show you my texts," she says defensively.

"Sorry," I say quietly, unable to come up with anything better, but desperately relieved to have my phone back. She does always show me all of her texts from her latest hook-ups and we usually scrutinize them for insights about underlying innuendo, or we laugh at the guys who are too eager. But Brandon is different. He isn't just a hook-up; and I can't have Jenna tearing apart his messages, because he's too good for that.

"I can't today," I tell her. "My mom wants me to come home," I lie. Brandon told me last night that he doesn't have any classes this afternoon, so I'm going to try to FaceTime him this afternoon; and I know my mom has class this afternoon, so I'll have the house to myself!

"I could come to your house?" Jenna offers.

I pause to carefully consider my answer before I respond. "I just remembered that my mom wants me home to babysit Izzy," I tell her.

"I've been there a million times when you've babysat," Jenna reminds me, pushing the issue, and pursing her perfectly glossed lips as she waits for my response.

"I know, my mom's just being really weird and I don't want to piss her off any more," I answer, relying on my standard excuse.

"Okay, whatevs," Jenna says, as we arrive at the door to my calculus classroom and separate as Jenna walks down the hall to her math class.

***

Back at home, I relish the silence and try not to feel too guilty about lying to Jenna as I get up my nerve to FaceTime Brandon. We've been texting non-stop since our date on Friday night, but this is completely different.

I inspect my makeup in the mirror one more time and use a tissue to blot my berry lipstick. I washed my face when I got home from school and re-did all of my makeup, but now I'm worried it looks like I'm trying too hard; oh well, maybe he won't be able to tell over the phone.

I dial his number and hold my breath while I wait to see if he answers…holy shit, it says it's connecting, I guess this is really happening!

"Hey," Brandon says as his magnificent face appears on my phone, with a heart-melting grin.

"Hey," I reply, returning his smile.

"What's going on?" he asks.

"Not much. I'm just doing some studying, but thought I would call you and say hi," I tell him. Considering that I thought about calling him all day, I should have planned something slightly more intelligent to say.

"Where are you?" Brandon asks.

"What?" I ask, my radar on high alert.

"Is that your dorm room? That's crazy – that doesn't look like the dorms at Fairfield!" Brandon exclaims.

I can't believe that I'm this much of an idiot! I look at my tiny reflection and see a portion of my bed with the mahogany headboard in the view, as well as the navy and white drapes in the background – there is no way in a million years that I could pretend this was a dorm room. And what if he asks to see the rest of the room, what would I do then?! Thankfully, much of what I told Brandon is truthful and I am able to think quickly with my reply.

"I'm actually at home in Westport. My mom needed my help with a few things, so I came home for the afternoon and I'm getting some studying done here. I'll go back to school after dinner," I tell him, praying it sounds believable.

"Man, I'm so jealous. It must be so nice to go home whenever you want and get dinner or get your laundry done," Brandon says.

"There are pros and cons," I tell him, trying to make a joke, and thrilled that I'm off the hook.

"If I lived that close to school, I know my parents would make me live at home," Brandon says.

"Yeah, I'm pretty lucky," I reply, not sure what else I can say. "Hey, where are *you*?" I ask, trying to change the subject.

"I'm outside the training room. We have conditioning practice today," Brandon tells me. "Actually, I should probably go. It starts in a few minutes and Coach gets really mad if we're late."

"Oh right, of course," I say.

"Hey, do you want to stop here on your way back to New Haven tonight?" Brandon asks. "We could just get a coffee or something," he says, grinning at me again.

For a minute, I forget that I'm not a freshman at Yale who's driving back to school tonight and I almost accept his invitation, but then I remember that it's a Wednesday night and there is no way in hell I will be able to make it happen.

"I wish I could," I say, desperately meaning it, "but I can't do it tonight," I tell him.

"Okay. We'll figure something out. Maybe this weekend?" he suggests.

"That would be great," I gush.

"I gotta go," he says.

"Okay. Talk to you later," I say.

"You too," he says, and then my screen goes dark.

Just as I'm about to obsess about how long I have to wait to text him or call him again, or if he really means that he wants to see me this weekend, my phone chirps.

Brandon: so nice to see your beautiful face. Only thing better would be to see it in person. I have a soccer game on Saturday – want to come to the game and then we can hang after?

Sydney: Yes!

I hug my phone to my chest and jump around my room, feeling the plush carpet beneath my toes as I dance to the nonexistent music. I wonder if I should apologize to all the girls that I mocked for years for being so annoyingly happy and smug – I just didn't get it until now!

***

"Do you want to get together this weekend to study?" Chelsea questions, as we pack up after chemistry.

Chelsea isn't in my regular group of friends, but none of my other friends are taking AP chemistry. Although we've only ever hung out together to study, she's actually much cooler than I thought she would be. Although now I feel terrible that I ever thought that, because I know it was only because Jenna and Naya used to make fun of her. In middle school she was a little awkward, but now she has totally found herself, or whatever you call it. She wears tight black clothes, is constantly changing the color of her hair, interns somewhere in the City, she's brilliant, really funny *and* I'm convinced she is going to get into Oxford (her first choice for college) and probably everywhere else she applies.

"I don't think I can," I tell her, as I shove my massive textbook into my oversized black LL Bean backpack, and grumble to myself about the insane number of books we are expected to carry around every day. It's taking all of my willpower not to tell her that the reason I can't study with her tomorrow is that I have a date with Brandon! I don't think it would do much harm to tell her, but our friendship isn't really like that; so I have to keep it inside, even though it's killing me!

"Alright. Let me know if anything changes. I'm kind of worried about the test on Monday," Chelsea says.

"You ace *everything*," I remind her.

"Not everything," she says modestly, although I don't think she's ever even gotten an A minus. "But thermodynamics is a little harder, at least for *me*," Chelsea says.

Oh God, I haven't even started studying for the test yet, and if Chelsea thinks it's hard, then it must really be tough. "I might be able to do something on Sunday," I tell her, "but I'm supposed to do my SAT prep work on Sunday." I say, remembering that I *do* have a lot of work to do this weekend.

"I'm going to be studying all weekend, so text me if you have time," she says.

"K, I'll let you know," I tell her, although all I'm really thinking about is that I will see Brandon in twenty-six hours.

***

My mom is sitting at the kitchen table, eating a bagel with cream cheese when I get home after school. This might not be that remarkable for most people, but my mom almost never eats bagels (because of the carbs and the empty calories and all of the other horrors) and she certainly never eats them as a snack at four-thirty in the afternoon! If she ever snacks, she eats berries, or a *handful* of almonds, or kale chips.

90

"Hey Syd, how was your day?" she says, between mouthfuls.

"It was fine," I reply, still somewhat in shock. "Are you okay?" I ask her.

"Yeah, I'm fine," she says unconvincingly.

"How's your bagel?" I ask, unable to resist.

"It's delicious," she says. "It sounded so good, that I stopped and bought a dozen on the way home from work. There's more on the counter if you want one," she offers.

"I'm good right now, maybe later," I reply, heading to the fridge to get a Diet Coke. "Do you want one?" I ask her.

"No thanks," she says, taking another big bite of her bagel and washing it down with a sip of orange juice.

"Mom, do you think I can borrow a car tomorrow?" I ask hopefully. I don't need a fancy car like Jenna or Katie, but I hate that I am at my parents' mercy every time I want to go anywhere.

"Why do you need it?" she asks.

"A few of us are going to go watch a soccer game at Fairfield," I tell her. Unlike last time, I gave this a lot of thought and decided to stick as close to the truth as possible. Obviously, I can't say I'm going alone, because that would be too weird, but if I stick close to the truth, there is probably less of a chance of getting in trouble.

"I thought *everyone* had their own car," my mom says, clearly mocking me. She takes the last bite of her bagel and pushes back her chair to get up and immediately put her plate and glass in the gleaming stainless steel dishwasher (at least her need to clean still seems normal).

91

"*Almost* everyone," I say. "I'm going with Chelsea and one of her friends," I fib. "You know, the girl I usually study chemistry with?" My mom has only met her a couple times and doesn't even know her last name, so this feels safe – all of my other friends *do* have their own cars and I don't want to use them as my alibi this time.

"What time do you need the car?" she asks.

"The game is at two, so I would probably leave here around one and then Chelsea knows someone on the team and said we might hang out for a little bit after, so I would be back by ten?" I ask. "Please!" I plead with her, before she even gives me her answer.

I don't know why it is taking her so long to think about it, but she appears to be rummaging through the pantry while she holds my fate in her hands. She pulls out a package of Oreos and pulls two out of the package, and exclaims, "Aha! I thought these were in here!"

I feel like I am losing my mind as I watch my mom eat her Oreos over the kitchen sink. I want to ask if aliens have possessed her, but I don't want to ruin my chances of getting the car. She's still in her "work" clothes, sporting tiny black Athleta leggings and a turquoise open-backed long-sleeve top with a black sports bra peeking through; but with a few chocolate crumbs stuck to her upper lip, she looks imperfect for the first time ever.

"I think we can make do with one car tomorrow," she says.

"Thank you! Thank you!" I scream.

"*But*, you still need to text me to check in, *and* you have to be home by ten, even though that's before your curfew. You can't be gone all day and stay out any later than that," she says.

"Okay, that's fine! Thank you!" I scream again, running up the stairs, taking them two at a time and flopping on my bed to text Brandon and confirm plans for tomorrow.

Chapter Twelve
Jack

Every time I think I've forgotten about it, I remember again. I get lost in work for an hour at a time, but then something happens and I think about the baby or Hailey, *or* that I haven't told Ellie about Hailey yet, and I feel like I can't breathe. Yesterday was better because I had back-to-back lectures most of the day, so I barely had time to think about anything other than work. But then I had office hours in the afternoon, and I jumped every time a new student knocked on my door, expecting each one to be Hailey.

I'm not sure why I'm so scared of her. She claims that she doesn't want anything from me. She only wanted to meet me and possibly get to know me (if that's what *I* want to do). But there's no way it's that easy. I know it's uncouth, but I had to ask her about money, and she swore that she has plenty and didn't want any from me. I guess Nikki's family was well off and although she's been orphaned, Hailey is not without funds. And I guess she isn't technically an orphan either...

"Hey Jack," Rob says, appearing in my office doorway.

"Hey Rob," I reply.

Rob is another economics professor; he came to Yale from the University of Chicago last year. He's younger than I am (my guess would be late thirties), but he is definitely a great addition to the department – not surprisingly, the econ department is not usually known for its charismatic professors.

"I'm heading out in a few minutes, want to grab a beer before you head home?" he asks.

"Yes!" I reply, almost too eagerly.

"I've had that kind of day too," he laughs. "I'll grab my coat and meet you in the parking lot in ten?" he asks.

"Sounds good," I reply.

Twenty minutes later and we are seated at the bar at Elm City Social, halfway through our first beer with smoked wings and deviled eggs on their way.

"Rough week so far?" Rob asks, taking a drink from his pint of Sam Adams.

"You have no idea," I reply, shaking my head and glancing around at the sparsely populated bar. Thankfully we are here on a Tuesday night; I've only been here a few times on the weekends, but it's impossible to get a seat, let alone have a conversation.

"What happened?" Rob inquires.

For a moment, I consider telling him. I contemplate what it would be like to tell him that an eighteen-year old girl showed up at my office last week and announced that she is the baby I conceived when I was blackout drunk during a bachelor party. Oh, and then I could tell him that my wife is also pregnant with our fourth child and I would be in my fifties when this kid starts elementary school. But instead, all I say is, "You know, just family stuff," and I drain my beer and signal the bartender to bring us another round.

"I totally get it," Rob replies. I try to listen as he retells a fight he had with his wife over the weekend about who was supposed to take their daughter to a birthday party.

"How old are the kids now?" I ask him, partly to keep the conversation going and partly because I honestly can't remember.

"Emma is four and Tabitha is one," Rob says. Before I even have a chance to reply, he takes out his phone and starts to scroll through pictures of the girls, narrating as he goes.

"They're adorable," I tell him, although what I'm really thinking is that Sydney, Max and Izzy were all much cuter than these kids even on their least photogenic days. I know that's a terrible thing to think, but objectively, we had adorable babies. Everyone used to stop us on the street to tell us how cute they were – Sydney was even asked to be a model as a toddler, but Ellie didn't think it was a good idea (I still think she could have been the face of Baby Gap).

"Thanks," Rob says, clearly beaming at the thought of his children, even though moments before he was complaining about his parental duties.

"How's your research coming on the new book?" Rob asks. "I was hoping to pick your brain on some thoughts for an article I've been working on," Rob adds.

Staring down into the remains of my lager, I can't help but wonder what another baby would look like. Would it be another girl? Would Max get a brother? Would he or she be brunette like Sydney, or have blonde hair like Max and Izzy?

"Everything okay?" Rob asks.

"Yeah, sorry, all good, what did you say?" I ask, trying to give him my full attention, and shake the images out of my brain; but it's proving harder than I thought.

Chapter Thirteen
Ellie

Is it possible that I'm already gaining weight and I'm not even six weeks pregnant? I wonder incredulously as I tug on the waistband of my favorite navy blue leggings and sense an unfamiliar tightness. I stare down at my stomach and it's still pretty flat, but I swear that I'm thicker than I was a few days ago.

Even if the weight is all in my head, or more likely, due to the carb-only diet I've been on for the past three days, it is the push I need to call the doctor and schedule an appointment. I told myself I would do it after class today, but then the same thing will happen that did yesterday and I will wait too long and the office will be closed.

Fortunately, someone picks up on the second ring, before I can lose my nerve. "Hi, my name is Ellie Miller and I need to make an appointment to see Dr. Vasquez," I tell her.

"Are you an existing patient?" the receptionist asks.

"Yes, I've been seeing her for years," I say.

"What's the appointment for?" she asks, in her no-nonsense tone.

"Um, well, actually," I falter. I really wish I could tell this lady that it's none of her business and I'd rather speak to Dr. Vasquez privately, but I know it doesn't work that way. "I'm pregnant," I say quietly, even though I'm home alone, and it's only the two of us on the line.

"Congratulations!" she says, perking up a little bit. "Do you know how far along you are?" she asks.

"I think I'm between five-and-a-half and six weeks," I tell her.

"Oh, well, okay. That's a bit early to see the doctor. Why don't you call back in a couple of weeks? Dr. Vasquez will want to see you for an appointment when you're twelve weeks," she tells me, ready to hang up the phone.

"No, wait. I need to see her now," I say. "I need to speak to her about my, um, about my options," I say, feeling the knots in my stomach curl even tighter with each word I utter.

"Oh," she says, her opinion coming through the phone loud and clear in a single word. "Let me check her calendar," she proceeds to say, without any trace of warmth.

"The next appointment I have is on November 10th," she says.

"But that's weeks away!" I panic.

"I'm sorry, that's all she has available. Do you want me to book the appointment for you?" she asks, clearly annoyed with me.

"No, thank you, I'll figure it out," I say, ending the phone call before she can say anything else.

I sit there in shock for a moment, trying to grasp what just happened. Although Jack and I need to talk about this, my head is swimming as I try and think through what a baby could mean for me at this point in my life. I am legitimately trying to figure out what my options are and if I don't want to keep it, then I have a very small window in which to make that decision and this person, this gatekeeper, thinks she can go ahead and make a decision for me by not letting me see my doctor for the next month?!

I'm not one for social media, other than what I have to do for the studio, but suddenly I have the urge to share my outrage on all possible platforms. I want to scream about the unfair treatment and the judgment. But of course I won't do anything, since I don't want anyone to find out I'm pregnant - if that's how the receptionist thought of me just for considering an abortion, imagine what others might think!

While I'm still angry, I look up the number that Dr. Vasquez gave me a few years ago after I had a mammography scare, but I never ended up needing it. It looks like I need it now.

Ellie: Hi Dr. Vasquez, it's Ellie Miller. I'm sorry to bother you on your personal number, but I have a very serious issue and I tried to schedule through your office, but the soonest they could get me in to see you was in November. Is there any way you could see me this week?

I have no idea how long it will take her to respond to my text, since she's probably in with patients, or she could be delivering a baby for all I know, but I have faith that she will write back.

Unfortunately, my call has put me behind schedule and if I don't hurry I'm going to be late for my ten o'clock class. As I run down the stairs, I notice that no one even attempted to tidy their rooms or make their beds this morning, but I don't have time to do anything about it; honestly, it's probably time I stop cleaning up after them anyway.

I find my gray overshirt on the back of the kitchen chair and I'm about to run out the door, when my phone chimes. I used to be able to resist the urge to look at every text the second it appeared, but now that Sydney and Max only communicate with me via text, I assume every message is from them, and that it is a life threatening emergency.

Dr. Vasquez: can you come in today at four?

I'm so excited by her reply, I practically cheer. Obviously this doesn't change anything, but at least I'll actually get to talk to a doctor today and maybe she'll provide some clarity.

Ellie: Yes! I'll be there! Thank you!

Of course this means Max is going to have to "babysit" for Izzy, since Sydney has soccer, and both Max and Izzy hate that, but there's not much I can do about it. It's all part of the juggling act of having three kids and being a working mom - some days it's nearly impossible to manage. I send Max a quick text letting him know that he's in charge when they get off the bus, text our next door neighbor so she knows (in case she starts to see flames or anything) and then send Sydney one as well, so she knows to come straight home after practice.

As I get in the car, I applaud myself for getting everything sorted and still getting to the studio on time; but as I'm driving, it hits me that all I've done is arranged *one* doctor appointment and made a plan for childcare for *one* afternoon. I pass dozens of moms and nannies pushing strollers and wrangling small children as I pass through the idyllic streets of Westport and suddenly it feels comical that I could have a baby. How would I manage four children *and* run my own business? Would I expect Max to babysit for an infant? We say he's in charge when he's there with Izzy, because he's in seventh grade, but we all know that he's playing video games and if something happened, Izzy would be the one calling 911. I know I wanted to talk about my options with Dr. Vasquez today, but it's feeling like there's only one option that makes any sense.

***

Maureen is sitting behind the desk chatting amicably with Lara when I make my way into the studio; I wave hello to attempt to disguise that I am slightly winded from running down the block.

"Are you feeling okay?" Lara says, never one to miss the chance to pounce on a wounded animal.

"I'm feeling great," I reply, feigning a smile, and taking a sip from my lilac S'well bottle with the "Body & Soul" logo printed on it in silver.

"You look a little peaked," she says, giving me another once-over and pausing for an instant too long on my mid-section. Actually, I'm sure it was my imagination, but there's no way I'm taking my overshirt off now.

"We've got ten today," Maureen informs me, trying to be helpful. "Everyone's already in there," she says.

"We're just waiting for *you*," Lara says, in a tone that she pretends is cheerful, but is filled with contempt. Class isn't due to start for another four minutes, so I'm not even late, but she has to make it seem like I've kept them all waiting. I plaster a smile on my face and say, "Then, let's get going!"

To Maureen I say, "I'll see you tomorrow, thanks for everything," and throw her a tiny wink.

"I'm going to stay and take your class today," she informs me cheerfully, unzipping her hoodie to reveal a miniscule floral sports bra and matching capris. I know it shouldn't, but it always makes me slightly nervous when Maureen, or any of my fellow teachers, take my classes. Even though I own the studio, am a certified Yogi, and have been doing this for *years*, there is a part of me that still feels like I am a social worker pretending to teach yoga. I know these things only happen in bad dreams, but it doesn't stop me from envisioning Maureen getting up in the middle of my class and telling everyone that I'm doing it all wrong. However, it does bring me a little joy to watch Lara look at Maureen's defined abdominal muscles and cross her arms over her own stomach; it's completely petty, but still…

The three of us walk single file into the studio and I quickly try to get into the right mindset to lead a sixty-minute yoga class. I focus on the blonde wood floors as I walk to my position at the front of the room and take deep cleansing breaths as I weave between my students, each patiently sitting on their rainbow colored mats waiting for instruction. I turn to face them and promise myself that I will clear my head for the next hour and think about nothing but yoga.

***

Even though I've come to this office every year for the last nine years for my annual gynecological exam, when I pull into the parking lot of Dr. Vasquez's Greenwich practice, all of the flashbacks I have are to the pre-natal visits I had leading up to Izzy's birth. It was 2010, and we had only been living in Westport for one year at that point. I wanted to keep my doctor at NYU, however, Jack (and all of my new friends) convinced me that I would be crazy to drive back into the City for all of the check-ups, *and* that I would love Greenwich hospital. Reluctantly, I abandoned my OB in the City and found Dr. Vasquez. It only took one trip to the luxurious hospital in Greenwich, with a piano player in the lobby, for me to stop missing the crowded halls of NYU, but it was Dr. Vasquez who really won me over. With her no nonsense attitude, black hair pulled back into a tight bun and unwavering policy on organic food, I was prepared not to like her; but as soon as I cracked through her tough exterior I learned that she is as loving as she is smart, she takes the time to get to know every patient, and she remembers *everything*! I never had to remind her about a pain I had at the previous visit, or something in my family history – she just knew it. And now that I only see her once a year, she still remembers it all. I used to joke that I was going to have another baby so I could keep seeing her every other week, but that was a long time ago, and now it doesn't seem like a very funny joke.

The waiting area of the office has changed slightly over the past ten years; the pastel floral fabric on the armchairs has been replaced by a more sophisticated gray and white design, the carpet has been replaced with dark hardwood floors (this is a big improvement) and the old, clunky television has been upgraded with multiple sleek, smart TV's. The staff has obviously come and gone over the years as well, but my two favorite nurses are still here, and it's such a joy to see them once a year for a quick catch up. There are three other doctors who practice out of this office, but other than a couple times when I was pregnant with Izzy, I never had to see them.

"Miller?" one of the nurses calls from the entrance to the waiting room.

I haven't even been sitting here very long, but I'm thankful to get into an exam room and get this over with. Heavily pregnant women have surrounded me for the last ten minutes and they all look young and happy, even with their swollen bellies and ankles – I need to get away.

"What brings you here today?" the nurse asks, as she closes the door to the exam room.

Just like on the phone, I find myself wanting to tell her that it's none of her business. Especially because of what happened on the phone, I feel like I should say that. But I know that it doesn't work that way, and I need to explain the "purpose of my visit" to the woman with the tablet. Oh, that's another thing that changed, there used to be actual paper charts, and people had pens, and now this twenty-something nurse has an iPad that looks like what Sydney uses for homework.

Begrudgingly, I quietly mutter, "I think I may be pregnant."

Unlike the bitchy receptionist, the young nurse seems to sense that I'm not ecstatic about the news, and gives me a half smile and a kind look with her warm brown eyes.

"Do you know the date of your last period?" she asks, ready to type away on her mini computer.

"Sometime in the middle of August, so I think that would make me about five-and-a-half or six weeks. I know it's still early, but I *need* to talk to Dr. Vasquez," I say, defending my right to this appointment.

"Of course," she says, making me feel a little silly about my outburst.

"Let me get your blood pressure, I'll weigh you, and leave you this cup for a urine sample and then you can change into the gown and the doctor will be in to see you shortly," the nurse tells me as she hands me a familiar soft, pink gown.

When I'm back from the bathroom and alone in the room, I strip down, and fold my clothes neatly before placing them on the chair. The gown is gigantic, since it is meant to fit women of all shapes and sizes throughout their nine months of pregnancy – there is so much fabric that I wrap it around myself twice before I step up onto the exam table to wait. Although the waiting room has changed, these little rooms look exactly the same as they did ten years ago. I guess they put the whole budget in one place. I perch on the edge of the table with the crinkly paper underneath me and my legs crossed tightly; just staring at the cold, metal stirrups makes me cross my legs that much tighter. There are pictures on the walls of babies curled upside down inside the womb, reminders to get mammograms, and charts on what to eat and what to avoid when you're pregnant. This isn't a shock, but if there's somewhere I wanted to go to avoid thinking about my current predicament – this isn't it!

A soft knock on the door is a welcome interruption to my education on the benefits of 3D mammograms. "Can I come in?" Dr. Vasquez asks.

"Yes, of course," I tell her.

"Good to see you, Ellie," Dr. Vasquez grins. "How have you been? How's the studio going? How's Jack?" she asks. In addition to remembering everything, I'm convinced that she has a soft spot for Jack, even though she hasn't seen him since Izzy was born.

"It's okay. The studio is good. Kids are good. Jack is good. But there's a bit of a problem, which is why I texted you," I tell her. I know that she knows something's wrong, due to my emergency text earlier today, but I appreciate that she is taking her time and making this feel like a regular appointment and not like she had to squeeze me in.

"What seems to be going on?" she asks, looking at me intently with her soulful, dark brown eyes. In addition to her thick, dark hair (similar to Sydney's and Jack's), Dr. Vasquez has the kind of flawless skin that completely conceals her age (she is one more thing that looks exactly the same from ten years ago.) When I first met her, I told her there was no way she was old enough to be a doctor, but she promised me she was thirty-five. I supposed that means she's forty-five now, but her smooth, lightly tanned skin doesn't even reveal a hint of a crow's foot or laugh line. She told me once that she owed her complexion and flawless skin to the combination of her Chinese mother and Puerto Rican father – it's truly a stunning combination. I'll never forget waiting for Izzy to make her appearance after eighteen hours of labor, and Dr. Vasquez spoke to one of the labor and delivery nurses in perfect Spanish and then turned around and said something to another doctor in Chinese (apparently a joke) and they both started laughing. Then without missing a beat she asked me a question about my contractions in unaccented English. I was already in awe of her medical knowledge, compassion and bedside manner, but even in my late stages of labor I had a new respect for her mastery of languages – especially since I barely managed a C in high school French. That was when I learned about her background and how her parents were very strict about education and desperately wanted her to be an engineer, but she fought them and went into medicine. She joked that they were only *kind of* proud of her.

I take a deep breath and my eyes well up with tears for the hundredth time this week as I say, "I'm pregnant."

"Okay," she says, smiling at me.

"I'm forty-three!" I exclaim, as if she doesn't know every detail about me.

"I know. You are a healthy forty-three year old woman," she says.

"I'm done having kids. I have a junior in high school! And Izzy is already nine!" I yell at her.

"Alright, I hear you," she says, always calm and collected.

Her words hang in the air, as I stare into my lap and try to think carefully about what to say next, but she speaks first.

"The urine sample confirmed the pregnancy, but before we go any further, let's do an ultrasound and see what's going on, okay?" she asks.

"Okay," I nod.

"I'm supposed to send you over to the hospital to do this at radiology..." she says.

"No! Really? Can't you do it here?" I plead, eyeing the machine in the corner, and dreading the idea of making an appointment at the hospital and having to come back on another day and doing the ultrasound with a random technician.

"Yes, that's what we are going to do," she says, and I feel my heartbeat return to a slightly more normal pace. "Scoot down," she instructs, gesturing to the end of the table with the unfriendly stirrups.

Moments later, I hear the familiar whooshing noise in the background that I once thought was the heartbeat, but then learned was just the noise made by the machine. Dr. Vasquez is staring intently at the screen, taking measurements and moving the wand to get the right images; I couldn't see anything if I wanted to because the screen is facing away from me, but my eyes are shut so tightly it wouldn't matter anyway.

"You're measuring six weeks and 3 days, does that sound right?" Dr. Vasquez asks.

"Yes, that could be about right," I say quietly, my eyes still firmly shut.

I'm waiting for her to ask if I want to see the screen; and I don't know what to say. I've never had an ultrasound this early, I think I was at least eight or nine weeks with the other three and then we came in to hear the heartbeat. At those appointments, Jack and I squinted at the images and pretended that it looked amazing, but honestly it just looked like a tiny dot and the technician had to show us where it was because we were clueless – even with Izzy.

"All right, I think everything looks good for six weeks, but it's still early," Dr. Vasquez says, turning on the light.

As if reading my mind, she says, "There's not much to see." My heart swells with gratitude for her in that moment – such a small, momentous kindness.

"I want to talk about my *options*," I say, too embarrassed to actually say what I mean – what if I don't want to have this pregnancy? And I can't even begin to form the word "abortion" with my lips. In this moment, I feel pain and empathy for teenagers, underprivileged women, abused women and the list goes on. I am an adult with an education and money, sitting here with a doctor that I respect and trust, and still I feel ashamed and uncomfortable having this conversation.

"Why don't you get dressed and meet me in my office?" Dr. Vasquez offers yet another kindness, so that I don't have to have this discussion without underwear.

"Thank you," I reply.

I arrive in Dr. Vasquez's office before she does, and attempt to make myself comfortable while I wait, although it's nearly impossible. I've only been in here a couple times. The first time that I met her, I came in here before I had my exam and then when Jack came for the first time, I think we both spoke with her in here, but other than that I am always in an exam room. Her diplomas from Johns Hopkins are displayed proudly on the wall, surrounded by hundreds (maybe thousands) of baby photos and holiday cards and birth announcements. She seems to have made a wallpaper collage of sorts out of everything that people send her and it covers every square inch of wall space (other than the diplomas).

"Sorry to keep you waiting," Dr. Vasquez says, as she enters her office and closes the door behind her.

"That's okay. Thank you again for seeing me today. And for doing the ultrasound here," I add.

"You're very welcome," she smiles, and then looks at me and waits for me to continue.

"I just don't know if I can have another baby," I say.

She nods, but says nothing.

"If I decide not to keep it, what do I do? I mean, how long do I have? I need to do it right away, right?" I ask, fumbling over my words.

"You do have options if you decide that you do not want to keep the pregnancy. I can preform a D&C, which would be done under a twilight anesthesia, or you can take a combination of pills, one in the office and then another at home, that would cause you to have a miscarriage and you would in essence terminate the pregnancy at home," she says, all business.

"Oh, I didn't realize there was a pill. I mean, of course I had heard about it I guess, but I didn't really know...." I ramble.

"There are pros and cons to both," she says.

"But I would want to do it as soon as possible, right?" I ask again.

"If this is what you decide, then I personally don't like to do a D&C before seven and a half weeks, and the abortion pill isn't usually given until eight weeks but can't be taken after ten weeks," she says.

"What?" I exclaim, incredulous. "Why would I need to wait, wouldn't the point be to do this as soon as possible?" I ask, starting to lose my cool.

"I know," she says sympathetically, "but it has to do with the lining in the uterus, and the safety of the procedure. This is my recommendation for the optimal time, even if other doctors or clinics would do it at a different time," she says.

"Ughh," I exhale at this confusing news.

"Ellie, just take a deep breath," she says. "You came in here saying that you weren't sure what you wanted to do. You have a little bit of time to think about your options, okay?" she says.

"Talk to Jack, talk to a friend," she continues. "Here is some information on both of the methods I told you about," she says, handing me two pamphlets.

"If I want to do the D&C, what do I need to do to schedule?" I ask.

"You can call my office and they will set it up for you. I operate on Wednesdays and Fridays, so I could do it next Friday," she says, glancing at her calendar. "If you want to schedule it on your way out, you can do that, and then you can always cancel it, as late as you need to," she says.

"Maybe I'll do that," I say, feeling like that will give me flexibility and then hating myself for thinking of this like it's any other appointment. "Thanks again," I say, getting up to leave, suddenly desperate to be in my car and on my way home.

"Ellie," Dr. Vasquez calls, as I'm almost out the door, "either decision will be the right decision - you and your family will be great, no matter what you decide," she says wisely.

"Thanks," I say feebly, although it sounds impossible to believe.

When I get in the car I have an overwhelming desire to call my mom and get her advice, which is crazy since she passed away twenty years ago. This used to happen all of the time, it was almost like I forgot she was gone and I would literally pick up the phone to call her and then as I was dialing our home number, it would hit me and the grief would be overwhelming. It happens very rarely now that she's been gone for so long, but if there were ever a time I could use her guidance, this would be it.

Chapter Fourteen
Sydney

"I'm a little disappointed in some of your test scores," Mrs. Lechter says, as she weaves her way around the room, passing back our chemistry tests from earlier in the week. "It's clear that many of you used the extra materials I provided, but a few of you didn't seem to study *at all*," she says, as she plunks my exam face down on my desk.

I am terrified to look at my grade, because I know it can't be good. Although I don't regret one minute of my time with Brandon on Saturday, I certainly didn't get any studying done. I hoped that the hour or two I spent looking over my notes late Sunday night would be good enough, but I knew right away during the test that I was in trouble. It's foolish to think that I will be able to get any sort of A (although as nerdy as it is, I am sort of proud of my 4.0 GPA), but maybe I could still get a low B and then I can just balance it out with A's the rest of the semester.

I slowly turn over just the top corner of the exam, trying to make sure that no one in the neighboring seats gets a look at my grade. I've watched other kids do this and always laughed to myself, as I turned over my varying shades of A's without a second thought. My breath catches in my throat as I see what looks like a six, and then another six, and then a giant red D! Oh my God – I got a fucking D!

"How'd you do?" Chelsea says, sneaking up behind me, and tapping me on the shoulder.

"Oh, um, okay, but not my best," I say, trying to laugh it off. "Definitely need to study with you for the next one," I joke. "What about you?" I ask.

"I did pretty well," Chelsea says modestly, which totally means she got an A.

"Congrats," I say, only slightly jealous, but I know she spent all weekend studying, while I definitely cannot say the same.

"Thanks," Chelsea says. "Hey you said you were doing SAT studying on Sunday, do you want to study together one day? Or maybe this weekend?" Chelsea asks, hugging her stack of notebooks to her chest.

I wince slightly as she mentions the SAT prep work, and I replay the weekend in my head. Saturday was a blur of excitement watching Brandon play in the soccer game and then celebrating after with his friends. He scored two goals and played the entire game – it was amazing to watch him out on the field with such grace and confidence handling the ball; after watching *him* play, I would die if he ever saw me play soccer. The whole team went out to a bar in Fairfield for beer and pizza after the game. A couple of the guys were like what I expected college athletes to be (making gross, offensive jokes, pounding beers and being super dumb), but most of them were more like Brandon and really nice and fun to hang out with; and they were all so much better than the assholes in high school that I deal with every day.

I was having such a great time that the afternoon quickly slipped into the evening and it was nine-thirty before I knew it. When Brandon walked me out to my car he kept apologizing that we didn't get to spend any time alone together and he wanted to make it up to me, so I agreed to meet him on Sunday in New Haven for brunch and a movie. He said he didn't want me to have to drive again, so he would come to Yale. In theory, it was a sweet gesture, but in reality, it was a nightmare to coordinate. However, there was no way I was going to turn him down, so I concocted an elaborate story about study groups to my parents and they barely even noticed as I left the house at nine in the morning and took an Uber to the Westport train station and then took the train to New Haven to meet Brandon for brunch at Claire's. We lingered for two hours over our omelets and coffee cake and I learned about his younger brother (who is *only* sixteen) and his desire to be a physical therapist after he graduates. I told him that even though I think I want to go to med school, I was already starting to think about all of the other possibilities. I tried to keep as much of the academics as close to Ainsley's as possible, so I didn't get stuck in my lie. Although *she* isn't wavering from pre-med, I *am* starting to seriously reconsider that choice, even though I've told everyone I've wanted to be a doctor since before I can remember. We decided to wander around the campus instead of seeing a movie, and I excelled in my role as tour guide due to the years of tours forced upon our family by my dad.

I had prepared an elaborate excuse for why we couldn't go back to my dorm room, but I never needed to use it. We held hands the whole day and snuck long kisses when we found ourselves alone on a bench or in a deserted archway, but around three o'clock Brandon said he needed to get back to study and I admitted I needed to do the same, although what I really needed to do was haul ass to make the train home. I got home a couple hours later than planned and I was ready for a fight with my parents, but it seemed like neither of them even noticed I was gone! When I finally got around to looking at my books for the first time all weekend it was after dinner on Sunday night and I reviewed a few SAT vocabulary words and a little chemistry and then texted with Brandon for an hour before going to sleep with a gigantic smile on my face.

"Everything okay?" Chelsea asks, waving her hand in front of my face. I've gotten lost in my daydream and realize I've just been staring blankly at the empty desk in front of me.

"Yeah, I'm fine, sorry," I say, blinking a couple times to bring myself back to the reality of the chemistry classroom.

"I've got to go, but text me later if you want to get together this weekend to study," she says. "Can't believe this is the last weekend before the test," she says, opening her mouth and pretending to scream, and then turning it into a laugh as she walks out of the room into the hall.

Alone in the classroom, I turn my exam over and get a good look at the gigantic D glaring up at me and all of the red notations scrawled over the pages pointing out every error I made. It's somewhat surreal to see this type of grade on a paper with my name on it, and I'm already doing the math to figure out the highest grade I can possibly get this semester if I get perfect scores on everything else, and then trying to calculate how that will impact my GPA. But at the same time, I'm not as upset about it as I would have been a few weeks ago.

I shove my binder and disgraceful exam into my backpack and extract my phone at the same time. I want to text Brandon about my grade, but I can't figure out quite what to say; it's not like I can tell him that I failed my AP Chem test. I'm slumped in my seat in the dark, empty classroom, with my thumbs hovering over the keyboard as I try to figure out what to say, when a message pops up on my screen.

Brandon: on my way to class – thinking about you ♥

Sydney: thinking about you too ♥♥♥

Sydney: I just got back a grade on a chem quiz, didn't do so well – probably should have studied more this weekend ☺

Brandon: sorry – that's my fault ☺

Sydney: not a big deal – I'd rather be with you ♥

I know there is a huge, dopey smile on my face as I watch the three little dots and wait for his reply, but I don't care. I glance out the window onto the main lawn and feel slightly guilty that Jenna is probably wondering where I am, since we always meet after fifth period and walk to lunch together, but I'm just not in the mood to watch her flirt with Sebastian and then deny that she likes him.

Wait, where did the dots go? Brandon was writing back and now there's nothing there! I must have scared him by saying that I wanted to be with him – ugh, I knew it was too much. Maybe, I should write something else? Maybe I should say I was just kidding? Just as I'm about to destroy everything with another message, he writes back and saves me.

Brandon: me too - K gotta go to class ttyl ♥

Sydney: bye ♥

"There you are!" Jenna says.

"Holy shit, you scared me!" I yell at her. I didn't see or hear her come in, and she just showed up right next to my desk.

"I waited for you forever at your locker," she says, "so I finally had to come look for you," she accuses, although she doesn't seem that upset. Jenna looks amazing as she always does for school, she is wearing a pair of ripped skinny jeans and a purple peasant top; it's probably from Anthropolgie, super soft and flowy and would make me look twenty pounds heavier, but on her it just makes her look soft and fragile – two words that generally don't describe me.

"Is everything okay? Why are you sitting here by yourself in the dark?" she asks, looking around at the empty desks and abandoned lab stations in the back of the room.

I feel a pang of guilt for leaving her waiting alone in the hall *and* for the thoughts I was having about her. She's still my almost best friend; it's just that I don't feel connected to her recently.

"Totally fine. I was finishing something," I tell her, grateful that my test is tucked away at the bottom of my bag. As much as my friends tease me about being the only "cool nerd," it is a title I have come to be proud of, and I would be humiliated if Jenna or the other girls learned about my grade.

"Okay, then let's go," Jenna says, as she starts to back out of the room, motioning for me to follow her. "I told Naya to tell Sebastian that…"

I completely tune out the rest of her diatribe as we walk toward the lunchroom because I already know what she's going to say, or at least the general flavor of it, and I'd rather spend my time thinking about what I'm going to do to fix my chemistry grade, find time to study for the SAT's, and most importantly, when I'm going to see Brandon again!

Chapter Fifteen
Jack

Work is usually a respite from any issues going on at home. I am able to lose myself in the energy and optimism of the students or engage in spirited debates with colleagues and grad students over my research on the cycles of economic crisis. But even when I forget about the baby for a few minutes, the orange post-it note on the corner of my desk is glaring at me, and reminding me of the other disaster I haven't dealt with. It says "Hailey" in loopy, curly letters (totally different than Sydney's or Izzy's) with her ten-digit cell phone number. It's not fair to call her a *disaster*, but that will certainly be what becomes of my life when Ellie finds out.

Every day I promise myself that I will call Hailey or text her, since it is the right thing to do, and I *am* technically her father, but I'm not sure what to do or what to say. Although the conversation was a blur, she was quite mature in her handling of the situation (once she got up off the floor). I'm guessing she prepared her speech, and I clearly had no preparation, but if she used some sort of guide on 'how to tell some strange guy he's your dad and give him as many outs as possible,' then she certainly did a great job. If she's telling the truth, she's just curious to meet me. She said she had a happy, albeit less-traditional childhood, growing up in a gated community in Austin and now her grandparents left her with a very sizable trust fund and her aunt is filling in; although she hinted that Nikki's older sister is not terribly parental.

I peel the post-it note off my desk, as I have done every day since Hailey came to visit, and I stare at the curly letters and look for an answer. Before I can give it more thought, I pick up my phone and dial the numbers, which is probably what I should have done days ago.

She picks up on the third ring, and I realize I'm slightly surprised, I had been expecting it to go voicemail.

"Hello?" Hailey says. Her voice is a little deeper than I remember, but maybe this is her normal voice and it was higher because she was nervous. There is also a distinct drawl, even in her one word greeting, and it brings me back to all the southern girls I knew at school.

"Hi. It's Jack Miller," I reply. I consider making a joke and saying something like "you know, your dad," but I don't think that would be appropriate.

"Oh, hi," she says, seemingly caught off guard.

"I'm sorry it's taken me a few days to call you," I tell her. "I've been trying to figure it all out," I say.

"That's okay," she says. "It's probably a lot to take in," she says, kindly excusing my behavior.

"I wanted to see if you'd like to meet for coffee or lunch or something?" I ask her. "I'd like to get to know you," I say, and then cringe as I hear how trite that sounds.

"That would be awesome," Hailey replies. "I'm not doing much during the day, so I could come back and meet you on campus?" Hailey offers.

Although it would be convenient, I think it's best to keep Hailey away from Yale for now; until I figure out what's going on, I can't be seen wandering around campus with her.

"You don't have to come all this way. I can come meet you in the City," I tell her, mentally going through my calendar to figure out when I can possibly get into Manhattan to actually do that.

"Okay, or I could meet you in the middle?" she offers. "I've taken the train back and forth a few times now," she admits, "and it looks like there are a lot of places in between."

Hailey sounds so mature for her age. I know Sydney is two years younger, but I'm trying to imagine her having a conversation like this and it just seems impossible. Although that could be a result of Sydney's cocoon-like upbringing, while it seems Hailey hasn't had things quite so easy – my chest burns a little as I realize that I am partially responsible.

"If it's really okay with you, then let's meet in Greenwich," I tell her. "But if not, I'll come meet you in New York."

"Greenwich is fine," she says, pronouncing the town's name with a lovely little twang, although it would kill most of the residents in that town to hear.

"Can you meet tomorrow morning?" I ask, opening the calendar on my computer to look at my schedule while I wait for her response. I have appointments with a couple of grad students before my eleven o'clock class, but I'm sure I could move those.

"Like I said, I'm pretty free. Other than pretending to help my aunt in her gallery and wandering around the West Village, I don't have a lot going on," Hailey replies.

"Um, great. Let's meet at Le Pain Quotidien at nine. I can text you the address. It's close to the train," I tell her.

"I'm sure I can find it," she assures me, with the same slightly condescending tone Sydney would use.

"I'll see you tomorrow then," I tell her, not sure what else to say.

"See you then," she says, hanging up the phone, thereby ending any question I had about whether there was more to discuss.

I had been dreading that call for days, but now I'm looking forward to seeing Hailey tomorrow. Just in the span of that three-minute phone call, I've come up with twenty questions that I want to ask her. Glancing around at the piles of paper and books that adorn my desk, I still have no idea how I am going to break the news to Ellie, especially given our current situation, but I know that ignoring Hailey isn't the answer.

***

On my drive home, with The Killers blasting on the alternative rock station, and the fireball of a sunset practically blinding me, I go over all of the possible alternatives for telling Ellie about Hailey, but none of the outcomes are good. If only the night with Nikki happened *before* Ellie and I were together; or at least before we were *living together*! I know it will be a lot for her to take no matter what, but I feel like she would be supportive if the timing were different – and then of course if she weren't pregnant.

When I pull into the driveway forty minutes later, the only viable option I've come up with is to keep my mouth shut. I take a moment longer than necessary with the car still idling to appreciate our white and red brick Georgian style home with an actual white picket fence. At three thousand square feet, it is one of the smallest houses on our cul-de-sac, and it is less than half the size of many of the homes in Westport, but Ellie and I were so excited when we bought it ten years ago. As is the case with most of the McMansions around here, our house looks similar to many houses in our neighborhood, but we have made a few changes and improvements over the years and we've certainly made it our home. Moving from our crowded two-bedroom apartment in the City, this house felt like a mansion. Sydney was six and Max was only two and we couldn't imagine ever having enough furniture to fill up the house, and now there are days when I feel like we've completely outgrown the space. I try to picture what it would be like to add a baby to the current picture and it's not easy to do, but for some reason, after talking to Hailey today, it's no longer impossible.

***

Since it's not even six-thirty, I expected everyone to be in the kitchen, but when I enter the mudroom, there's complete silence.

"Hello?" I call out, taking off my overcoat and putting down my briefcase. "Where is everybody?"

The white marble countertops and the kitchen table are spotless, no sign of dinner (either previously eaten or being prepared). I know it's ridiculous, but I have a brief moment of panic that something terrible has happened – it's like a scene out of one of those terrible horror movies that Max likes to watch.

Just as quickly as they came, my ridiculous fears are allayed as Izzy walks into the kitchen and her face lights up when she sees me. "Daddy!" she screams, running over to wrap her arms around my waist and bury her face in my shirt.

"Hey sweetie," I say, hugging her back. "Where is everyone?"

Izzy takes a step back so she can look me in the eye, I can tell that she wants to make sure she has my full attention. She puts her hands on her hips and clears her throat before she begins –

she must have something good to share, as the youngest child, Izzy relishes her role as tattletale and chief gossip.

"So, Mom said she didn't want to make dinner tonight and she took us all to McDonalds!" Izzy announces, her brown eyes shining with delight.

"What?!" I ask, stunned by her revelation. Ellie is not a *complete* health food freak, but she despises fast food; I'm pretty sure the last time she ate at McDonalds was when she was high in college.

"Did Mom eat there, too?" I ask, still trying to picture my family sitting on the molded plastic chairs with their trays – I can't believe I missed out!

"Mom got fries and a vanilla shake for dinner, but then Sydney only wanted a couple bites of her hamburger and mom finished it!" Izzy tells me, loving her role as the reporter.

"What did you get?" I ask, trying to get the full picture.

"I got chicken nuggets and fries. Max got a cheeseburger and fries," Izzy tells me.

"Did you like it?" I ask.

"It was okay, but it actually wasn't as good as I thought it would be," she confesses. "But the milkshake was amazing!"

"Where's everyone now?" I ask, laughing at her recap.

"Max is in his room," Izzy says, giving me that look that says, 'isn't that where he always is?' "And Sydney went over to a friend's house to do homework or something, and Mom went to go lie down because she's tired. And I'm right here," Izzy adds, grinning up at me.

"Thanks for the detailed report. I'm going to go check on Mom, okay?" I say to her, holding out my hand for a fist-bump and hoping that's still a cool thing to do.

"I'll go watch some TV," she says, bumping my fist and running off to the family room.

I walk by Max's room and contemplate going in to check on him, but then reconsider and continue down the hall to the master bedroom. I open the door and Ellie is curled on the bed paging through a magazine.

"McDonald's, huh?" I say, starting to laugh.

"Don't judge me," she says playfully, picking up her magazine to throw it at me, but it only makes it to the end of the bed. "I had all the kids in the car and then I drove by and it seemed like a good idea. It was inspirational," Ellie says, laying back down on the pillow and moaning softly.

"Is it still feeling quite as inspirational?" I tease.

"It's not sitting quite so well, but it tasted a lot better than I thought it would," she admits. "It must be the hormones."

"How *are* you feeling?" I ask.

"About the same. I'm really tired, and I'm not at all nauseous as long as I'm eating carbs or fat. I think I've already gained ten pounds," she says tugging on the waistband of her jeans.

"That's ridiculous. You haven't gained any weight. You look exactly the same," I tell her, although this is a tiny bit of a lie. I didn't think it was possible this early, but her boobs are already bigger. It didn't happen the other times until further along, unless I'm not remembering correctly, but she doesn't need to hear that from me.

"Do you want to talk about it?" I ask her, crossing the room to sit at the foot of the bed.

"Not really. But we can't just keep avoiding it," Ellie says, pulling herself into a seated position and leaning back against the mountain of pointless white throw pillows on the bed.

"I don't think we've gotten any younger since last week," I try to joke.

"Ha-ha," Ellie says, not finding my comment amusing, but still cracking a smile.

"And I think we still have all the same obstacles," I say.

"You're right. It just doesn't make sense," Ellie says, cutting me off.

"What?" I ask her, surprised at her reaction.

"I met with Dr. Vasquez today," she says.

"I would have gone with you," I tell her, surprised and a little hurt that she went on her own.

"It's fine. I just needed to go and get it over with. And I think what you said is right. It just doesn't make sense. I mean how can we have a kid in college and one in diapers? It would be ridiculous. And I'm too old," she adds.

"That's not exactly what I said," trying to remember how I phrased it.

"I made an appointment for a D&C next week," she says.

"An abortion?" I ask.

"Well, yes. Although I still find the term less desirable, even though I suppose I should be fine with the word if I am okay with the actual procedure," she says, rubbing her eyes, as if to confirm her exhaustion.

"And it has to be next week?" I ask.

"I would rather it be *this* week. If we are going to do it, then it should be as soon as possible," she says sternly.

"Right, of course. It just feels so sudden," I say.

"I would say this whole *thing* is a bit sudden, don't you think?" she says, raising her voice.

"Yes, right, of course. I'm sorry," I tell her. "I just wasn't expecting you to already have an appointment," I stumble.

"Do you want another baby?" she asks staring at me.

"Not exactly," I say quietly.

"Then unfortunately this seems to be the option," Ellie says, looking drained and miserable.

"But what if I'm not sure? What if we aren't sure?" I ask her. "The other day you were excited, weren't you?"

"Yes, for a little while," she concedes. "But I hadn't really thought about it. Now that I've thought about what it would do to our lives and to the kids' lives, I realize that it's impossible. I mean, how would we possibly manage a baby?" she asks.

"If we were to do it, we would need to get a lot of help, but if we had enough help it could be possible," I muse.

"We would need a full time nanny, and that's just a tiny part of it. Do you know how expensive that is?" she asks.

"I'm just saying it's something to consider. And my new book deal should be pretty big," I say, trying to think through how this might work.

"But it's not just the money, that's only one element," Ellie urges.

"I know, but money can solve some of the problems," I reason.

"Why are you suddenly doubting this, when you also don't want to have another baby?" she demands. "It's not like this is an easy decision, and I don't understand why it's suddenly only *my* decision," she says angrily.

"It's not. Of course it's not. I still can't imagine having a baby right now. I just don't want either of us to make the wrong decision," I tell her. "Do you want to talk to anyone else about it?" I ask her.

"Whom would you suggest?" she asks, looking at me skeptically.

"One of your friends? Jillian?" I offer, thinking it's the obvious answer.

"No way," she shoots back.

"Why not?" I question.

"Because then it will always be out there, if I decide not to keep the baby, then she'll always know. And I'll have to see her all the time, and it will just be hanging there," Ellie says.

"But you and Jillian went to a pro-choice march together a few years ago," I remind her.

"That's not the point, and just because she's in favor of choice in general, doesn't mean she won't judge me – this is not as clear cut as it looks, I promise you," Ellie says.

"Okay, if you say so," I reply, not sure she is correct. "But I still think you should talk to someone. And if we have until next week…" I say, trailing off.

"I'll think about it," Ellie says, clearly upset and annoyed with me.

"By the way, I have a breakfast meeting in Greenwich tomorrow, so I can take the kids to school and help out in the morning," I tell her, trying to ease my guilt with this offer.

"That would be wonderful," Ellie replies, leaning over to give me a hug, and lay her head in my lap, her blonde hair cascading across my navy suit pants in stark contrast.

I remind myself that I'm protecting all of us. Nothing good would come from telling her about Hailey right now, but I still feel like an asshole as Ellie cuddles up to me for comfort.

Chapter Sixteen
Ellie

Even with Jack's help, it's still chaos getting everyone out the door, but with Jack taking everyone to school, I do have an extra thirty minutes before I have to leave for work. I force myself to make a green smoothie, even though every cell in my body is craving toast with cinnamon and sugar.

Halfway through gathering ingredients from around the kitchen, I lose some of my resolve and determine that I can only tolerate a fruit smoothie. I gleefully swing open the stainless steel door of the fridge and toss the kale and spinach back in the produce drawer and take out a container of strawberries instead. As I toss the berries, orange segments and frozen banana in the blender, I replay the conversation from last night in my head. I can't believe that Jack is having second thoughts, especially after he was so sure it was a terrible idea, but it's forcing me to think through it all again. I do wish there was someone I could talk to, but it *can't* be someone in Westport. As much as these women are my friends, I can't bear the judgment if they don't agree with my decision. There *is* one person that would understand, maybe the only person I could really talk to about this, but we've drifted so far apart over the last ten years, I don't know if I could call her now.

I met Erica the first day of my MSW program at NYU. She was ten minutes late to the first lecture and came running into class, plopped down next to me and announced loudly to the entire class, "Sorry I'm late, this building is so fucking confusing, it's impossible to find anything!" I grew up in Atlanta and I had just spent four years at school in Austin, so to hear someone speak like this in a class was shocking to say the least, but it was a good introduction to New York – and Erica was definitely a New Yorker.

Even though I was momentarily traumatized by her outburst, I was impressed by her style and confidence and she took me under her wing. Every memory of my first few months in New York revolves around Erica; we studied together, went out together, and of course she was there the night I met Jack – or met Jack *again* as it happened to be. Jack was a senior at UT when I was a freshman, and it's a massive school, but I met him a couple of times in Austin and then four years later I ran into him in Manhattan, but in my memory the night is almost as much about Erica as it is of Jack.

I catch sight of the clock and realize that the thirty-minute cushion I had is nearly gone and I need to pour my smoothie in a thermos and get to the studio. On my way out to the car, I scroll through my contacts just to make sure Erica is still in there. I can't imagine I would have deleted her, but every few years I go through some massive purge and clean out closets and desk drawers and last time I also decided to electronically purge as well and I deleted files and photos and contacts. I breathe a tiny sigh of relief when I finally get down to the W's and I see "Erica Weston." I can't imagine what she would say if I texted her or called her after ten years – especially after how things ended last time, but I may have to find out.

***

My mood improves when I see Dorothy walk through door. I vow once again to try to forget about my troubles for the next sixty minutes, and focus only on my students, especially now that Dorothy is here.

"I've missed you," I say to Dorothy as she approaches the gray oak bench against the wall to hang up her cardigan and have a seat to take off her sensible walking shoes.

"I wanted to come to class last week, but my body had other plans," Dorothy jokes as she places her shoes and pom-pom socks under the bench and rises slowly to follow me in her bare feet into the studio.

"I'm sorry to hear that," I say, placing my hand gently on her arm. I don't want to pry, but I want to know if she's okay and who's taking care of her. "I hope you're feeling well now," I say.

"Just being here around you young people makes me feel good," Dorothy laughs.

"I'm happy you like it here," I tell her. "If there's anything I can do to help you, please let me know. I'm happy to give you a ride to class, or whatever would be helpful…" I say, trailing off and realizing from the look on her face that I may have overstepped my boundaries. I don't know what it is about Dorothy, but I'm oddly drawn to her. I can't imagine offering unsolicited rides to any of my other students, but here I am overstepping social norms right and left.

"That's very sweet of you, but I'm all set," Dorothy says, smiling at me to make me feel less awkward.

"Shouldn't we get started? I think it's nine," Lara calls from her spot in the front of the room. She must have walked in while I was talking to Dorothy. I could never *actually* do this, but I desperately want to suggest that Lara find another yoga studio if she has so many criticisms about the way I run mine. Jillian would never forgive me, and the gossip would run like wildfire through Westport, which wouldn't be good for business, so instead I will smile and suck up to a woman who clearly thinks I am beneath her, but still takes my yoga classes at least three days a week.

Twenty-six poses later and all fourteen of my students are lying on their mats in corpse pose with their eyes closed, taking their last few deep breaths to end the class. I may not have thought about being pregnant for at least ten minutes of the class, which is somewhat of an improvement. Since my doctor appointment yesterday that's the first ten minutes I haven't spent obsessing over it.

"Namaste everyone, thank you all for coming, and have a great day," I say to the students, signaling that the class is over and they can open their eyes and get on with their days. There is a chorus of "namaste" and "thank you" from the group as they pick up their mats and move toward the entrance to get their shoes and bags.

"Do you want to grab some *tea*?" Jillian says to me, as she's rolling up her mat, and then she winks at me to let me know she clearly means coffee. Jillian knows my coffee secret, although in my current condition I don't know what I'm drinking. I usually love the chance to catch up with Jillian, especially on Tuesdays when I don't have another class to teach and Lara has to go straight to her tennis lesson so she can't join us. But I don't know if I can sit across from my friend for an hour today and make idle chitchat when I only have one thing on my mind.

"Sorry, I can't today," I say apologetically.

"Oh, okay," Jillian says, looking visibly disappointed at my response and making me feel selfish and guilty.

"If you have a few minutes, we can talk while I clean the extra mats?" I offer, trying to make it up to her.

"Okay," Jillian says halfheartedly, sitting back down on her mat to stretch. She releases her long red hair from the bun on top of her head and combs her fingers through it and then puts it back in a loose ponytail before continuing her straddle.

131

I grab the bottle of cleaning solution and a roll of paper towels from the supply closet and drag the stack of mats out to the middle of the floor next to Jillian so that I can clean while we talk. Somehow this seems more manageable than going out to get coffee – and I needed to do it anyway.

"Is everything okay with Sydney?" Jillian asks.

"Yes," I reply adamantly. "Why would you ask?"

"Sorry. It's just that Katie said something the other day, so I wanted to check," she says.

Katie and Sydney have been friends since the girls were six and we first moved to Westport. More often than not, it's great that our daughters are friends, but in the last couple of years there have been moments where it makes things more difficult and I'm guessing this is about to be one of those moments.

"What did Katie say?" I ask, focusing on wiping the teal foam mat, so I don't have to make eye contact.

"I'm sure it's not a big deal, but Jenna was over and the girls were mentioning that Sydney had been ignoring them recently," Jillian says, it seems like she's trying to choose her words carefully.

I stop cleaning to think for a minute about how I want to reply. Sydney's been in a great mood recently. Her snotty attitude has almost disappeared and although she is still a teenager, she is generally pleasant to be around. I've been so wrapped up in my own issues, that I haven't given it much thought, but maybe she is distancing herself from those girls and is hanging out with new friends. I love Jillian, but I think Katie has grown quite spoiled over the past few years and I've never thought Mary and Jenna were great influences. I try to recall something Sydney told me and remember that she's been spending time studying with her friend Chelsea.

"I'm sure it's nothing, you know how kids are. But I know that she's been studying a lot with that girl Chelsea, so I bet that's all it is," I tell Jillian. It's not what I mean, but what's also implied is that Chelsea is in the honors and AP classes with Sydney, and Katie is not.

"Oh right, I'm sure that's all it is," Jillian says smiling, but with a little less warmth than usual.

***

On the drive home I stare at every woman pushing a stroller and try and picture myself doing it all again. When I pictured it the other day, it seemed impossible, but now after talking to Jack last night, I'm letting my mind wander and trying to see what it would look like. A smile spreads across my face as I picture myself teaching yoga classes with a sleeping infant in a baby bjorn on my chest, but it's only momentary as I remember that none of my other children would have agreed to that – that only works in the movies.

I don't even take off my shoes or coat when I get home. I walk straight into the living room, pull all three photo albums off the shelf and take a seat. An hour later I'm barely through Sydney's album and I've just started my journey into Max's baby years. I don't know if this is punishment or a daydream, but I am now firmly in limbo staring at pictures of my little babies and imagining the possibility of doing it all over again.

Jack is right about one thing – I do need to talk to someone; but the only person I can talk to about this is Erica. I don't even know if she'll talk to me, but I have to try.

My hand is shaking as I find her name again in my contacts and press her number. I clutch Izzy's baby book to my chest for comfort while I wait. After three rings, she picks up, and I hold my breath, since I'm still not sure what I'm going to say.

"I've missed you so much," Erica blurts out the instant she picks up the phone.

Chapter Seventeen
Jack

I arrive at Le Pain Quotidien early and secure a table for two in the back corner. Ellie loves the communal tables here, and has been known to spend most of our meals talking to the strangers seated next to her, but I think that my breakfast with Hailey requires as much privacy as possible. I select the chair facing the door so I can see her when she comes in, but also so I'll know if I recognize anyone else who walks through the door. It feels a bit ridiculous and cloak and dagger; but I don't need news getting back to Ellie that I'm having breakfast with an eighteen-year old girl in Greenwich – I'm pretty sure those scenarios might be worse than the truth.

Hailey walks through the door at exactly nine o'clock and she is even more attractive than I remember, although I quickly chastise myself for even viewing her as *objectively* attractive. Apparently, I'm not the only one who notices, because multiple people in the restaurant turn and watch her tall, lithe body weave through the tables, dressed in ripped jeans and a fitted camouflage long sleeve shirt. Her long dark hair is piled on top of her head today in a messy bun that looks like something Sydney might wear, but she is wearing a lot of black eye makeup, something that I've never seen Syd wear – and it seems a bit much for Tuesday breakfast, but I guess that isn't my place to decide.

"Thanks so much for coming. Did you have any trouble finding it?" I ask Hailey, as I stand to greet her. I'm not sure if

I should hug her or shake her hand, or what qualifies as a proper greeting in this circumstance, so I simply sit back down once she reaches the table.

"It was easy to find," she says, as she pulls out her chair to sit, and slings her large leather bag over her chair.

"Great," I say, at a loss for words.

"Have you ordered yet?" Hailey asks.

"Just coffee," I tell her, gesturing to my oversized latte mug.

"What are you going to get?" Hailey asks, picking up the small eggshell colored menu.

"I don't know. Probably fruit, or the oatmeal," I tell her.

"Oh come on, live a little. The pastries looked good. Let's get some of those," she prods.

"You like pastries?" I ask, although it sounds somewhat foolish after it comes out of my mouth, they're not an unusual food to like.

"Love 'em," she replies.

"What else do you like?" I ask, desperate to hear her answer, mesmerized by this stranger who shares half my DNA.

"You mean food?" she asks casually, not seeming to grasp how badly I need the answer to this question.

"Sure, food, let's start there," I say. I lean back in my chair and try to seem less desperate.

"I have a crazy sweet tooth - cookies, candy, cake, you name it. I love Mexican food, I'll eat some vegetables, but I hate them.

136

Fruit's okay, but I'm a little picky about which fruit," she says, taking a big sip from the glass of water in front of her.

I can't help but laugh at the brutal honesty of her answer, and how at ease Hailey appears compared to the other day in my office.

"What is it?" she asks, smiling with her perfect white teeth, but unsure of the joke.

"Sorry, I don't mean to laugh, I just wasn't expecting your answer. Also, I know this is probably inappropriate, but you don't look like you survive on a diet of pure sugar without any fruits and vegetables," I say, hoping I haven't overstepped.

"I'm a runner," Hailey says, as if it needs no further explanation.

"Oh. You like to run?" I ask.

"I *love* to run," she replies.

"How often do you run?" I ask.

"I run every day. I *have* to run," she explains.

"How far do you run?" I ask her, intrigued by each piece of new information.

"It depends on the day. I have to run a minimum of six miles, but I try to run eight to ten," she says casually, looking around for the waiter, and clutching her empty water glass.

"Eight to ten miles!" I exclaim, trying to grasp this development. "When did you start running?" I ask, bewildered at her dedication.

"I started running with my mom when I was seven or eight. My mom was a runner, did you know that?" she asks.

I wince as I am forced to reply that I had no idea Nikki was a runner.

"Yeah, she was really good. She was a distance runner. She even ran track at UT her freshman and sophomore year, but then she had to stop," Hailey says.

"Why did she have to stop?" I ask.

"Because she got pregnant during her junior year," Hailey says, looking at me like I am the dumbest person alive.

"Right, of course," I say, feeling like an asshole.

Hailey continues her story, and we both try to pretend that I'm not a total moron. "My mom was a young mom and she didn't always do all of the typical mom things with me. My grandparents did a lot of that stuff, but she loved running and that was something we could do together. I knew that I had to be fast and have stamina to keep up with her, or she wouldn't let me come with her, so that was what I did. And then when my mom got sick and couldn't run anymore, I kept running to take my mind off it, and now I can't imagine my life without it," Hailey says.

"That's amazing," I tell her, although I wish I had something more profound to say.

"I don't know that it's so amazing, it's just what I do," she says nonchalantly. "But it does mean that I'm pretty hungry, since I ran nine miles this morning, and I haven't really eaten breakfast yet," she says, continuing to search for a waiter.

"Oh my God, let's get you something to eat," I say, waving my arm frantically until someone comes to the table to take our order.

As discussed, we order an entire basket of pastries, and Hailey also gets two poached eggs and bacon, and I get the fruit salad – I didn't run nine miles this morning and Ellie's influence is strong.

As we wait for our food, Hailey tells me more about her love of running and shares a funny story about her only attempt to run competitively when she went out for the cross-country team in high school. She didn't like the course they laid out, so she led her team on another path and they all got lost and finished last.

One apple Danish and two croissants later, Hailey's phone vibrates on the table and I see a glimmer of anxiety cross her face. She answers the phone, and only says a few words, ending with, "Okay, I'll be there soon," and then looks up at me, and says, "Sorry, I have to go."

"Is everything okay?" I ask, concerned about her sudden change in demeanor.

"Yeah, it's fine. I just need to get back to help my aunt at the gallery," Hailey says.

"Oh, okay," I respond. I also need to leave to get to New Haven, so it's probably for the best, but I feel inexplicably sad at the thought of Hailey leaving, when I have hundreds more questions to ask. "Maybe I could come meet you at her gallery next time? I'd love to meet your aunt," I suggest.

"No!" Hailey says, practically shouting. "Sorry, I just mean that you've got so much going on, and I barely have anything to do. Well, other than right now," she laughs.

"Maybe I could come back to Yale, and you could show me around?" she suggests. "I've spent so much time on campus in Austin, and I'll be there next fall, but Yale seems so old and different," she says.

"That would be great. Although I'm pretty jealous that you have four years ahead of you at UT, I've got some great memories there," I say, and I cringe as soon as the words are out of my mouth.

"I should go, it's going to take a little while to get back to the City," Hailey says.

"Thanks so much for coming. This was great," I say, getting up as she rises and standing awkwardly next to the rustic wooden table.

"I'll text you about lunch next week, okay?" Hailey asks.

"Great!" I reply. And then Hailey leans over and gives me a quick hug, grabs the last croissant from the basket and turns to leave, waving over her shoulder as she walks away.

I know the two aren't related, but I can't help drawing a connection. I missed eighteen years with Hailey, and although it's absurd to think about having another baby right now, I feel like it's another opportunity that I shouldn't miss out on.

As I'm walking to my car, I send Ellie a quick text:

Jack: I know we'll need a lot of extra help to make it work, but maybe we could do it

Chapter Eighteen
Sydney

I rearrange the Yale blanket one more time and straighten the two Degas posters that I have stuck to my wall and inspect the area for the fourth time. I've spent the last hour trying to turn the corner of my bedroom into a plausible dorm room and it's somewhat disastrous. Brandon wants to FaceTime tonight and I can't say that I'm home in Westport *again*. The last few times I ran out to Starbucks, but I think he's starting to wonder why I'm never in my room. It's probably ridiculous to think that this will work, but it's also ridiculous to tell him that I don't want to FaceTime – especially since I would never turn down the chance to see him.

The telltale chime lets me know he's calling; I position myself in front of my staged background and accept his call.

"Hi," I say, as soon as his dark hair, green eyes and sexy smile appear.

"Hey beautiful girl," Brandon says, grinning at me, and I can feel my heart melt, even though I didn't know that was possible.

"How are you?" I ask, waiting for him to comment on my bizarre surroundings.

"I'm good. Really tired. Practice today was really long, and then I have a paper due tomorrow that I haven't started," Brandon complains, lying back on his bed.

"I'm sorry," I say, wishing I could wrap my arms around him.

"How was your day?" he asks, yawning right after he asks. "Sorry," he says.

"My day was fine. Nothing too exciting," I tell him, which is pretty much the truth, talking to him is by far the highlight of my entire day! I could tell him that I spent thirty minutes studying for my SAT's, but then I stopped so I could prepare my room for our call...

"I think the rest of my week is going to be pretty busy too," he confesses. "It looks like we have a chance of making it into the NCAA tournament," he says proudly.

"That would be amazing!" I tell him.

"I know! It would be huge. But that's going to mean a lot of extra practice time. It's a long shot to make it into the top sixteen, but Coach thinks we have a chance with our record," Brandon says.

"That's so exciting!" I squeal.

"I know, but I don't think I'm going to have any time to see you this week," he says sadly.

"Oh," I say. I'm trying to hide my relief that I won't have to find a way to see Brandon on a weeknight, but it's also mixed with an immense thrill that he wants to see me! "What about this weekend?" I ask.

"I'm not sure, but I could probably do Saturday night, would that be okay?" Brandon asks.

I don't know who is watching over me right now, but I'm saying a million thank-yous right now. With the SATs on Saturday morning, that is perfect timing!

"Yes, Saturday night would be great!" I tell him.

"Oh wait, I can't do Saturday. Could you do Friday instead?" Brandon asks. "I forgot that we have some team thing on Saturday," Brandon says.

"Friday?" I say, while thinking 'SHIT' to myself.

"You can come here, or I could come to New Haven, whatever you want," Brandon says.

"Yeah, I think I can do that. Let's text later this week and we can figure it out, okay?" I say, trying to keep calm.

"Okay, great, can't wait to see you," Brandon says.

"You too," I say, "have a good week."

"Thanks," he says, and then he actually blows me a kiss before he closes his screen! I know it's ridiculous, but I feel like I'm in one of those dumb rom-com movies, and the worst part is that I like it!

Chapter Nineteen
Ellie

"You'll never guess who I talked to today," I say to Jack the second he walks in the door, without even giving him the chance to take his coat off or put his bag down.

"I don't know," he says sounding tired, then placing his bag on the ground and walking back into the mudroom to hang up his coat.

"Aren't you going to guess?" I ask excitedly, from behind the marble island where I am chopping zucchini and squash for ratatouille.

"Talia?" Jack guesses, as he walks past me and grabs a can of craft beer from the fridge. He cracks the top, letting out a loud popping noise and then pours it into one of the cold mugs that we keep in the freezer. My mouth starts to water as I watch the ritual and he catches my eye and then shrugs as if to say, "sorry, not sorry" before he takes a sip and settles himself at a barstool facing me.

"Not Talia, but that's a good guess. I haven't talked to her in a long time either, I should give her a call," I think to myself. Talia and I worked together in the same clinic at NYU as social workers, before she went into private practice and I moved to Westport and gave up social work for a career in yoga. Talia and I will exchange texts once or twice a year, and the obligatory holiday card, but our lives have also gone in opposite directions.

"No, you'll never believe who I talked to," I tell Jack.

"Are you going to tell me, or are you seriously going to make me guess?" he asks, sounding slightly annoyed.

"Erica." I say, holding my breath and waiting for his reaction.

"Holy shit!" Jack says, which is pretty much the reaction I was expecting. "How did that go?" He asks.

I'm still replaying the conversation with Erica from this afternoon over and over in my head, and I know he doesn't want to hear all of it, but Erica actually played a critical role in the early stages of our relationship. Erica and I were roommates in Murray Hill when I met Jack, and the three of us spent countless nights together drinking way too much on our army-green futon.

"It was awkward at first, but then it got a little better," I say.

"Did you tell her about the baby?" he asks, not wasting any time.

I'm glad that I have my vegetable chopping and dinner prep to keep me busy, because I'm not in the mood for this discussion right now. "No, I didn't. I actually called her thinking that I wanted to talk about that, but I couldn't bring it up. We have some other issues to cover before we can talk about that," I remind him.

"Right, I guess that makes sense. So how is she? Is she still with that guy?" Jack asks smugly, draining his beer.

"She's doing well. She has two kids," I start to say and Jack interrupts me.

"Really? She has kids?"

"Yup. A three-year old and a one-year old," I tell him.

"Wow. I never saw her having kids," he says, shaking his head. "So who's the father?" he asks, raising his eyebrow.

"It's not Paul," I tell him, answering the question he's really asking.

"What happened to that asshole?" he asks.

"We didn't get into it. After ten years of not speaking because of him, it didn't feel appropriate for me to ask what happened to the married guy that she was having an affair with, who was also her boss," I say. I move the bowls of vegetables aside to start chopping spinach for the salad that I know all of the kids will complain about.

"I hope he's divorced and unemployed, that's what he deserves," Jack says, getting up to get himself another beer.

"Erica got married five years ago to some guy named Walter. They are still living in the City, and now they have kids. I'm going to meet her on Thursday, so maybe I'll learn more about Paul then, but honestly, it doesn't really matter, I'm going to try and move past it," I say, more to myself than to Jack.

"You were a great friend, don't sell yourself short," he says. "Wow, so you're going to see her? Do you think you want to talk to her about the baby? She doesn't live here, so you won't have that issue. And it sounds like she just had a baby," Jack says, his voice trailing off, but his implications are obvious.

"Yes, I think I will talk to her about it. It's all I thought about today, well, almost all I've thought about every day, and I'm so confused," I say to Jack.

"I know," Jack says sympathetically. "Maybe you should try not to think about it for a day or two, just come back to it. I tried to put it out of my head the past two days at work, and until I got home just now I don't think I thought about it at all," Jack says, smiling at me.

"I'm going to go change and say hi to the kids, be back down in a bit," Jack says.

I stare after him as he walks upstairs and my breasts hurt just from their own weight. I'm quite certain the smell of the ratatouille in the oven is going to make me nauseous, and I think how nice it must be for Jack to get to 'take his mind off it' when I have to live this twenty-four hours a day.

***

I knock lightly on Sydney's door after dinner, hoping she is still in a good mood. She was surprisingly pleasant after school and at dinner, but I know from experience that this can change without warning.

"Come in," Sydney calls out in a chipper tone, without even asking who's at her door – this certainly bodes well.

I crack open the door, and take a small step into her bedroom, but leave one foot in the hall for a quick getaway. "Hey sweetie, how's it going?" I ask.

"It's good, just doing some homework," Sydney replies. She's sitting on her bed surrounded by books and loose pieces of paper, with her laptop perched on her knees.

"Sounds good," I say. I've stopped asking Sydney about her homework and even her classwork. She does really well in school, and if she ever has a question or needs help she is quick to ask for it, although she usually asks Jack, but I try not to let that bother me. It seems that Max isn't going to be quite as easy to manage as a student, but this is one area where I know Sydney excels.

"I wanted to check and see if you can babysit on Thursday night?" I ask. "Your dad has to stay late at work and I have to meet someone in the City, so I probably won't be back until nine or ten. I know you have the SAT's on Saturday, but is that okay?" I ask hopefully.

"Sure, that's fine," Sydney says cheerfully. "What time are you leaving?"

"I'll leave right after you get home from soccer," I tell her.

"Fine with me. Have fun," Sydney says.

"Thanks so much," I say, grateful for the ease of the conversation.

"By the way, I'm going to do some last minute studying with Chelsea on Friday night," Sydney says.

"Of course! That's a great idea. Does she want to come over here?" I ask.

"No, I'm going to go to her house, but maybe next time," Sydney says.

"Okay, whatever you want to do sweetie," I say.

"Thanks Mom," Sydney says.

"I'll let you get back to your homework," I tell her, pulling the door closed behind me. I know I have so many issues that are still unsettled, but it's like the universe knows I can't handle anything else and at least I can cross Sydney off my worry list.

***

I spot Erica immediately when I walk into the restaurant. Even though it's a crowded Thursday night at Grand Central Oyster Bar, Erica's five-foot-ten frame, model-worthy figure and waist-length red hair are almost impossible to hide in any setting. It's been ten years since I've seen her, but she still looks like Nicole Kidman's doppelganger dressed in a stunning Trina Turk jumpsuit. She sees me seconds later, and holds up her glass of wine in lieu of a wave. With one last deep breath, I make my way over and hope that this reunion isn't a gigantic mistake.

"She just told me our table's ready," Erica says, as soon as I approach. "Unless you want to sit at the bar?"

"A table would be great," I reply.

"Follow me," the maître d' says, picking up two menus and turning on her heel as she takes off through the sea of red and white checked tablecloths.

Erica and I both fall in line behind her, and I'm thankful for the momentary physical distraction. We reach our table in the back of the restaurant and are left with two menus and a promise of a server who will be back shortly to take our orders.

"I didn't know if I'd ever hear from you again," Erica says, as soon as the maître d' is out of earshot.

On the train ride here I was wondering if we would gloss over the past and just try and start fresh, but this answers the question.

"It was a long time ago," I say, trying to figure out how much I really want to get back into it. "I should have called sooner..."

"It's my fault, we both know that," Erica says, with tears brimming in her green eyes.

"Hey, don't do that, or you'll make me cry," I say feeling my eyes well up, reaching over and instinctively taking her hand, even though a few minutes ago I wasn't sure I was ready to give her a hug.

"You were right about everything. Paul dumped me and..."

"We don't have to talk about it," I say, cutting her off. I've wanted to hear those words for so long, and now they seem meaningless.

"No. I want to talk about it. I don't think we can just pretend like it didn't happen," Erica says. She takes a graceful sip from her wine, and I desperately wish that I could have a glass or four. "Oh my God, you don't even have a drink! Should we order a bottle?" she asks.

"No. I'm good with water," I say. "I'm teaching tomorrow and I don't like to drink before I teach," I lie.

"Wait, what do you teach?" Erica asks.

"This is so weird. Ten years is a long time," I say. "I own a yoga studio," I tell her.

"What? Really?" she asks.

"How did that happen?" Erica asks. "Wait. We have so much to catch up on, but I want to get through the hard part first, okay?" she asks.

"We really don't have to," I assure her.

Erica takes another sip of wine and plows ahead. "I was too in love with Paul to really understand where you were coming from. I think deep down I always knew that it was wrong, but he said all the right things and I really thought we had a future together. I know now how naive I was to think he would leave his family for me."

150

Erica pauses and I wonder for a minute if she's done with her explanation. I'm trying not to let my anger resurface, but I'm hoping she realizes that her naiveté was not the only issue.

"I should never have put you in such a terrible position," Erica says, looking at me with more tears in her eyes.

I know I said that I didn't want to get into it, but now that we're here, I can't help myself. "I was married, and pregnant, and you lied to me over and over and you made me lie to Paul's pregnant wife," I remind Erica.

"I know," she nods. "I'm so sorry."

"And all those horrible things you said," I say, because now I can't stop.

"I'm so sorry. I didn't mean any of them. I should have chosen you over Paul. I made so many mistakes," Erica says, staring down into her lap, not even bothering to wipe the tears or trying to salvage her mascara as it drips down her cheeks.

"I know," I tell her. I dig through my oversized Furla tote bag for tissues and hand her the entire pack to wipe her face.

"Thanks," she says, with a small smile, trying to wipe the black makeup from underneath her eyes and her cheeks. Lucky for Erica, there's not much that can ruin her appearance, and even hysterical tears don't seem to have a lasting impact on her beautiful complexion.

"So, tell me about Walter," I say, signaling the transition to a new topic.

"He's great," Erica says, beaming purely at the mention of his name. "I'm not sure I deserve someone so amazing," she says.

"Of course you do," I protest. It's worthless to dwell on now, but I wish Erica would have realized years ago that she was worthy of someone wonderful and perhaps we wouldn't have wasted the past decade.

"You and Jack would love him!" Erica says. "I don't know if we're there yet, but I would love for you both to meet him sometime."

"That would be nice," I reply, trying to imagine a double date with Erica. We were always a quirky threesome and then there were the few times we went out with Paul, *before* she told us who he really was – so this would be new territory.

"How is Jack?" Erica asks.

"He's good. He's doing well. Actually, it's kind of the reason I called you," I tell her.

"What do you mean?" Erica asks, suspiciously.

"Look, I have to tell you something, and I know it's a lot, especially given that we are just seeing each other for the first time in forever, but you are the only person I can talk to," I tell her.

"Is everything okay?" Erica asks, looking worried.

"I'm pregnant," I say, biting my bottom lip as soon as the words come out and looking at her for a reaction.

"Wow?" Erica says, making it sound like a question, which feels appropriate.

"I know. It's pretty crazy. I can't quite get my head around it. It doesn't feel real," I tell her.

"That would be a pretty big change for you," Erica says, taking a generous sip from her wine, and then looking at me as if to apologize for imbibing.

"I think that's an understatement," I say to her, laughing in spite of myself.

"What are you thinking?" Erica asks, looking me in the eye, the tone of the conversation has quickly gotten more serious.

"I really don't know," I tell her, shaking my head.

"What does Jack think?" Erica asks.

"His current thought is that we should have the baby."

"Hmmm," Erica says, nodding along, but not saying anything else.

"He didn't think so the night I told him, but he seems to have changed his tune and now he thinks with enough help we can do it. But let's be honest, his world won't change nearly as much," I say.

"And what about you?" Erica presses.

"At first I was shocked, but kind of excited. And then I remembered how old I am and that Sydney is sixteen and that I don't have enough time or energy for my three kids as it is now. This will literally change our whole lives forever and now I'm not sure. I made an appointment for a D&C for next week," I say in a whisper.

"Wow, really?" Erica says.

"I know," I say quietly.

"Do you think you could really do it?" she asks, her green eyes staring at me.

"I don't know," I say, shaking my head and staring down into the napkin on my lap.

"You're not old," Erica says, leaning over and placing her glossy manicured hand over mine. "I'm a year older than you and I have an eight-month old," she says.

"I didn't mean that we're *old*. But I was thirty-three when I had Izzy, and she was my third!" I rationalize.

"There are a lot of women our age and older having babies. I mean, there are also a lot of younger women I saw in the hospital whose skin and metabolisms I would have killed for, but still, it's not so bad," she jokes.

"I'm pretty sure even the twenty-five year olds were jealous of you," I tease. "But it's not just that. Izzy would be going to college in seven years and then Jack and I would be starting the next chapter of our lives, and a baby would mean we would be starting *all over* again," I say to her.

"I'm not going to pretend that I know a lot about your life right now, although I hope that maybe we can get back there at some point. But are you and Jack really ready to leave Westport and retire in seven years?" Erica asks.

"Who said we were retiring? I didn't say we were moving to a senior center in Florida and playing shuffleboard," I say indignantly. "I'll barely be past fifty!"

"Exactly," Erica says.

We take a moment to look at each other and try and determine which of us just won the point – I'm not sure it's entirely clear, and I think "win" is the wrong word.

"But I was going to be just over fifty with three kids in or out of college and Jack and I could work a little less and travel more. But if I have a baby, then I'll be over fifty and helping Sydney plan her wedding while organizing girl scout cookie boxes in my living room!"

"There are worse things you could be doing," Erica says.

"Why are you pushing me toward a baby?" I ask her, slightly annoyed.

Erica takes a deep breath and then says, "Because I don't think you can handle it if you have another D&C."

"It's not the same," I whisper.

"Of course it's not the same. But isn't that why you wanted to talk to *me*?" she asks.

I let the question sink in, and I know that she's right. I told myself that it was because she was an old friend and didn't live in Westport, but this is the real reason it had to be her.

"I never thought I would have to make this decision again," I remark.

"Well, it wasn't too much of a decision last time. You got pregnant the first night you slept with Jack and you'd been on three dates," Erica says, as if I could ever need reminding.

"Pregnant from broken condoms twenty years apart, what are the odds of that..." I wonder aloud, not looking for an answer.

"I know I am overstepping, since I have lost my place to even *have* an opinion, but I don't know if you could go through it again," Erica says.

At that moment, the twenty-something waiter appears at our table with a sense of purpose and delight that can only mean he has been on the job for fewer than three months. "Can I share the specials with you ladies?" he asks happily.

"Come back in a little bit," I reply, without even picking up my head to glance in his direction.

"And please bring me another one of these," Erica says, handing him her empty glass and dismissing him with a wave before telling him what was even in the glass.

"What do you mean by that?" I ask, immediately returning to the conversation.

"I think you made the right choice and I would have made the same one, but, well..." Erica says, pausing as if looking for the right words, "It took you a long time to get over it," she reminds me.

Silence hangs over the table as we both remember the months after my abortion where I struggled to regain normalcy, and the pain of pretending everything was fine when Jack was around since he didn't know about it.

"I don't regret it," I say clearly. "But I've tried hard to forget about it. I'll go weeks and sometimes months where I don't think too much about it, and then something will happen and it all comes flooding back," I say to Erica.

"Maybe that's why Jack changed his mind. Maybe he feels like it would be too hard for you," Erica tells me. She's trying to focus on me, but I can see her casually searching for any sign of the waiter with her wine, and I definitely don't blame her.

"I don't think that's it," I say.

"Why not?" Erica asks.

"Because I never told him about it," I admit, exhaling as I confess the terrible truth.

"Oh," Erica says, because really, what else is there to say.

Chapter Twenty
Sydney

I can hear Izzy and Max laughing hysterically from downstairs while watching some idiotic show, but at least they aren't fighting or bothering me – although I would welcome a distraction right now. I am staring at the flashcards that I missed when I quizzed myself, and I still can't get them right. "Austere, ignominious and promulgate aren't words that anyone really needs to know anyway," I complain out loud, although there is no one there to hear me. I roll over onto my stomach and stack the cards again, putting the three offenders to the side and start going through them again. I know I haven't studied as much as I should, but I'm secretly hoping that I get a great score on Saturday anyway so I won't have to take the test again and I can put this behind me. I realize that most kids take it at least twice, if not more, but I also know my parents are expecting me to kick ass the first time, because that's just what they expect.

My phone buzzes and for a full thirty seconds I ignore it like I promised myself I would while I was studying, but that's all the willpower I have. Besides, it could be Mom or Dad trying to get in touch with me...

Brandon: Just found out my roommate is out of town tomorrow night, so maybe we hang here instead of going out?

My heart skips about five beats and the swirl of activity in my stomach feels like I'm at the top of a rollercoaster. Of course I knew this *could* happen, and *would* happen, but I just didn't know *when* it would happen or that it would be tomorrow night! I try to compose myself before I text back, so he doesn't sense my excitement and utter anxiety through the phone.

Sydney: sounds good

I read it back and worry that it doesn't sound like I'm excited enough so I quickly add something to my message.

Sydney: can't wait!

Brandon: meet at 7? Text me when you get here and I'll come down and help you find a parking spot. Gotta go. xoxo

Sydney: xoxo

I glance over at my flashcards, but it's quite clear there is no way I'm going to learn the meaning of promulgate tonight when all I can think about it losing my virginity in less than twenty-four hours!

***

I thought today would drag on endlessly, but it was exactly the opposite. Every time I checked my Apple watch, another two hours seemed to have vanished and suddenly it was five thirty and I was almost late to get in the shower and pack my overnight bag. My parents barely noticed when I grabbed the car keys and said a quick good-bye. At the last minute, my mom seemed to remember the SAT's are tomorrow and gave me a kiss on the cheek and a flippant good-luck. They are both acting pretty weird lately and basically ignoring me, but I suppose it's working in my favor so I won't complain.

The butterflies fly more rapidly around my stomach with every mile I get closer to Fairfield, and as I see the exit for the university I worry my shaking hands won't be able to turn the wheel. But miraculously I make the appropriate turns and end up double parked in front of Brandon's dorm.

Sydney: I'm here

Brandon: I'll be right down

Brandon must have been waiting for me, because he appears at the passenger door less than two minutes later. He opens the door and arranges his body in the passenger seat and then leans over and puts his warm hand on my jaw and kisses me gently on the lips and I feel much of my anxiety slip away.

"Take a left up here, and then your next right. There's a faculty lot up here that you can park in on nights and weekends," he advises.

I follow his instructions and we drive into the partially empty lot without incident. I know it's silly, but I love the feel of Brandon in my car. I'm imagining the two of us taking a trip together – maybe going apple picking or to the beach or anywhere else romantic that college couples go together. Then I remember that I'm not actually the college student I'm pretending to be and a wave of sadness crashes over me. It's ridiculous, but lately I've gotten so caught up in my story, that I keep forgetting that I'm in high school. I try to push that aside, and the lie that I am getting in deeper and deeper every time we're together, and focus on the epic nature of the night ahead.

As we walk back to Brandon's dorm, it seems that we are both focused on the night ahead, because neither of us can come up with anything to say. Finally, Brandon breaks the silence by asking if I want to order pizza and it sounds like the best idea ever.

I've only seen his dorm room before on FaceTime and it looks pretty much the same, although there is a weathered blue couch against the wall that I hadn't seen before, and I decide that's the best place to sit – opting for that over Brandon's extra-long twin bed or his desk chair. My pulse is starting to race again and I cross my legs in my too-tight skinny jeans as I lower myself onto the couch and wait to see if Brandon comes to join me.

Brandon quickly answers my question as he kicks his shoes off in the direction of his closet and flops down on the olive green comforter spread over his bed. I breathe a tiny sigh of relief as I realize that *it* is not going to happen immediately. "Do you like anything on your pizza?" Brandon asks, looking up from what must be the delivery menu on his phone.

"Plain, I mean just cheese is fine. Or whatever you want," I tell him.

"I usually get anchovy and extra onions. Is that okay?" Brandon asks, without the hint of a smile.

"Oh. Um, I guess so. I can probably just pick around them," I tell him.

"Syd, that's disgusting," Brandon says, his face erupting into a huge grin. "Did you really think that's what I would get?" he asks, laughing.

"I don't know," I say, blushing slightly while looking around for something to throw at him and finding nothing that wouldn't cause serious injury or damage.

"Plain cheese it is," he says, still smiling. "Alright, that's done," he announces, putting down his phone. "Do you want to watch a movie while we wait?"

I hadn't realized that there was a specific time he had in mind, but I guess it makes sense that he would want to have sex a little later. I almost wish I could ask him what time he was aiming for, so it would be less of a surprise when it started – although maybe it's supposed to be a surprise...

"Is everything okay?" Brandon asks.

"Yeah, of course, why?" I stammer.

"You were just mumbling something and looking at your watch, but I couldn't quite understand what you were saying."

Oh my God! I can't believe I said any of that out loud! At least it was mumbling, although now he thinks I'm crazy! "No, I'm totally fine. We can definitely watch a movie while we *wait*," I tell him, trying to pull myself together.

"Okay," Brandon says, giving me a sideways glance. "The pizza should be here in about forty minutes. What do you want to watch?"

He meant wait for the pizza! Holy shit, I am a world-class loser! I can't believe he hasn't figured out what I freak I am and kicked me right out of here. He's just sitting there on his bed smiling at me, looking at me like he actually wants me here, perhaps a little confused, but it's like he enjoys it – his silly grin is because of me. I slip off my boots and take the six steps it takes to cross the room and I kneel down on the bed next to Brandon, and before I lose my nerve I say, "Maybe we can watch a movie a little bit later," and then lean over and softly kiss the corner of his mouth.

"Movies are overrated," Brandon says, finding my lips and eagerly returning the kiss. I've put so much thought into this exact moment, but now that it's here, thinking is the last thing that's happening. I've taken off my bulky sweater, but I still have on my tank top and jeans. Brandon has everything on, but just lying on top of him, kissing on his bed and knowing what's going to happen next, makes this the best night ever.

Not that I have a ton of experience, but usually by this point in a hook-up, the guy is tearing at my shirt and pawing forcibly at my chest, like in the hook-up manual it says, "after one to five minutes of kissing you now get to grab the girl's boobs even if you don't know what to do with them." But Brandon is so different, he's kissing my neck and then kissing my lips again and sometimes it's slow and then it's more urgent, but he's not in any hurry. I surprise myself as I sit up and pull my tank top over my head and un-hook my own bra and throw it on the ground – it's like I can't take it for one more minute if Brandon doesn't touch me (which is quite a new experience).

"You're so beautiful," Brandon says, as he smiles up at me, and I honestly feel like I am. I reach down to help him take off his t-shirt, and then lay back down to feel his warm skin against my own. I don't know if this is the right time to ask, but my face is right next to his ear, so I whisper quietly, "Do you have anything?"

As Brandon tries to raise his head to look at me and adjusts himself slightly under me, I realize what I said, or what it might have sounded like, and I say much too loudly, "Oh my God, that's not what I meant! I just meant, do you have a condom, not like do you have a disease or anything!" I bury my face in the hollow part of his neck and refuse to move.

Brandon starts laughing so hard that our bodies are both moving from the vibrations of his amusement. I'm mortified, but in spite of myself, the laughter is contagious and I roll off of him and Brandon has to catch me to keep me from rolling off the narrow twin bed and landing on the floor.

"I guess I kind of ruined the moment," I declare, leaning my head against his shoulder and staring up at the soccer (or football, since they are European) posters, which cover the ceiling.

"Not at all," he says, shifting his chin so he can kiss the top of my head. "Actually, your timing was kind of perfect, because there was something I wanted to talk to you about."

I don't know what he's going to say next, but I know that it isn't good. Maybe he has another girlfriend? Or maybe he *does* have a disease? Or maybe he found out I'm actually in high school??? These thoughts run through my head as I scan the floor for my tank top; whatever he has to tell me, it feels like I shouldn't be sitting here with my boobs on display.

"What's up?" I ask, trying to sound casual, even as my insides are withering in panic.

"I really like you," Brandon says.

"I really like you too," I reply, although I already hear the "but" coming at the end of his confession and it kills me.

"But I want to take this slowly," Brandon says, staring at his comforter while he speaks and then glancing up to gauge my reaction. Although there was a "but" it definitely wasn't what I expected.

"That's okay, we can take it slowly," I reply. I've never had a mature conversation about a relationship before, so these are definitely unchartered waters, but this is a lot better than some of my previous conversations with lines like "wanna fuck?" and "I'm out." No wonder I didn't want to be with any of those assholes from school; Brandon is better on every level.

"I feel like I owe you more of an explanation," Brandon says, pulling himself up to a seated position. I try not to drool as his tanned abs flex and ripple with every motion, but it's virtually impossible – I'm not sure if I want to touch them or have them for myself; either way, they are a thing of beauty and he barely seems to notice they are there. If I had abs like that, I would wear a bikini or crop top every day and I would constantly touch my own stomach, or maybe practice bouncing things off of it. I try to remember what Brandon just said, but his half naked body makes it difficult.

"You don't owe me an explanation, we can go slowly. I'm just happy being here," I tell him, which is completely true.

"I don't think it's fair to you otherwise. I know it's a little weird that the guy is asking to wait, but I want you to know why," Brandon says.

"Okay," I reply. A wave of equal parts relief and disappointment crashes over me as I realize that I'm definitely not having sex tonight, and I can't decide which part of the wave is stronger.

"I dated someone for a few years," Brandon begins.

"Oh," I say.

"No, no, it's not like that. We're totally broken up; this has nothing to do with her. Well, I mean it has *something* to do with her, but there's nothing there anymore," Brandon tells me.

"Does she go to school here?" I ask, praying he doesn't say "yes."

"No, she was my girlfriend from home," he tells me.

"When did you break up?" I ask hesitantly, not sure I want the answer.

"At the end of the summer. But it hadn't been good for a while. The distance is really hard. She's at school in Vermont, and it got really complicated," Brandon says.

"So what happened?" I ask, leaning back on my heels and pulling the pillow in front of my chest for protection – I'm not sure if I want to hear about the love of his life, but it seems like that's out of my control.

"Freshman year was fine, it was hard being far away, but she came to visit and I visited her, anyway that's not really the point. Last year was a lot harder and soccer took up a lot more time and it felt like we were fighting more, and it wasn't working," Brandon says.

164

"Oh, that sounds tough," I say. It doesn't sound different than any other long-distance relationship I've heard about, but it's sweet, and maybe a tiny bit weird that it makes him want to take it really slow this time.

"It was, but really it's just what happens with college and long distance I think. We were essentially broken up by last spring. We weren't really talking much, and we barely saw each other and then we both ended up home at the beginning of the summer and we slept together once, just out of habit," Brandon says and then quickly follows up with, "sorry."

"You don't need to be sorry," I tell him, although I kind of wish he would wrap up the story, or that the pizza would come, or something.

"Anyway, she called me a few weeks later and told me that she was pregnant," Brandon says.

"Oh shit!" I blurt out. Now I realize that this story may be taking an entirely new and unexpected direction. "Sorry," I say, now it's my turn to apologize.

"No worries, that's exactly the right reaction. It was definitely my reaction," he tells me.

I desperately want to ask him what happened, and I'm hoping that the story doesn't end with him telling me that he is about to be a dad and that's why we can't have sex, but I assume he didn't tell me this much only to stop now, so I guess I need to be patient and let him finish.

Brandon reaches over and takes a sip of water from the Fairfield thermos that is sitting on his night table and then looks back at me to continue the story. "For weeks we went back and forth about what to do and how we were going to handle it and those were the worst weeks of my life."

Brandon pauses again and I am literally biting my tongue to prevent myself from screaming out, "So what the hell happened?" Instead I smile, in what hopefully conveys some sort of compassion or understanding of a situation I cannot begin to comprehend and will him to complete the story before I explode.

"She ended up getting her period almost three weeks late, so they assume it was a miscarriage, but she could have just been late. We stayed together for a little bit longer because it didn't feel like we could break up right after that, but then it was obvious that we were over," he says.

"Wow. I can't even imagine that. I'm so sorry," I tell him, reaching out to wrap my fingers around his hand and letting the relief sweep over me that Brandon isn't the father of a baby in Vermont.

"I know it isn't logical to think that it will happen again, but all I could think about was my life being over, and her life too...." Brandon trails off.

"Were you using anything?" I ask.

"She was on the pill," Brandon says, shaking his perfect head in disbelief. "That's supposed to be like a hundred percent effective."

"Wow, that's a nightmare," I say in total shock, thinking that his story is probably the best birth control ever because now I was planning to use a condom and those aren't even as safe as the pill!

"I really like you Sydney," Brandon says, leaning forward and putting his hand gently behind my head and kissing me softly on the lips and then slipping his tongue inside and lightly biting my lip in a way I couldn't have imagined liking a few months ago, and now I can't imagine kissing any other way.

He makes his way down to my neck and whispers quietly in my ear, "and it is killing me to take this slowly, because you're all that I think about."

"It's fine. I understand. I promise," I whisper back. "Besides, there are other things we can do," I murmur into his ear, shocking myself with my confidence.

"I don't deserve you," Brandon sighs as he repositions himself next to me on the bed and reaches over to turn off the light.

Later that night when I'm dozing off to sleep wearing one of Brandon's Fairfield t-shirts, and lying nestled in the crook of his arm, I think this is the happiest I have ever been in my entire life, even though sleeping with Brandon turned out to be just sleeping together in the same tiny bed.

***

"Where are you going?" Brandon asks, as he rubs his eyes and looks around for his phone to check the time. "What time is it?"

"It's seven ten," I practically scream as I run back over to the couch to try and find my second ankle boot.

"Why are you up so early? Is everything okay?" he asks, sitting up and letting the covers slip to the floor to reveal only his tight gray boxer-briefs. Even in my state of utter panic, I take a second look because the sight is too magnificent to ignore.

"I'm really late," I say, shoving my phone in my bag and running over to kiss him. "I had a great time, I'll text you later," I say, as I run out the door. The heavy institutional door slams behind me, probably waking everyone on his hall – I silently apologize as I run down the hall and say about fifty prayers that I can find the parking lot and my car. Then there is the gigantic prayer that I need to say that will let me get to the high school by seven forty-five before the doors close and I'm not allowed in to even take the test, but I'll wait to find the car first – I'm totally screwed!

Chapter Twenty-One
Jack

"Did you see Syd after she got back from the SAT's?" Ellie asks me. It is early Saturday evening, and between Max's soccer game in Chappaqua, Izzy's field hockey jamboree and getting rides with friends all day since Sydney had one of the cars, we are only now seeing each for the first time all day.

"I've been back for an hour or so. I think she's in her room. I should have checked to see how it was," I reply, feeling extremely guilty that I totally forgot she even took the test this morning.

"I'll go check on her. I need to get up to pee anyway," Ellie says, lifting her petite frame off the sofa. I don't think anyone else would even notice, but because she is so small, there is already a miniscule bump showing underneath her belly button; it essentially looks like she ate too much at lunch, but combined with the size of her breasts, it's impossible not to recognize the changes that I've seen her go through three times already. I never thought we would be here again, but just watching her *be* pregnant brings back all of the memories from Sydney, Max and Izzy and it's hard not to think about the possibilities.

"She doesn't want to talk about it," Ellie reports as she comes back down the stairs and quickly returns to her spot on the couch, grabs the yellow blanket off the back and wraps it around her legs.

"I'm sure it was fine. You know she'll do really well," I say confidently.

"I know. And I hear that most of the kids take it again to improve their scores, but I'm sure she won't need to," Ellie says, fidgeting with the tassels on the blanket.

Silence descends as the main topic hangs in the air. Last night we were too tired to talk about it, so we pushed it to tonight. I know I would be fine pushing it off another night and I have a feeling Ellie would be too, but all of the kids are occupied and we should just get on with it. I glance at the bar in the corner and wonder if it would be poor form if I poured myself a scotch; I don't know if Ellie has changed her thinking much this week, but I think a drink could help regardless.

"Jack, have a drink, it's fine," Ellie says. Clearly, my glance toward the bar wasn't disguised.

"Can I get you anything? I mean water or seltzer or juice?" I offer.

"I'll have some ginger ale, thanks. I think there is some in the kitchen," Ellie instructs.

"Sure, I'll be right back," I tell her.

I return with two identical crystal tumblers full of ice and golden liquid, the scotch and ginger ale are slightly different shades, but other than that our drinks are almost identical. "You can barely tell the difference," I say, handing her a glass.

"Thanks," she says, taking a sip and then resting the glass in her lap on top of the blanket.

"So..." Ellie says.

"So..." I reply.

"What are you thinking?" she asks.

"Right now?" I ask.

"About the baby," she says, slightly annoyed.

"Oh right, sorry," I reply. "Just making sure that was what we were talking about."

"What else would we be talking about?" she asks.

"Nothing. I don't know," I reply. "Well, I think I still feel pretty much the same. I think it's mostly crazy to have a baby at our age with kids in middle school and high school, and I think it will change our entire lives, but I still think it feels like the right thing to do," I tell her.

Ellie looks at me, takes a sip of her drink and then looks around the room and I have no idea what she is going to say.

"I can't believe I'm saying this, but I think I agree with you," Ellie says, looking up at me with her big brown eyes.

"Are you serious?" I ask, stunned at her response.

"I think so," she says, nodding her head. "I think we are completely nuts, and I don't know what I'll do about work or the studio and the kids may kill us, but I think it feels like the right thing to do," Ellie says, a big smile spreading across her face.

"Oh my God, I can't believe we're going to have a baby!" I say, the news starting to sink in for the first time. "I know four kids is a lot, but I have tenure now and I'm making a lot more money than I ever have before, and this book deal is going to be huge. Just the money from the book deal alone should pay for the extra help that you need to take care of the baby, even if you don't work at all. I need to run the numbers, but everything is going to work out," I tell Ellie, placing both of our drinks on the coffee table so I can reach out and scoop her into my lap for a proper hug.

"I can't believe we're going to be a family of six!" Ellie says into my chest, the joy, excitement and apprehension unmistakable in her voice.

For a minute I wonder if this would be the time that I should come clean and tell her that we're actually going to be a family of seven and tell her about Hailey, but I can't figure out how to do it.

***

"How was your weekend?" Ginny asks, as I approach her paper-strewn desk on Monday morning. I didn't get out the door until nine, so I'm later than I'd like to be, but I'm in a great mood on this crisp autumn day, so it doesn't bother me like it usually does.

"It was really good. How was yours?" I ask, pausing in front of her desk to listen to her reply.

"Oh, you know, nothing too exciting. Marvin took all the screens out and put up the storm windows. And I made a chicken pot pie on Sunday night," Ginny tells me.

"Sounds delicious," I respond, slowly backing up toward my office.

"I could bring some in for you tomorrow for lunch?" Ginny offers, her face brightening at the idea.

"I wouldn't want to trouble you," I tell her, and then happily remember a conflict. "Actually, I have an appointment tomorrow at lunch."

"Oh, I didn't see it in your calendar," Ginny says, getting back to a more business-like tone.

"Sorry, it just came up. I'll add it to my calendar right now," I tell her, taking the final step into my office, and closing the door behind me.

The conversation with Ginny killed a bit of my morning "high" but I find myself whistling as I skim through my emails and jot down additional notes that I want to incorporate into this afternoon's lecture. I know we have a long road ahead of us, but after our discussion on Saturday night, it felt like we both landed in the same place. It's hard to explain, because we've done this three times, but this feels even more exciting in some ways, maybe because it's so crazy, but we're taking this chance together. I know that I need to determine what to do about Hailey, but I'm still figuring out what to do about it myself. I don't want to throw that on Ellie (especially now) until I have a plan.

I make myself a reminder to text Hailey later today to schedule lunch for later this week and hopefully that will help me get closer to figuring out what to do.

I return to my inbox and get lost in the endless questions that have come in from students over the weekend. Even though they are supposed to direct questions about the upcoming midterm to the teaching assistants, these questions always seem to find their way to me. I attempt to triage as quickly as possible and forward the simple or stupid ones on to my assistants, but there are some students who have put a great deal of time and thought into their work and it only seems fair that I reply.

The shrill sound of the office phone interrupts my eloquent response to a question on planned obsolescence.

"Sorry to bother you," Ginny says, before I can even say hello. "Greg is on the phone and he said he needs to speak with you," she apologizes.

"Of course, put him on," I reply.

I haven't heard from Greg in a few weeks. When we were selling the textbook, I spoke with him several times a week, sometimes multiple times a day, which apparently is quite natural for an author-agent relationship. I sent the first two chapters of the textbook to my editor last week, and she should be calling any day now with feedback. I glance nervously out the window at the picture-perfect blue sky and wonder if there was something wrong with the pages and that's why Greg is calling.

"Hey Jack," Greg's voice comes over the line, before I can wonder for too much longer.

"Hey Greg, how are you?" I ask him.

"Can't complain," he replies.

"Good to hear it," I tell him, drumming my fingers on the desk as I wait to hear what he has to say.

"How's the book coming?" Greg asks. "How much have you written?"

"I'm right on schedule, don't worry about it," I assure him. "I sent the first two chapters last week and I'm already working on the third one," I tell my agent.

"Okay, well glad you haven't gotten too much further," Greg says, and then lets out a sigh.

"What is that supposed to mean?" I ask him, pulling my shoulders back and straightening myself to my full height in my leather chair, even though Greg can't see me.

174

"We've gotten some bad news from the publisher," Greg begins.

Immediately I slump backwards in my chair as if the words have done physical damage. "What does that mean?"

"They've cancelled the book deal. I'm so sorry Jack," Greg says, his words ringing with sincerity.

"How can they do that? We had a deal! We had a contract!" I say, raising my voice.

"We had both those things, but in the fine print, they are allowed to cancel it," he says.

"But why? Why do they want to cancel it? Is it the chapters I sent?" I ask, with a mix of confusion and anger in my voice.

"It's not you, it's nothing you did. You know Professor Rainer from the University of Chicago?" Greg asks.

"Is that a hypothetical question? He won the Nobel prize in economics last week; the entire world knows him," I reply.

"It turns out that he has also offered to work on a textbook, and the publisher decided that they would rather have his name on the cover. I'm so sorry Jack," Greg says.

"This guy is going to have time to write a graduate level textbook and continue his Nobel prize research? Are you kidding me?" I say.

"I'm not really sure how he will do it. We both know that he'll probably have other people do most of the writing, but there's nothing I can do. I tried," Greg apologizes.

"But what about the payment? And the advance?" I force myself to ask.

"That's the good news," Greg says. "I did negotiate that you could keep the $50,000 advance and you won't have to pay any of that back," he says proudly.

"Thanks," I say feebly. The publisher wrote me that check nine months ago, and I've already paid taxes on it and it was absorbed into our bank account, but most of it has already been put toward the exorbitant daily cost of living in Westport. I can't imagine what would have happened if I had to pay that back.

"I'm really sorry about this Jack. Like I said, it has nothing to do with you, this guy just has the name right now and they're hoping that more schools will replace their books if it has his name on it," Greg says.

"What about a new undergrad textbook? Could you pitch that?" I ask.

"I can try. But I was thinking you could come up with some ideas for general business books that we could sell to the mass market. Those are really hot right now. If you give me a few ideas, I can take those back to the publisher and see what I can do, okay?" Greg asks.

"Sure," I reply, although I already know the odds aren't in my favor. The market is completely saturated with business books and the ones that sell are by CEO's and people who have already made their fortunes - economic theory isn't what a sales manager is looking to read on his flight from Detroit to Akron.

"Let's be in touch next week. And again, I'm really sorry about this Jack," Greg says.

"Yeah, me too," I say, as I hang up the phone.

I'm not sure what it feels like to be in shock, but this must be pretty close. I can't believe that fifteen minutes ago I felt like I was king of the world, and now I want to curl up in a ball under my desk and disappear. I know there are no guarantees in life, but this was a done deal. We had a contract and I was already writing chapters! I was supposed to be on the syllabus in every MBA program and graduate economics program in the country within the next five years!

The clock says eleven-thirty. I should be preparing for class and finishing my emails, but I can't help myself and I open the excel file titled "book projections." I've run dozens of scenarios based on the number of institutions that would take the book and the number of classes, but at the lowest end the $95 textbook was supposed to provide an additional $200,000 income each year, every year for the next ten years, and at the high end it could be as much as $500,000 a year in royalties.

I stare at the numbers that I've looked at and manipulated so many times before, each time trying to imagine what the money would mean for our family. It's not that we aren't comfortable right now, but living on a professor's salary in a town of bankers and lawyers is a losing battle. It's not that I want my teenage daughter driving around in a Porsche - I certainly don't need to be that jackass - but it would be nice not to worry about money, and not to worry what will happen if Sydney doesn't want to go to Yale, or somehow doesn't get in!

Then I open the spreadsheet that I started to put together the other day – the one labeled "#4." It's only a draft, but I just wanted to run the numbers on a fourth kid, with college and nannies and retirement planning and everything else we have to take into account, and although it's expensive, it was all okay because of the book. But that's not the case anymore...

Chapter Twenty-Two
Ellie

"Mom? Mom, are you listening?" Izzy asks.

"Sorry, sweetie, what did you say?" I question, trying to smile through clenched teeth. I know I should be listening to Izzy, but all of my energy has been focused on restraining myself from laying my full body weight on the horn and scaring the shit out of the silver Range Rover in front of me in the drop off line. I have a pretty good idea of who it is, and she seems to think that drop-off is the ideal time to have an in-depth conversation with her best friend on the curb, so everyone is stuck behind her – unable to drop off their own children or get on with their own days.

"I was just asking if I could have a play-date after school today," Izzy says quietly.

"Sure, that's fine. Sorry, I'm not mad at you, I just don't want you to be late and I don't want to be late to class," I say, drumming my fingers on the steering wheel.

"I can just get out here," Izzy offers.

"No!" I yell. "Sorry, sweetie, it's not your fault. But remember, they get mad if you get out before you get to the curb," I sigh. "We have to move up a few more feet and then you can get out," I tell her.

"Why don't you honk?" Izzy offers.

"Oh don't I wish," I say, shooting daggers at the two hundred thousand dollar vehicle blocking my path.

"Huh?" Izzy says.

"Never mind," I tell her.

"They're moving," Izzy announces joyfully, as the car finally starts to roll forward, allowing the rest of us access to the designated walkway.

"Hallelujah," I mutter, as I take my foot off the brake and roll forward as far as I can to let the car behind me in as well.

"Have a great day," I say, trying to find my cheeriest voice.

"Thanks Mom, you too," Izzy says, as she grabs her purple sequined backpack and dashes out of the car.

"I'll try," I say to the empty car after she slams the door.

***

Maureen is sitting at the desk when I walk in; she's intently focused on something on her phone and if I were a betting woman I would guess it's her Instagram profile. Although I barely know how to use it, the last time I checked, she had something like five thousand followers. I know she posts daily yoga and barre poses, health tips and pretty much anything she's thinking about; and then all of these strangers tell her how amazing she is.

"Good morning," I say loudly.

"Oh, hi!" Maureen says, slightly startled. "I didn't hear you come in," she admits. The front door is made of glass, it's seven feet from the desk and there is a tiny bell on it, but it's not worth it to point that out to her. Sometimes Maureen feels

179

more like a daughter than an employee, but she brings in a lot of students, and I need her.

"How was the early class?" I ask.

"It was good. Pretty full. I think we had thirteen or fourteen," she informs me.

"That's good. How many are signed up for the nine o'clock?" I ask her.

"I don't know," she says.

"Can you check?" I ask, taking a deep breath and motioning toward the computer screen that is directly in front of her.

"Oh right," she laughs, like I made a joke. "It looks like we have seventeen," she says, looking up from the monitor.

"Ugh," I groan and sink down onto the bench and put my head in my hands.

"Are you okay Ellie?" Maureen asks, in her irritatingly youthful voice.

"I've been better," I admit, hoping she won't ask for additional details. "Hey, do you think you could teach this class for me? I'll stick around out here, but I'm supposed to teach at nine and eleven, and I'm just not feeling it today," I tell her.

Maureen's blonde ponytails (yes, there are two of them today), bob up and down, and I think that means that's a yes.

"So you can do it?" I confirm, making sure we are on the same page.

"Of course Ellie, I'm happy to help you out," she says, putting her hand over her fuchsia sports bra, as if she's pledging me her allegiance.

"Thanks Maureen, I really appreciate it," I say. I know she can be flaky sometimes, but she means well. Maybe I should be easier on her, at least in how I mentally treat her. She is only twenty-five; at her age I was a newlywed and in my first year as a social worker, but from what I understand, these days, twenty-five is basically still a teenager.

"I'll go get set up for class," Maureen says, and gets up from behind the desk to reveal matching fuchsia hot pants in the place of where any normal person would be wearing tights or yoga pants. "Do you like them?" she asks, looking down at her miniscule shorts.

"They look great," I offer, because no matter how I feel about them, there is no question that she looks great in the outfit, "but I wouldn't think to wear shorts to class," I say, trying to be as diplomatic as possible.

"I'm teaching a hip hop class this afternoon, and I thought it would be fun to wear it here. I mean, who says you have to wear pants for yoga, right?" she laughs as she turns and takes her Victoria Secret worthy figure into the studio.

I don't have time to dwell on Maureen's outfit or wonder what the Westport ladies will think when they watch her demonstrate downward facing dog with a one inch inseam, because right then four ladies walk in the door. Even though I'm no longer teaching this class, it's still my job to chat and gossip and play my role as 'yoga hostess with the mostest.'

"Morning!" Jillian says, coming over to give me a kiss on the cheek as she dumps her brand new Valentino tote on the floor like it's a Nike duffle.

"Hey there," I say, returning her kiss.

"I thought *you* were teaching today?" she questions, looking at Maureen stretching on her mat in the middle of the studio.

181

"Sorry. I was going to do the nine, but Maureen is going to take it for me so I can get some paperwork done," I tell her.

"Okay. I know I'll get a good workout," Jillian laughs. "Although what is going on with that outfit?" she asks.

"I'm not quite sure. But it looks like you've got something new too?" I ask her. I don't actually keep track, but I rarely see Jillian wear the same outfit twice. It happens occasionally, but there seems to be endless shopping trips and a limitless Lululemon and Athleta budget. It's not that I'm jealous, although I could use a few new outfits, I just don't know what happens to all of her clothes – does she donate them? Does she think they are disposable? These are the kinds of questions that keep me up at night, but no matter how close we are, I can never ask.

"Do you like?" Jillian asks, spinning around to model her pastel green fitted tank top and off-white capri leggings with matching pastel green trim.

"I love it!" I exclaim. Her outfit is flattering, and this is also our pattern. Jillian shows me her latest purchase and I fawn over it – it's just what we do.

"Thanks," Jillian says, reaching down to get her S'well bottle out of her three thousand dollar purse.

"Oh, by the way. Is Sydney going to do her make-up test next weekend at New Canaan? It's pretty lucky that there's another one so soon and close by," Jillian comments.

"What are you talking about?" I ask, looking at her with utter confusion.

"The SAT that she missed last weekend when she was sick," Jillian says, giving me a look that says I'm the one who's crazy.

"Oh right. Of course – yes, the timing was terrible, but she'll be able to take it next week I think. It's New Canaan, right?" I say with a smile so forced my cheeks may split. I can feel the heat in my face and I'm trying to control my breathing, but even with years of training, I barely remember how to exhale right now.

"Oh my God, also, did you hear about Alana?" Jillian asks.

"No, what happened?" I inquire, my head still spinning.

"She's pregnant! Can you believe it!" Jillian whispers.

"Oh wow," I reply. Alana also has a daughter in the high school with Katie and Sydney, although she is a couple years younger, and I believe she has a son in elementary school.

"Can you even imagine? What a fucking nightmare! Clearly an accident! You couldn't pay me enough money or give me enough help to go through that again, right?" Jillian asks, rolling her eyes.

"Oh yeah, totally," I say, trying to laugh at this joke that is anything but funny. Although I guess it's good to get a preview of what everyone will be saying about me in a few months...

"I better get in there, it looks like Maureen is about to start," she says.

"I'll see you after class. Have fun," I say, giving her a little wave, and trying my hardest to speak in my normal voice.

When the glass doors to the studio finally close, I wipe the phony smile off my face and attempt five deep breaths before I do anything completely reckless. I'm just going to ignore the comment about Alana – there's nothing I can do about that, although all it does is add to my already upset stomach. My first thought about the test is that Katie is lying to Jillian and she doesn't know what she's talking about. But as much as I want to believe that, I don't see this as something Katie would lie about, even though she has become a bit of an entitled brat.

It's nine o'clock, which means Jack is either still on his way to New Haven or he just arrived on campus and Sydney is at school. I desperately want to call Jack, but he was already running late this morning, because he drove Sydney and Max to school and he said he had a hectic day. Besides, there isn't anything he can do about it right now and all this will do is ruin his day – he was in such a good mood this morning, the least I can do is let him enjoy his day and wait until tonight to wreck it.

My finger hovers over Sydney's name in my 'favorites' as I contemplate calling her at school. I know she can't pick up her phone during a class, but she checks that damn thing between periods and I could leave her a voicemail that would certainly get her attention. I'm formulating the message in my head, when I realize the error in my plan. If I leave her a message, or send her an irate text, she will have time to come up with an excuse. As much as it kills me to wait, I need to hold off and confront her in person after school so I can see her reaction. I need the element of surprise so she can't cover up her lie anymore than she already has.

Although paperwork wasn't the reason I'm not teaching this class, it isn't a lie that I have 'busy work' to catch up on. The next fifty minutes seems like the perfect time, if I'm not going to be using that time to interrogate Sydney. But before I can get to the invoices or the November schedules, I notice the names for the nine o'clock class open on the monitor and see that Dorothy signed up for the class, but it's already ten after, and she's not here.

I know that this is outside of my duties as a yoga teacher or studio owner, but I tell myself that I merely want to ask Dorothy if she would like a refund for today's class or if she would like me to credit her for a future class. Of course our official policy is that if you don't cancel within twenty-four hours, you don't get your money back at all, but that's not my concern right now.

To: dorothy973@gmail.com
From: ellie@bodysoulyoga.com

Dear Dorothy,

I noticed that you signed up for this morning's 9am yoga class, but you were not able to make the class. Would you like me to refund the money for today's class back to your card on file, or would you like to apply the credit to another class?

I hope that you are feeling well and that everything is okay. I also offer private yoga classes if you would like me to come by for a class – the charge would be the same.

Best,
Ellie

I press send before I can change my mind or even re-read the email. I know that it's poorly written, and we certainly don't give private yoga lessons to other students, but there's just *something* about Dorothy.

I'm sure a therapist would say I'm searching for a "mother figure" and Jack would likely take this opportunity to remind me that three therapy sessions may not have been enough to help me get over my grief; but I'm a licensed social worker and I think I'm perfectly healthy. Or else I'm in denial. But either way, I don't have to defend my affection for Dorothy.

Less then a minute later, my inbox chimes:

To: ellie@bodysoulyoga.com
From: dorothy973@gmail.com

Dear Ellie,

You are so kind to check in on me. I don't need a refund for my lesson, I think that goes against your cancellation policy, and I'm not sure I'm up to a private lesson, but I would love if you would come over and join me for tea. How does that sound? It's the house at the point on Hillspoint Road, you can't miss it.

Sincerely,
Dorothy

A smile spreads across my face as I think about spending the afternoon with Dorothy having tea and butter cookies in her living room. It certainly doesn't fix anything, but it sounds like the perfect distraction to the disastrous issues with Sydney and the rest of the problems in my life.

To: dorothy973@gmail.com
From: ellie@bodysoulyoga.com

Dear Dorothy,

I would absolutely love to join you for tea. Please tell me what day and time is good for you, and I'll be there.

Best,
Ellie

Dorothy is about twelve years older than my mom would have been now. It's hard to picture what she would have been like in her late sixties, since she never made it past fifty-two. Sometimes it's still hard to accept that both of my parents have been gone for such a long time. My dad died from an aneurysm when I was in high school and then my mom died when I was in my early twenties. So maybe this *is* why I care a little bit more about Dorothy, or maybe it's just because Dorothy is a fascinating older woman and one of the only women I seem to interact with these days who has her priorities straight.

I have to shake my head at this last thought, because as much as I don't want to admit it, my priorities are just as fucked up, if not more so.

***

Thankfully, the day didn't get any worse after this morning's bombshell. One could argue it improved, because I helped Max with his homework, managed Izzy's playdate and somehow I found time to get to the grocery store, make lasagna, *and* the smell of the meat, sauce and cheese bubbling together in the oven isn't even making me nauseous. As I dry and put away the Dutch oven and wipe down the counter, I half expect someone to burst through the door and give me a medal for my outstanding work in the field of parenthood, home management and general life skills.

Moments later, the back door opens, but it's only Jack, and from the look on his face, it doesn't appear that he will be giving out any medals. Seeing him reminds me that I need to tell him about the Sydney SAT debacle and my temporary sense of triumph deflates. In the ten hours since Jack left this morning, his mouth has gone from shit-eating grin to an ogre's scowl – I wonder what happened today?

"Hey honey," I say cautiously, sensing his mood from the moment he opens the door.

"Hey," he says. Jack drops his bag on the mud room floor with a thud, and I wince even though I know his laptop is well padded.

"Are you okay?" I ask. It's possible that it's better to avoid him altogether and let him march into his study and come out when he's ready, but his chocolate brown eyes don't look angry, they look like a lost puppy dog.

"I've had better days," Jack says sadly.

"Do you want to talk about it?" I ask, pushing the hair back from my face that's come loose while cooking, and trying to catch Jack's eye.

"Not right now. I'm going to go change first and get a glass of wine. Let's talk about it after dinner, okay?" he says, shuffling through the kitchen.

"Okay," I reply. "We need to talk about Sydney too," I call after him, but I don't think he hears me.

***

"Thanks for dinner, sorry I didn't help clean up," Jack says, as I crawl into bed a few hours later. He is under the covers watching CNBC, where he has been since dinner ended.

"It's okay," I say, although I don't quite mean it. I felt like superwoman making my homemade lasagna, but when I was still in the kitchen four hours later cleaning up the mess by myself, I was tired and annoyed and no longer feeling quite so super.

"So what's going on?" I ask Jack, lying down next to him and propping my head on my hand, trying to convey as much concern as I can muster. He disappeared immediately after dinner and we didn't have a chance to discuss Sydney's SAT lie, and now she has also gone to bed. I don't want there to be a serious problem, but Jack better have a good reason for this type of drama.

"The book is dead," Jack says, staring at the ceiling.

"What do you mean?" I ask, wholly confused.

"I mean, Jorge Raines is going to be writing the new textbook, and I am not," he says.

"But that's not possible. You have a contract!" I say indignantly.

"That's what I said," Jack says sadly, still refusing to meet my stare.

188

"This is bullshit! We'll get a lawyer! I never liked Greg anyway, or that crappy publisher!" I say, raising my voice.

"It's not Greg's fault. And a lawyer has already looked at it. It's in the fine print. I get to keep the advance, but the rest of the book is dead," Jack repeats, seemingly resigned with the outcome.

Now I'm not sure what to say. This is all Jack has been talking about for an entire year. I don't know much about economics textbooks, but I can't imagine they will have another brand new one coming out soon. I'm pretty sure this chance won't happen again for a long time.

"I'm so sorry," I say, reaching over and stroking his bare arm.

"Yeah, me too," he laughs, but I know the situation isn't amusing.

I'm not sure if I should say it, but I say it anyway, "Don't worry about the money. It was going to be really nice, but we don't need it," I tell him.

Jack is very quiet for a minute and then he rolls over and looks at me for the first time since I got into bed. "Ellie, we *do* need that money. I've looked at the numbers all day. If we are going to have another baby we need that money," he says.

"Oh," I reply.

"I know it sounds awful, but I don't think we can afford to have a baby without the money from the book," Jack says, turning back over and staring up at the ceiling so he doesn't have to face me.

I've spent nearly every moment in a state of gut-wrenching turmoil since I saw the word "pregnant" appear on that stick; but until now I was worried about the impact on our family's daily life, being the "old" mom on the playground and three more years of diapers. I know that we aren't one of the wealthier families in town, but I never thought we couldn't actually afford to have a baby - that just seems preposterous. I'm still wrestling with the idea of going through this again, but somehow, the idea of upper-middle class financial strain makes my current discomfort even worse.

"Jack, there are families that make less than fifty-thousand dollars a year and have five or six kids, we can obviously afford to have a baby," I tell him.

"Ellie, is that really who you want to compare us to? I don't think that either of us are looking to have that kind of lifestyle, so lets be honest here," Jack says, sounding frustrated.

"Sorry, that obviously isn't a fair comparison. I just meant that it doesn't seem right to say we *can't* afford a baby, when we both have good jobs and we are very comfortable," I argue.

"Yes, we can afford to have a baby, but not in the style we are currently living. It will mean that we can't take the vacations we take right now. And we *aren't* going to be able to afford a nanny. I'm not even sure what type of childcare we will be able to afford, but we can't afford for you not to keep working full-time. And speaking of working, I'm going to need to keep teaching until I'm about eighty to pay for all four kids to go to college," Jack says.

I need a minute to process what Jack just said. I know we decided to have the baby, but I still feel like I'm weighing the pros and cons, and one of the factors in that decision was going back to work (either at the studio or somewhere else) and having full-time help to be able to do that. I just told myself that it was crass to let finances influence this kind of decision, but maybe it's naive not to. Ugh, but then I think about what Erica said and although I try never to think about those dark weeks after the first procedure, I'm honestly *not* sure I can do it again.

"So what are you saying?" I ask Jack, looking for some clarity in this muddy conversation.

"I don't know what I'm saying. But maybe we should think about our options again now that we know we won't have this money coming in. I know what I said before, but maybe that's not the smartest choice. There's still time, right?" Jack says, not wanting to say any of the taboo words.

"Yes, there's still time. Let's give it another day or two and then we can talk about it again," I tell him.

"Okay, goodnight," he says, still staring at the ceiling.

"Goodnight," I reply, firmly rooted to my side of the bed.

Even when we've had a fight, one of us always makes the effort for a perfunctory kiss or cuddle, or some show of affection before we go to sleep, just to let the other person know that it's *only* a disagreement and we're stronger than whatever petty issue came between us. There are no good night kisses or cuddles tonight.

Chapter Twenty-Three
Sydney

For a split second when my alarm goes off, I lay in bed in that groggy haze before I'm fully awake and all I think about is the amazing phone call I had last night with Brandon. We talked until one in the morning about everything and nothing and all topics in between. We shared so much about our families and I told him about the warped relationship I have with my mom. He's such a great listener that at one point I almost told him the truth about my age and Yale and everything. But then I thought about what would happen when he realized I'd been lying about my age, and it didn't seem worth the risk.

Now, as I stumble across the room to silence the god-awful rooster alarm, which is the only noise I won't sleep through, the disaster of Saturday's SAT debacle comes crashing back and wipes out all the warm fuzzy memories of last night's phone call. The only positive is that my parents don't know and they are so fucking out of it lately, that they won't even notice when I take the make-up this weekend and get my scores from the test in New Canaan a week after everyone else.

Last night when I was on the phone, I picked out my outfit for today and hung it neatly on my closet door so I wouldn't be rushed this morning. However, the tight, ripped white jeans and fitted black v-neck sweater that looked stylish at midnight, now only look tight and uncomfortable. Instead I grab a pair of black leggings from my drawer, a gray tank top and a super soft white hoodie. One glance in the mirror and I know my mom is going to say that it looks like I'm wearing pajamas, but I don't understand why she can prance around town in yoga clothes and I can't wear the same thing to school (and my clothes cover a lot more skin). I turn away from my reflection before I start to focus too closely on any particular aspect of my body or start to make the inevitable comparisons and conclude that my mom just looks better in her Athleta clothes and that's why she's *allowed* to wear them. I quickly throw on an extra coat of mascara and my new Nars lip-gloss and start to pack up my backpack when there is a knock on my door. Before I can ask who it is, or even say, "Come in," my mom appears in my room (dressed in an almost matching black and white outfit – although hers is tighter, of course).

"We need to talk," she says sternly, as she walks into my room, shuts the door behind her and sits down on my unmade bed.

"What's up?" I ask her, trying to sound as casual as possible, although my heart is beating a mile a minute.

"Where were you on Saturday morning?" she asks, speaking slowly and deliberately.

Oh. Shit. I wonder what she knows, or how much she knows. Or maybe she just thinks she knows something and she's fishing for an answer. There's no way I can tell her the entire truth, but she knows enough to ask the question, so if I lie straight to her face and she has proof, then I'm going to be in even more trouble. I wish I had time to figure out what she knows, but I'm pretty sure I don't have that luxury.

"I'm so sorry," I say to her, tears coming almost immediately to my eyes. I'm not a good actress, so I couldn't fake tears like this, but I really *am* sorry about missing the test, so it isn't hard to show remorse.

"What happened?" my mom asks, her tone is still firm, but there is a slight softening in her delivery.

"I panicked. I hadn't studied enough, I was really worried about getting a high enough score for Yale and I didn't feel ready to take it," I tell her. Although this clearly isn't why I missed the test, it *is* true that I wasn't ready.

My mom sighs and exhales loudly, and then takes another deep breath. I'm not sure if she is doing yoga breathing exercises or if she is just breathing like that so she can take her time before she responds.

Finally, she looks at me and stops her weird breathing and says, "You should have told us."

"I know. I'm sorry I didn't say anything, but you've been so busy lately," I tell her. "I didn't feel like I could talk to you and I didn't want to bother you."

She flinches like I hit her and then I can see that she is trying to hold back her own tears; she blinks several times to keep herself from crying, "You can always talk to me and your dad. I know we've been busy lately and I'm really sorry about that. We'll be better, I promise."

I know it's a low blow, and it's kind of shitty considering the actual reason I missed the test, but they *have* both been totally pre-occupied recently.

"That's okay. I'm going to take the test in New Canaan on Saturday," I tell her.

"Okay. Let me know if you need help studying or anything," she says as she gets up from my bed and starts moving toward the door.

"I'll let you know," I tell her.

"Crap, we have to hurry," she says, looking at her watch.

"Can't Dad drive me?" I ask.

"He left early today," she says.

"What? He never leaves this early," I reply, grabbing my bag and following her down the stairs where I can hear Max and Izzy fighting over which of them gets to read the back of the cereal box while they eat.

"I guess he needed to be in early today," she says, but her answer is incredibly unconvincing.

"Come on everybody, hurry up, we need to leave in ten minutes," my mom says, absentmindedly pouring me a bowl of cereal, even though I rarely eat breakfast at home in the morning.

I take a bite of the flavorless rice puffs and sneak a look at the text message that came in while my mom was in my room – that didn't seem the best time to check my message.

Brandon: thinking about you –have a great day ♥

I re-read it at least five times before I put the phone back in my bag, and I have to keep myself from hugging the phone to my chest. I'll write back to him when I get to school – I want to think of the perfect reply, but I know that whatever happens today, or tomorrow, or with the SAT on Saturday, it's all going to be okay as long as I have Brandon.

Chapter Twenty-Four
Jack

I'm sure I'm just imagining it, but it feels like there was a campus-wide memo to all faculty members letting them know about the demise of my textbook. Only Charles, the department chair, mentioned something outright, but I swear I have been getting looks of pity for the past two days. Even faculty from other departments have been staring and pointing like I'm an animal from the zoo, although those two French professors may have been pointing to the new library entrance, but it was hard to decipher with all their gesturing.

Ordinarily, my office or anywhere on campus is where I come to escape, but this new turn of events adds an unwanted twist. I've come in unusually early the last few mornings to avoid conversations with Ellie at home, although that's not what I said to her. I can't be at home, I can't be at work – that doesn't leave me many options.

I know our relationship isn't quite to this point, but on a whim, I decide to text Hailey. We said we would try to have lunch soon – maybe she's free this afternoon, I could cancel my office hours and head into the City to meet her. Just the idea of a trip into the City and seeing her brightens my mood.

Jack: Hi there. Any chance you are free this afternoon? Late lunch maybe or coffee? I could come into the City...

I see the three dots appear almost instantly to show that she's replying, similar to when I text Sydney – kids this age have a response time of under ten seconds, it's astonishing.

Hailey: Hi!

Hailey: I have to work for my aunt this afternoon – sorry

Jack: I could come see the gallery and meet your aunt

The dots appear quickly, and then disappear, then they reappear again a few minutes later.

Hailey: I don't think that will work. Could you have lunch on Saturday? I can come to Yale.

Now it's my turn to pause. Saturday is definitely family time and that is hard to juggle, although that's quite ironic since Hailey is certainly family. I'm sure I am supposed to be driving to a soccer game on Saturday, but I can't say no to Hailey, it's too new and fragile.

Jack: sure – let's meet at my office at noon?

Hailey: sounds good! Have a good week!

Jack: You too ☺

I don't have a clue how I'm going to manage the logistics of getting to New Haven on Saturday and what I'm going to tell Ellie, but I'll have to make it work. It's only two o'clock and I have no reason to cancel office hours or to leave campus now that I'm not meeting Hailey, but I just can't sit here anymore.

I toss my laptop and a stack of papers in my bag, grab my camel hair blazer from the back of my chair and for the first time in my professional career, I leave early just because I feel like it.

"Ginny, please cancel my office hours, something came up and I have to go. I'll see you tomorrow," I say as I swing by her desk, not giving her enough time to respond.

***

It's only when I'm speeding down I-95 (there's virtually no traffic at two-thirty on a Wednesday) that I realize I have no idea where I'm going. I can't go home. It's too early to go to a bar; I don't want to be the lonely guy in a bar on a weekday afternoon. I could go to the gym, but I don't have any of my stuff with me and then I'd have to go home and explain why I'm playing hooky. I'm getting closer and closer to the exit for Westport and I still haven't figured out what I'm going to do for the next three hours.

Without a fully formed plan, I take the exit twenty-nine for Bridgeport and continue straight on Seaview Avenue and about half a mile up the road there is a Starbucks pretty much exactly where I remembered it. I've only been here once before, when I was taking Max to work with me and he had to go to the bathroom so badly he couldn't hold it another five minutes to the easily accessible rest stop, let alone the twenty-five minutes to my office.

Although all Starbucks have a similar look and feel, which is part of their billion-dollar brand, the Bridgeport Starbucks definitely lacks a little something compared to my home-field Starbucks in Westport. As I wait in line behind an octogenarian and his caregiver, I'm trying to figure out exactly why it feels so different; the basics are the same, although this store only has tables and chairs, no comfy couches and armchairs, but then the key difference hits me. This store is quiet and virtually empty, whereas at home, it sounds more like a club and it is almost impossible to get a table at any hour of the day. The seats are occupied by groups of women with babies and toddlers on their laps and hordes of teenagers spending their parents' money on eight-dollar cashew milk lattes, hovering over the few patrons with laptops urging them to leave.

I accept my grande latte and cranberry scone and select a table by the window, where I can sit and figure out my plan for the afternoon. I've already acknowledged that it's more than likely I will sit here for a few hours and work and then go home a little earlier than normal, but first I'm going to enjoy my coffee and see if I can think of anything better before I accept my fate.

I'm only a few sips in, when I hear crying, quickly followed by a woman's voice saying, "It's okay, let's get you something to eat, shhhh, shhhhh, it's okay."

I glance over my shoulder to see a sturdy, heavily made-up woman (that's the nicest way to say it), holding a baby and struggling to pull a high chair off the top of the stack of high chairs at the back wall. If they have noticed, it does not appear that either of the baristas are going to come to her aid, so I put down my coffee and walk over to assist.

"Can I help?" I ask, as I approach the woman and her crying baby.

"Thank you so much," she says, releasing her death grip on the sticky high chair.

With two hands, I easily lift the chair off the stack. "Where would you like it?" I ask her.

She surveys the seating area and then points to the table directly next to mine. "Over there by the window would be great. Thank you so much," she says, readjusting the bag on her shoulder and the baby on her hip and ambling toward the table.

I wish I could suggest she choose a different location, or perhaps just carry the highchair to a different table, but it's not my place to tell her where she can sit, and I'll look like a jackass if I get up and move as soon as she sits down. Maybe the kid will stop crying when it gets something to eat – hopefully she's right and it's just hungry.

"Thank you again," she says as she straps the baby into the high chair and we all sit back down in our seats.

Ellie is the one who is good at this sort of thing, but I would guess that the kid is about ten or eleven months old; although it's been so long, it's hard to remember what that looks like.

I pull out an issue of the Economist from my bag and try to focus on the cover story and my buttery scone, but it's impossible not to be distracted by the thousand decibel shrieking taking place four feet away.

The mom takes a gulp of her venti Frappuccino and then starts to unpack her massive diaper bag onto the table. I assume (or at least I hope) she is searching for food, or a pacifier, or something that will make the baby stop crying! Eventually she finds a jar of something orange, a spoon and a bib, and she attempts to put the bib around the kid's neck with minimal success. She tosses the bib and digs into the orange mush and offers it to the baby. I can't help it, but I'm now watching this more intently than a Red Sox game. I'm waiting for the greedy little bugger to chomp down on the spoon in delight, but instead it spits out the orange mush and starts crying even louder. The mom rummages some more in her bag and finds a similar jar, but filled with green goo. She goes through the same motions, and the kid has the exact same reaction. I want to turn away, but I can't. She tries Cheerios and the little monster throws the whole container on the floor, crying louder than I thought was humanly possible.

She takes another sip or two of her Frappuccino in between feeding attempts, and although I think I judged her before, now I'm just impressed that she isn't also in tears. Finally she takes a bottle out of her bag and puts powder inside, gives it a shake and hands it to the kid, who takes a few deep pulls on the bottle and the entire store goes quiet. I don't want to get involved, but

I almost feel like I should give her a high five. But then the magic spell wears off and the kid throws the bottle on the floor and starts screaming again. The mom sighs and starts piling everything back in her bag again, including the items she has to bend down for and grab off the floor. With her bag on her shoulder and her half-drunk milkshake in her hand, she scoops up her screaming child and gives me a look that might as well say, "I can't believe this is my life," and she walks out the door.

***

"You're home early," Ellie remarks, when I walk in the door a little after five-thirty. I find her in the living room with her laptop open next to her on the sofa and an untouched glass of iced tea next to her on the end table.

"Yeah, I wrapped up early today and wanted to get home," I tell her.

"Hmmm," she replies, picking up her laptop and resting it on her thighs. This conversation is the longest one we've had since we talked the other night in bed, and it's going downhill quickly. I know I have been avoiding her *and* this conversation, but I think we have to talk about the elephant in the room – I mentally breathe a sigh of relief that I didn't say that out loud.

"Where is everyone?" I ask, taking a seat on the leather club chair to her right.

"Do you mean our children?" she asks, tight lipped, not moving her eyes from the screen.

"Those would be the ones. Unless there are others I should be aware of?" I ask, trying to make a joke.

"Max is at a friend's house, he needs to be picked up in half an hour. Izzy is in the basement watching TV and Sydney is upstairs doing homework," she answers.

"I'm sorry if it seems like I've been avoiding you," I say, combing my hands through my hair, a nervous habit I can't seem to shake.

Ellie slams her laptop shut and tosses it to the side where it lands with a dull thud on the navy, velvet cushion. "You *have* been avoiding me, it doesn't just *seem* like it," she accuses, now staring directly at me with her angry hazel eyes.

"You're right. I'm sorry," I concede. "I've needed time to think, but I shouldn't have ignored you," I apologize.

"So, have you come to any conclusions?" Ellie asks, she still seems upset, but my apology appears to have mollified her somewhat.

I slump back in the chair and wonder if I can really say what I've been planning the entire drive home from Bridgeport. I came up with several different versions, but none of them are good. "I know that this isn't what I said before, but I've been thinking about it, and the money is definitely part of it, but it isn't *just* the money." I pause, take a breath and look around, because once I say this, there's really no going back, "I don't think I want to have another baby."

The words hang in the air, and I'm waiting for Ellie to catch them, or add to them, or do something, but she just sits there.

After an uncomfortably long silence, she replies, but not the way I expected, given her initial reaction. "I'm still having a hard time accepting this as well, but I don't think I can have another abortion," she says quietly.

"What do you mean, *another* abortion?" I ask, assuming I misunderstood her, but all my senses are on high alert for fear that I did not.

"I have no idea how to tell you this. It all happened so fast and we barely knew each other. I always planned to tell you and then I didn't say anything, and then too much time had passed and I *couldn't* say anything," she says, fumbling to get the words out, and overusing her hands to make her point the way she does when she's flustered.

"Are you trying to tell me that you got pregnant with *our* baby and you had an abortion?" I ask, my voice raising to a dangerous level for having two of our three kids in the house.

"It was the first time we slept together," she tells me, looking like she's about to cry. "We had only been on three dates, well two and a half really. I still don't think frozen yogurt counts as a date," she says, making a poor attempt at lightening the mood.

"And so you made that decision without me?" I ask. "Look, I get that it's your body and I'm sure we would have decided to do the same thing together, because neither of us was ready for a baby then, but why wouldn't you tell me?" I ask with disbelief.

"I was terrified. We didn't really know each other, and I didn't want to ruin everything or change things, I just wanted it to go away so things could go back to normal," she tries to explain.

"So what about after that? When we got serious? Or when we got engaged? Or married? Or maybe sometime over the last eighteen years when we had three children and built a life together? You didn't think there was a good time to tell me then?" I ask, unable to keep from raising my voice again.

"It felt like it was too late. The only person who knew was Erica, and then it just felt like it was my awful secret. I know you don't understand, but even though it was definitely the *right* decision, I had a really tough time afterwards. That was the two-week trip I took to visit my sick aunt in May. I didn't go away, I just couldn't leave my apartment or get out of bed, so Erica made that up," Ellie says. There are tears streaming down her cheeks now, but she's not making an attempt to wipe them away, they are washing the mascara off her lashes and creating black rivers down her cheeks. It's hard to watch her cry like this without offering some level of comfort, but I'm too angry to think about giving her a hug or even getting up to fetch her a tissue.

"So you and Erica have kept this from me for twenty years? Are there other things you are keeping from me? Other children I should know about?" I ask cruelly.

"That's not fair. I know I shouldn't have kept this from you. I was scared and twenty-three and it was stupid not to tell you. But I think a lot more has happened in our lives that we can work past this," she pleads. "And I'm just as uncertain about this baby as you are," she says, resting her hand on her tiny stomach, "but I think we'll find a way to make it work," she says, with about as much conviction as I currently feel.

Ellie grabs her condensation coated tea glass and silently exits the room, leaving me alone with my thoughts, which is a dangerous place to be. I try to think back to our first few months together in the summer of 1999 in Manhattan. Although much of it is now a blur, I'll never forget our first time, on the black canvas futon in my studio on Mercer Street. I vaguely remember that she went out of town to visit someone a few weeks later, but I was in the depths of my PhD thesis, so as much as I was into Ellie at the time, a couple weeks of separation didn't really mean much to me. But now I find out that I was naively enjoying our first great months together and she was home curled up in bed, alone and miserable – too scared to tell me about it. I'm still furious, but I also feel awful for that young girl – barely older than Sydney or Hailey...

And that transgression isn't lost on me, but I didn't even know about her until a few weeks ago – it isn't the same thing. Although, the incident at Richie's bachelor party is a different story altogether. I just need to get more comfortable with the relationship with Hailey and then I will figure out the right way to tell Ellie. I have to get control over something in my life.

Chapter Twenty-Five
Ellie

I pause to check my outfit one more time in the full-length mirror inside the hall closet. When we installed this mirror, Jack said it was a ridiculous place to put it, but I think I use it more than the one in our bedroom. I'm still not quite sure what to wear for tea with Dorothy, and unfortunately my usual dress clothes don't have forgiving waist-bands like the rest of my wardrobe, but I did find a navy empire waist dress that looks tasteful, but doesn't look too frumpy or like a maternity tent. My arms and legs are still toned, even if they have lost their entire summer glow, so I look like myself, or a version of myself playing dress-up. I found a pair of low navy heels in the back of my closet and put on gold hoops and a matching necklace that I haven't worn in years. The overall look is somewhere between fifties housewife and something I swear I saw in one of the windows downtown last week, so maybe it will suffice for tea.

When I get in the car, I dial Erica's number and put in my Air Pods as I back out of the driveway. She picks up on the first ring.

"Hey, how are you?" she asks, out of breath.

"Is this a bad time?" I ask her.

"No, it's fine," she assures me, as I hear her gulping down water.

"Where *are* you?" I ask her.

"I'm home. I just got off the Peloton. Bruce kicked my ass again today," she exclaims.

"I don't get the whole spinning thing," I say. "Especially, doing it in your living room."

"It's just because you haven't tried it yet. You'd love it, I promise. And I can do it while the baby is napping," she brags.

"Hmmm," is all I say.

"But you didn't call to get a sales pitch on a super expensive bike, so what's up?" she asks.

"It seems Jack has had a change of heart," I tell her.

"What does that mean?" Erica asks.

"He lost out on this opportunity at work, which is going to mean a lot less money coming in and that really freaked him out. But then he said it wasn't just the money. He's been thinking about it and he doesn't want to have a baby. He thinks I should have an abortion," I confide.

"How does that make you feel? Did the two of you discuss that as an option?" she asks, in her best therapist voice.

"I also told him about the D&C when we first started dating," I explain.

"Wow, how did he take it?"

"He was really upset. This happened last night and he slept on the couch in his office after I told him. He was already gone this morning when I left for work," I tell her.

207

"I'm so sorry. That's a lot for him to process, especially with what's going on right now. And that's a lot for you to deal with," she says sympathetically.

"It's all just so shitty. I have no idea what to do," I admit.

"Do you have a gut feeling?" Erica asks.

"The only reliable feeling I have is that I wish I could re-wind the clock and not be in this situation. I'm not sure about having a baby right now, especially if Jack isn't on board! But I really don't know if I can go through the procedure again – and with every day that goes by I'm running out of time!" I say, my voice catching in my throat as my composure begins to crumble.

"I'm sure Jack will come around in a day or two and then you can talk again," she assures me.

"I'm not sure it will happen that quickly, but I'm going to give him a few days of distance and then I'll have to do something," I say, more to myself than to her.

"Okay, I'm here if you need me," she promises. Although we had a ten-year hiatus, we have fallen back into a regular pattern of texting and phone calls since our reunion, but we are both still treating the friendship with kid gloves.

"Thanks. Okay, I gotta go, I'll talk to you later."

"Bye, hang in there," Erica says, hanging up the phone.

***

My call with Erica ended at just the perfect time as I pull up in front of massive stone walls at the spot where the GPS told me I "arrived at my location." I knew I was heading toward Compo Beach, but I didn't realize Dorothy lived in a compound surrounded by water on three sides – perhaps I didn't need to be so worried about Dorothy's well being.

I pull my five-year old Acura MDX over to the side of Hillspoint Road and look for a callbox or some other method of communication to let Dorothy know of my arrival. Just as I'm about to get out of the car to further investigate my options, the ten-foot-high steel gate begins to slowly slide open. I nudge my car into the driveway and get my first glimpse of the breathtaking ocean view property. I hope that the gate was opened for me and it wasn't just a coincidence, or this is going to be very embarrassing.

When I pull up to the front of the estate, Dorothy is standing by the oversized double-doors waiting to greet me. She looks smaller and more frail than she did when I last saw her, and I am dismayed to see a cane in her left hand, but there is a radiant smile on her face and she is waving eagerly with her free hand.

There is a woman next to Dorothy, who I would guess is in her early fifties, and although she isn't wearing a classic black and white maid's uniform like she stepped off the set of Downton Abbey, she is definitely wearing some sort of uniform and her graying hair is tied back in a tight bun. I'm trying to focus on parking the car on the beautiful Belgian block driveway without running off onto the immaculate lawn, but it's a difficult task as my mind works to reconcile this image of Dorothy with the unsuspecting older woman in velour pants from my yoga classes.

"I'm so glad you could make it," Dorothy calls out, as soon as I open my door.

"Thank you so much for inviting me," I gush, as I make my way over toward her. "Your property is stunning," I remark, glancing over her shoulder through the magnificent entryway and the living room in the distance with floor to ceiling windows and panoramic views of the water.

"They are lovely views," she says, in the way someone might say, "yes, these trousers are quite nice."

"Come inside, tea is ready," Dorothy says. Without a word, she takes my arm, and hands her cane over to the maid and I happily escort her inside.

I attempt not to gawk once inside, but this proves quite difficult. It's hard to tell, but the house doesn't appear to be nearly as large as some of the new construction in Westport - the ten and twelve thousand square foot homes that seem to go up overnight. However, Dorothy's home is certainly substantial and has the feel of something that was well built and each and every element was customized and crafted with care.

"How long have you lived here?" I ask Dorothy, as we make our way into the sunken living room, where a silver tea service and an assortment of scones and pastries are arranged on the coffee table.

"We built this house in 1978. Hard to believe it was forty-one years ago, I remember them pouring the foundation like it was yesterday," Dorothy says wistfully.

"That's amazing," I reply, craning my neck to look up at the skylights overhead in the two-story room. You don't see a lot of skylights like that anymore, but I suppose she did just say it was built in the seventies.

"Sometimes it seems silly that I still live here. One person doesn't need this many rooms or this much land, but I couldn't bear to leave all the memories," Dorothy says.

"I don't think *I* would ever leave if I lived here," I say to Dorothy, and then I wince as I hear my words out loud. "Sorry, I just meant that it's such a beautiful house and it's pretty hard to find this type of view or privacy anywhere else," I say, trying to recover.

"Oh, don't worry dear. I know I'm pretty fortunate to have this kind of real estate," she chuckles. "I just wish Norman was still here so we could enjoy it together," she sighs.

Although I've never heard her use her husband's name before, I'm going to take a leap and assume that Norman was her husband. "How long ago did he pass away?" I ask, hoping the question isn't too personal.

"It will be four years this December, God rest his soul," she says, and closes her eyes as if she's saying a little prayer. "That's about the time I met you if you remember," she says.

"I guess it was," I reply.

"I promised Norman that I would get out and try something new, and I had to keep my promise," she tells me.

"And yoga was your something new?" I ask, rather dumbfounded with this new piece of information.

"My first class was two weeks after the funeral," she tells me. "I only started it to keep my promise to Norman, but you were so lovely, and I found that I really enjoyed it. It's made such a difference for me. Ellie, *you've* made such a difference to me," Dorothy says.

"I had no idea," I say to Dorothy, struggling to find the right words. I knew that I felt a connection to her, but I had no idea the feeling was mutual.

"Where are my manners, can I get you some tea? How about a little snack?" Dorothy says, pointing to the array of goodies in front of us.

"Tea would be great, thank you. And I'll have one of these," I say, taking a golden colored blueberry scone from the tray that looks and smells like it just came out of the oven.

We sit in silence for a couple of minutes as Dorothy pours us each a cup of tea and then she puts one lump of sugar into hers and waits for it to dissolve and I put two lumps into mine and a healthy splash of cream – might as well get some benefit out of my current predicament. A quick glance around the room and I observe some framed photographs on the mantle that I didn't notice when I came in.

"Is that you and Norman?" I ask Dorothy, pointing to the photo on the end of a much younger woman and man on a beach, grinning with their arms around each other's shoulders.

"Oh yes. We were practically children when that was taken," she laughs. "Actually, I was probably about your age in that picture. It was a few years before we moved into this house. We were on vacation in California and I fell in love with the beach and the next thing I knew, Norman bought this land and soon after, he started building the house," she says, reflectively.

"Wow, so he bought the land on his own?" I ask, trying to follow the story,

"He was a real estate developer. We were living in Greenwich before that, but we weren't near the water and I said I wanted to live on the beach – I really said it as a lark. I didn't think he was going to do anything about it, but I should have known better, knowing Norman. Next thing I knew, he bought the land and was building me a house," Dorothy says.

"That's so romantic," I tell her, hanging on her every word. It's not quite what I mean to say. But just listening to her talk about her husband I can tell that he did it because he loved and adored her, not because he had a lot of money.

"Are those your children in the other pictures?" I ask her, glancing at the assorted photos on the mantel of young children and young adults.

Dorothy hesitates before answering, and I desperately hope that I haven't said the wrong thing, or upset her with my question.

"Yes. Those are my children and my grandchildren," she replies, her tone is much cooler than it was a moment ago.

"Do they live nearby?" I ask. I should probably close my mouth, but I have been desperate to know about her situation since I met her, and this may be my only chance to find out.

"My daughter lives in Seattle and my son lives in Melbourne," she replies.

"Australia?" I ask, as if I don't understand geography.

"That's the one. It's like it was a competition to see who could get further away from me," she says.

"Oh Dorothy, don't say that," I say, feeling terrible that I brought up the subject.

"It's okay. I've made my peace with it," she says, taking a small sip from her teacup and replacing it in its matching blue and white Spode saucer.

I know that we are in desperate need of a change of topic, but I want to ensure I pick something safe, now that I've made such a terrible blunder. I'm about to remark on the China pattern, since it is one I've always admired, and it seems about as benign as possible, when Dorothy starts speaking again.

"As a mother, you do the best you can, I mean, *you* know that, but it's hard to get it right. And then they grow up and they have lives of their own and they move on without you." She pauses and I wonder if I should comment, but then she picks right back up. "Of course they always know where to find me when they need money – they've never been shy when it comes to asking for money, but then they go back to their own lives without a second thought," Dorothy complains.

"I'm sorry Dorothy, that must be difficult for you," I say, sympathetically.

"Oh, it isn't just their fault. There are a lot of things I would change if I could go back and do it over," she says.

"What do you mean?" I ask.

"It wasn't like it is today, where parents are so involved in everything their kids do. Having kids in the late sixties and seventies was a different story," she says.

"But it was a different time, that doesn't mean it's better or worse," I tell her.

"I know you may find this hard to believe looking at me now, but I had quite the life back in my twenties and thirties. We had two nannies *and* maid and they were the ones who did everything with the children. It was the same for most of my friends. I never stopped to think that there was anything wrong with it. But looking back on it, I can't believe that's the type of mother I was," she says shaking her head.

"I'm sure you were around more than you think," I say hopefully, trying to make her feel better.

"I'm afraid I wasn't there when it counted. I was there for Norman. I was always there for the dinners and the trips and I waited up late at night for him, but my priorities were out of line. By the time I tried to make some sort of relationship with the children in high school, it was too late," she says sadly.

"I'm so very sorry Dorothy," I say again, reaching over and patting her arm, I know the words may sound hollow at this point, but I'm not sure what else I can say.

"Oh it's not your fault dear. And I know that *you* are a lovely mother. I always hear you talking about your children and all of the time you devote to them," Dorothy says, the wrinkles on her cheeks deepening as she smiles.

I try and digest this information and ignore the pit of guilt that is gnawing away at my stomach as I think about my recent absentee parenting and Sydney's SAT situation.

"Don't be too hard on yourself and don't give me too much credit, I'm not sure I'm doing anything right most days," I laugh nervously.

"Oh nonsense," Dorothy says, smiling again.

"Your grandchildren are lovely," I say, pointing at the picture of four tow-headed young children. I assume these are her grandchildren and hope I haven't stumbled onto another landmine; usually grandmothers can agree on the aesthetics of their grandchildren.

"That they are. They're much bigger now of course. The oldest just turned twenty-three and is working in Chicago if you can believe that! The two younger ones live in Melbourne, so I don't see them very often – that picture was taken at Norman's seventieth birthday, a rare time when we were all together. But the two older grandchildren do come visit once or twice a year and that's nice," Dorothy says, nodding her head, her coiffed silver hair bouncing ever-so-slightly.

"How nice," I say emphatically. I almost say that I wish my mother was still around for my children to visit, but when people find out about my parents it always creates an awkward silence and then sympathy, and I don't want that from Dorothy.

"I know you are a busy lady, and I'm sure you have other things to do with your day. I only wanted a chance to visit with you and let you know how much our yoga sessions have meant to me," Dorothy says.

"Thank you. I'm so honored. I'm happy to have played such a special role in your healing process," I tell her. "I hope that I will be seeing you back in class soon," I say expectantly.

"I hope so too," Dorothy says. "But my hip has been bothering me, and I'm just not sure if I will be able to make it to class anymore. I'll try, but I wanted to tell you in person, in case I can't make the classes anymore," she says.

I feel that aching feeling in my stomach for the second time today, and it's like I've lost Dorothy even though she's right in front of me. "I could come to the house and do a private low intensity class for you?" I offer.

"You're too sweet," Dorothy says. "Perhaps you could just come again for tea sometime," she offers.

"I'd like that a lot," I reply.

Chapter Twenty-Six
Jack

"It's good to see you," I say to Hailey as she approaches the bench where I'm waiting outside the economics building. I offered to pick her up at the station, but she insisted on taking an Uber from the train. Fall appears to finally have arrived in earnest, and Hailey is wearing jeans, a heavy gray turtleneck sweater paired with a sky blue down vest. I grabbed a canvas jacket when I left this morning to throw over my light sweater, but she *is* from Texas, so fifty-five degrees probably feels like winter to her.

"It's good to see you too," she says. It feels like she was contemplating leaning in for a hug or a kiss on the cheek, but instead she sticks both hands inside her vest pockets, so she isn't faced with the dilemma.

"How was the ride up here?" I ask.

"It was fine. I'm really getting the hang of Metro North," she jokes. "No one takes the train in Texas, everyone drives everywhere," she remarks.

"I remember," I say.

"Oh right, of course," Hailey says. Due to the nature of our circumstances, I would think that she would remember my ties to Austin, but each time I bring it up, it's as if she's completely forgotten our connection.

"What would you like to eat?" I ask her. "Although, unfortunately we are pretty limited, because almost everything is closed on Saturday, except brunch in the dining halls, and I don't think we want to do that," I laugh.

"Anything's good for me," Hailey says.

"Okay, we'll go to the Thain Café, that's one place that I know is open now," I say, pointing in the direction of Bass Library, where the café is located.

"Sounds good," Hailey says, reaching back to quickly secure her dark hair in an intricate bun on top of her head. I'm not sure if this is a learned skill, or something that is taught, but it seems all girls between the ages of fourteen and twenty-five have a secret bun code meant to baffle members of the opposite sex.

"Did you always want to be a professor?" Hailey asks, as we begin our stroll down the stone pathway through old campus. With the chill in the air, and the leaves a brilliant mix of red, gold and orange against the backdrop of the splendid gothic arches, Yale's campus looks and feels like the quintessential New England school.

"You mean once I figured out that I wasn't going to be a major league baseball player?" I joke.

Hailey cracks a small smile, but that's it.

"I don't think I knew that's what I wanted to do when I first started college. But I liked going to school, I liked my classes and I knew senior year when my friends were interviewing for jobs that I wasn't interested in doing that. So I applied to a PhD program at NYU, to delay the inevitable. I guess it was somewhere during the course of my PhD program that I decided I wanted to teach. I could have gone to work at one of the big banks as an economist, but that didn't sound very appealing," I tell her.

"Why not?" Hailey asks. "You probably would have made a lot more money."

I laugh at her brutal honesty and find it refreshing that she doesn't seem to care if her line of questioning offends me.

"Don't think I haven't thought about that many times over the years," I tell her, and I've thought a lot more about it in the last few days as my book deal slipped away. "Several of my classmates took those jobs and they make ten times what I do and they'll probably retire by the time they are fifty. So maybe they were the smart ones," I say thoughtfully.

"But why didn't you want to do it at the time?" Hailey probes.

"I thought this would be more fulfilling. I liked the idea of being in an academic environment with bright students and being able to do research and keep learning, not just using my power to help rich assholes make even more money," I tell her.

"And you don't still feel that way?" she asks.

"I do," I say, "It's just some days, it's harder than others to live here," I say gesturing to the ivy-covered buildings, "When the demands of the real world don't stop. Do you know what you want to do?" I ask her. I have to stop myself from saying "when you grow up," since she is eighteen-years old.

"I have absolutely no idea," Hailey says.

"Well, that's okay," I tell her. "You have plenty of time to figure that out," I say reassuringly, although I can't help but think how different it is from conversations with Sydney where she has always had a 'plan' even if it has changed over the years. Then it dawns on me that Hailey's lack of direction is likely due to her unstable parental situation and I feel responsible.

"Austin is awesome, but this definitely seems like what college is supposed to look like. You know what I mean?" Hailey says, pointing at the façade of the famed Sterling Memorial Library as we walk by.

"I know exactly what you mean," I tell her. "I've been here ten years, and I'm still in awe of the campus."

Suddenly over Hailey's shoulder I see a girl in a familiar olive-green army jacket, with almost waist-length chestnut colored hair, and my heart catches in my throat. It takes me a second too long to register what's happening because she's walking hand-in-hand with a good-looking older boy, or man! I don't know the right terminology, but he definitely is not someone who should be laughing and holding Sydney's hand! I'm about to yell just that, when I realize that doing so will bring attention to Hailey and Sydney heard me tell Ellie last night that I had all-day meetings – shit!

I grab Hailey's arm, a little harder than I mean to, and tell her to follow me without looking back.

"What's going on?" she asks, trying to keep up with my pace.

"Do you think they saw us?" I ask her.

"What are you talking about?"

"The girl and boy back there? Do you think they saw us?" I ask her, realizing I must sound somewhat deranged.

"I have no idea!" she bursts out. Hailey stops walking and crosses her arms over her chest. We've gotten far enough away, that I feel somewhat safe, so I stop a few feet in front of her.

"What's going on?" Hailey demands.

"I'm so sorry. I didn't know what else to do. That was my daughter," I try to explain, both looking and feeling sheepish.

"We had to run away so your daughter wouldn't see me?" she asks.

"Well, yes. But it's just because I haven't told my family yet," I tell her, cringing as the words come out.

"Look, I'm sure this isn't *easy* for you. But I don't need to be your dirty little secret," she says, lifting her eyebrows to express the perfect level of disdain.

"Hailey, that's not how it is," I plead with her. "I just need to find the right time and the right way to explain it to my wife and then tell my kids," I tell her.

"Don't worry about it," she says coldly. "I wanted to meet you. Now I've learned all I need to know. I told you that you didn't owe me anything and I'm keeping my promise. I'm sorry to have *inconvenienced* you," Hailey says sarcastically, turning around and walking away from me.

"Don't leave! This is silly!" I say, walking quickly to catch up with her.

"It's my fault. I should have known better," she says, shaking her head. "You ditched my mom, I don't know why I expected you would be any different with me," she says.

"It's not like that," I tell her. "Let's have lunch and we can talk about it," I plead with her.

"I don't think so," she says, as she picks up her pace and breaks into a graceful jog that she could probably keep up all the way to Manhattan, ensuring I will have no chance of catching her.

Chapter Twenty-Seven
Sydney

"Oh my God!" I nearly scream, when I see his trademark brown Barbour jacket only fifty feet away.

"What's wrong?" Brandon asks.

"It's nothing," I tell him, trying to twist my look of panic into a smile. "I thought I saw someone, but it wasn't who I thought," I tell him, hoping my vague answer and miserable acting job are convincing.

"Okay," Brandon says, drawing out the O for emphasis; however, he's still smiling and shaking his head like I'm slightly crazy, but in a cute way.

"Do you want to see my room?" I ask, hoping I sound casual, although the butterflies in my stomach are the antithesis of casual.

"I'd love to," Brandon says, squeezing my hand. "Are you just trying to show off how much better your room is than mine?" Brandon teases.

"I promise I won't rub it in," I joke. "It's this way, I say, pulling him in the direction of old campus and Branford College, where my cousin Ainsley lives.

In a moment of brilliance and perhaps sheer insanity, I called Ainsley on Thursday and told her about Brandon and all the lies I've told him about Yale. I was waiting for her to tell me I was stupid or childish; but instead she was thrilled for me and immediately moved into problem solving mode. And then she went above and beyond what any rational person would do and she asked her roommates (two of whom are drama majors) to cooperate and let me use her room today. She couldn't promise who would be in the suite at what time, but all three of them are in on it and they have promised to go along with it and say that I live there. Ainsley even got them to put my name on the door for the day – and this is why Ainsley is my favorite cousin and probably my favorite person in the whole world right now.

I'm having trouble focusing on exactly what Brandon is saying because I am so worried about what will happen if we get to the room and he figures out that I don't live there. And then there is the added concern – what if we get there and it all works out and he decides that he's over what happened with his ex-girlfriend and he's ready to have sex?! My brain is working so hard, it's amazing I am able to put one foot in front of the other. I tried to keep most of these thoughts out of my head when I took the SAT this morning, but I'd be lying if I said I was completely focused – ugh.

"This is it," I announce, as we walk through the archway that leads to my possible demise.

"Lead the way," Brandon says.

He walks closely behind me up the stairs and when I get to the top I hesitate for a moment before I remember if I need to turn left or right. I choose left, keep track of the room numbers and pray that my luck hasn't run out.

"Here we are!" I declare as I find the door sign on the appropriate room that shows my name next to the three other girls that Ainsley told me about. I will need to find a way to repay these goddesses.

I turn the doorknob, and as promised the door opens easily and I let out a huge sigh of relief.

"Hey Sydney," a girl calls from the couch.

"Hi!" I say brightly. I want to run over and hug and kiss her and scream "thank you!" but that will have to wait for some other time.

"You must be Brandon," she says, getting up from the couch to say hello. "I've heard so much about you," she gushes. "I'm Ava," she says, introducing herself to both of us, unbeknownst to Brandon.

"Nice to meet you," Brandon says politely.

"I'm the only one here right now," Ava says, giving me a sly look, "so you'll have to meet the other girls some other time," she says, with a big smile on her face.

"That's great," I reply. "I think we'll just hang out in my room," I say, quickly looking at the four doors surrounding the common area and hoping I can figure out which room belongs to Ainsley.

I don't deserve this much good fortune, but there, on one of the doors is a poster with my name on it. The paint may still even be wet, but hopefully Brandon's focus isn't on the door sign.

"See you later, nice to meet you," Brandon says again as we walk toward my room and he closes the door behind me.

***

It isn't until I'm home that night in my own bed that the events of the afternoon start to play back in my head. Initially, I was so worried about my dad seeing me, and then relieved to get away from him without being caught that I almost forgot about what I saw. And then I practically erased the whole thing after two hours in Ainsley's room making out with Brandon and learning some of the amazing things he knows how to do that don't have a chance of causing pregnancy, but which Jenna and Katie would still consider "taking it super slow."

But now in the pitch black, with only the familiar quarter-hour chime of the grandfather clock to interrupt the silence, all I can see is my dad walking way too close to a beautiful young girl when he told my mom he was going to be in all-day meetings, and I feel a sense of anger and betrayal toward him that I've never experienced. No matter how much I fight with my mom, she doesn't deserve anything like this.

It takes me over an hour to fall asleep, but as I drift off to sleep, I determine that I need to do something to help; I'm just not sure what that is.

Chapter Twenty-Eight
Ellie

"I have a doctor appointment tomorrow," I say to Jack, trying to sound like it isn't a big deal.

"For what?" Jack asks, although he barely sounds interested. After two nights on the couch in his study, he slept in bed the last couple of nights, but things are still quite frosty between us.

"It's because I'm old," I say, trying to make a joke.

Jack continues to concentrate on getting the perfect Windsor knot in his tie and doesn't respond to my comment, which would previously have been met with an argument for my ever-present youth, or at least a joke of his own, but today it's just crickets.

Not to be deterred, I continue. "The doctor wants me to do an ultrasound this week just to check on everything. I'm only eight weeks or so, but she doesn't want to wait until the usual eleven or twelve weeks due to my advanced maternal age." I put air quotes around this last term, but that still doesn't get a smile, so I give up.

"I have a full day tomorrow, I can't make it to Greenwich for any appointments," Jack says, slipping on his blazer.

"Of course not. I didn't expect you to be there, I was only letting you know," I tell him, trying to ease the tension.

"I'm going to get going," he says, crossing over the bedroom to where I am still sitting in bed, to give me a perfunctory kiss on the cheek.

"Have a good day."

"Thanks, you too," Jack says, and heads out into the hall and down the stairs.

I know I should be thankful that we are slowly getting back to normal, and I need to accept that he is angry because of a secret *I* kept all these years, but honestly, I have too much to do to walk on eggshells right now. I wish he would set a date and tell me that he would be mad up until that date and then it would be over, but it doesn't work like that. So instead, he will avoid me and speak in short sentences, and leave early for work and come home late, and I will just have to deal with it.

***

"Alright ladies, it's a beautiful fall day! Who's ready for some yoga?" I ask the fifteen women in front of me, in various shades and shapes of body-shaping performance fabric.

There is a chorus of "yeses" and I instruct them all to get into a sun salutation to begin the class.

"Aren't you going to be *hot* in that?" Lara asks snidely, referring to the lime green hoodie I've chosen to wear over my black leggings and tank top. Although the lump on my stomach is still almost nonexistent, my usually flat tummy is no longer flat, and these gossips would notice it instantly.

"I'm actually kind of chilly today," I say, plastering a smile on my face. "I'm not working hard like you ladies," I tell her, trying to appeal to her vanity.

"Hmmm," Lara says, switching legs and repositioning her hands to perfect her pose.

The hour drags a little, but mercifully class does come to an end and I am hopefully almost moments away from being able to take off my sweat-soaked hoodie. I'm almost in the clear when Jillian stops at the desk on the way out, where I'm browsing the confirmations for afternoon classes and counting the seconds until the studio is empty.

"Have a great day!" I say cheerfully, glancing up and then looking back down at the screen, trying to convey a message.

"Thanks, you too!" Jillian says, and then she pauses directly in front of me. "Hey, are you sure you're okay?" she asks.

"What? Of course I'm okay!" I say, with more force than is necessary. "Why do you ask?"

"You just seem stressed recently," she says, and then laughs. "That sounds funny, a yoga teacher who's stressed, right?" she laughs again, her perfectly blown-out hair shaking slightly as she does. "But seriously, you seem a little upset, or out of it, or something," she finishes; resting her freshly manicured nails on the desk – I notice they are a pretty shade of lilac this week.

"I promise I'm okay. But thanks for checking," I try to assure her. "You know how it is, everything is so busy and crazy. I know school basically just started, but I feel like I already need a vacation," I say, chuckling.

"Oh my God, totally," Jillian says. "Are you guys going away for Thanksgiving?" she asks.

"We're going to be here. I think Jack's dad and stepmom will probably come, but we haven't really thought about it yet. You know we have the smallest family ever," I remind her. "Are you going away?" I ask, trying to embrace the topic change.

"We are! My mom isn't thrilled, but we're going to Cabo. I don't think they have turkey there, but it will be nice not to have to deal with all the usual nonsense. Besides, we're hosting Christmas this year, and you know what an ordeal *that* is," she says, nodding her head.

"That sounds amazing!" I tell her, thinking four days at a sunny resort would be a dream.

"You guys should come with us!" Jillian squeals. "I'll have Tom call Jack and they can arrange it! We have room on the plane, so you don't have to worry about that. It's just the hotel, and that's nothing," she says, waving her hand, as if to dismiss the cost of the hotel into thin air.

When Jillian says "nothing" I'm pretty sure the rooms cost at least two or three thousand dollars a night. I know Jack would kill me for even thinking about it. "I'm pretty sure we need to do something with Jack's Dad," I tell her, "but I'll check with him and let you know," I say, knowing that I will never mention a word of this to Jack.

"Sounds good!" she says. "Oh, and how's Sydney? How was the make-up test?" Jillian asks, looking at me with a tiny bit of sympathy.

"She said it was great," I tell her.

"Tell her that the girls miss her. Katie said she hardly sees her anymore," Jillian says. "She heard she has some mystery boyfriend that's taking up all her time. Oh shoot, is that the time," Jillian says, glancing at the clock on the wall behind my desk. "So sorry, I have to run. See you later this week!" And just like that, she's gone, and my biggest immediate concern is no longer stripping down to my sweaty tank top.

***

I spent most of the afternoon debating the best way to talk to Sydney, considering she doesn't usually want to talk to me about much of anything. After much deliberating, I decided that getting her alone in the car and asking her point-blank is going to be my best option. Over the years, we've had some of our best talks in the car, and this way she can't run out on me. I briefly considered saying nothing, given that the source is Katie, and Sydney is almost seventeen *and* has every right to have a boyfriend. But then I reconsidered and decided that while she's living in my house, I deserve to know about anyone she's dating.

Ellie: Syd – I'll pick you up after soccer – I have to be out anyway. Meet me out front

Sydney: K

Only this generation would feel the need to shorten a four-letter word to one letter.

Unsurprisingly, Max is in his bedroom when I need to leave to pick up Sydney. I knock, but choose to speak through the door instead of entering. "Hey sweetie, I'm going to pick up Sydney at soccer. Izzy is being dropped off from a playdate at five thirty, but I should be home by then," I tell him.

"Okay," he replies.

"Are you done with your homework?" I ask hopefully.

"Yup," he replies.

"Everything okay in there?" I ask.

"Yup. Bye mom," he calls back.

"Bye Max," I sigh, shaking my head and walking away.

I arrive a few minutes early, but Sydney is already out in front of school waiting for me, her oversized backpack on the ground beside her and her Adidas soccer bag slung over her shoulder. She looks slightly annoyed that I've made her wait, but not too mad – maybe she realizes I'm actually early. She looks so strong and athletic in her full soccer gear - black umbros, black socks pulled up to her knees, fluorescent blue cleats, gray t-shirt stained with sweat and of course her mane of hair pulled into a ponytail on top of her head. I always looked too weak to play any serious sports. My attempt at swimming and volleyball were both disasters and I ended up on top of the cheerleading pyramid by default, but I wish just once I could have looked and felt like a proper athlete, like Sydney does right now.

"Hey," Sydney says, as she slides into the passenger seat.

"How was your day?" I ask her, wishing I had written down a script for this conversation.

"Fine," she answers.

"Good," I reply, as we pull out of school and I try to remember my opening line.

Before I can say anything, Sydney surprises me. "Mom, I don't know how to say this, but I have to tell you something," she says.

Wow, maybe she's going to confess about the mystery man before I even bring it up – she's doing my job for me, I think with relief. "What is it, Syd?" I ask, assuming I know what she's about to say.

"I think Dad's having an affair," she blurts out.

'What?!" I say, completely shocked at her words *and* how far off this is from my expectations.

"Dad is sleeping with one of his students and I think you should know. I'm so sorry," Sydney says, reaching over to pat my arm and likely also to make sure I don't lose control of the steering wheel.

Chapter Twenty-Nine
Jack

"Professor Miller, will you be available at office hours today?" a student asks hopefully, approaching me at my desk at the front of the lecture hall after class.

"Yes, I will be there this afternoon," I tell the bright-eyed girl with two blonde braids that seem more appropriate for someone Izzy's age than a college junior.

"Thank you so much," she beams. "I'm having a little bit of trouble with the neoclassical model of utility maximization and I want to make sure I'm ready for the midterm on Friday," she says, the stress apparent on her face. "I went yesterday and Owen was there, but I was hoping you could help me some more," she explains.

"I'd be happy to help," I tell her. "I'll see you this afternoon," I say, zipping closed my leather messenger bag and hoping she gets the signal that the conversation is over – she could also look around and note that she is the only student remaining in the auditorium.

"Great, thanks again Professor Miller, I'll see you this afternoon," she gushes, zipping up her own bag and making her way up the stairs, the heavy door closing behind her with a bang.

I know that I shouldn't be taking my distress out on my students, but it's hard not to let my personal life bleed over into my professional one with all that's going on right now. And no wonder that poor girl needs to come back for office hours again today. It's certainly not fair to provide Owen as my substitute – he's barely scraping by in the master's program, but he was the only one available yesterday at the last minute and I just had to get off campus for the afternoon. But today I will put it all aside for two hours and help Lisa (at least I think her name is Lisa) and any other students that need help getting ready for their midterms, and then tonight I will make a plan to figure out the shit-show that is my life.

***

Rob walks out to the elevator just as I'm pushing the down button to begin the journey home; I'm not particularly excited to head back to Westport yet, but I've had enough of my depressing office for the day.

"You heading home?" I ask Rob.

"That's the plan," he says, resting his backpack on the floor so he can put on his overcoat. Unfortunately, the weather in New Haven seems to have changed quickly, and coats are no longer optional.

"Do you have time to grab a quick drink?" I ask him, glancing at my watch as I ask. "It's only six fifteen," I inform him.

"I probably shouldn't," Rob says, turning up his palms in a way that lets me know he wants to, but it's not up to him.

"Oh come on, just one drink. You'll be home by seven," I promise.

"I don't know," Rob says, but I can tell he's starting to cave.

"You usually don't even leave here until six forty-five," I try to reason with him.

"Alright, alright," Rob says, laughing, as the elevator comes and we both get in. "But if Rayna calls, I'm handing you the phone," he jokes.

"It's a deal. I promise I'll tell your wife it was an emergency department meeting," I say.

I'm surprised it took Rob this long to bring it up, but he doesn't say anything until we start on our second round. "I'm sorry about the book deal, Jack. You got screwed," he says.

"Thanks," I tell him, taking a mouthful of Guinness.

"Something else will come along," Rob says confidently. "You should just write your own thing," Rob says, "you know, like a mass-market book," he says, nodding his head along with his great idea.

"It's not the same," I try to explain, but it doesn't seem worth it. "That is probably what I'll do. I just need to find the right angle – there's a lot of business books out there," I remind him.

"I'm happy to help out," he offers. "Not that you need it, or not that you would want my help," he says, trying to back-pedal.

"Rob, that would be great," I assure him. "Just give me a little time to figure out what I'm doing and I'll let you know," I tell him.

"Great," he says, looking enthused.

"Have you ever thought that you might have a kid out there that you didn't know about?" I blurt out, drastically changing the course of our conversation.

"What?" Rob asks, rightfully confused at both the question and the ridiculous non sequitur.

"I'm just saying, have you ever wondered if a long time ago you slept with a girl and got her pregnant and then you never saw her again, and she never told you about it and somewhere out there you had a son or daughter running around that you didn't know about?" I ask Rob, trying to impress upon him the severity of the situation that he (and all men) could be facing at this very moment.

"Um, actually, I've never thought about that," Rob says, looking at me like I'm insane, and then taking a quick glance at his watch.

"Well you should. It's something everyone should think about," I say a little too loudly, although it's still on the early side for Elm City Social, so the seats next to us are empty.

"Is everything okay?" Rob asks, looking quite concerned.

For a second, I think about telling him the whole story. Maybe Rob has the answer, or at least he has some advice on how to tell Ellie, or how to get Hailey to talk to me when I've fucked it up so badly. But once it's out, there's nothing I can do to put the genie back in the bottle, and honestly how well do I really know Rob? I've probably said far too much already.

"Everything's fine," I assure him. "It was a story I was reading about. I can't remember where I read it, but the statistics were quite frightening," I tell him.

"Ah," he says with a chuckle and an obvious look of relief. "I think I'm pretty safe. Or at least I hope I am. If I have any random kids out there, Rayna would kill me! You know what I mean?" Rob laughs, finishing the rest of his beer.

I smile weakly and take another sip of mine, "Yeah, totally," I reply.

236

"Alright, I gotta get going. I'll see you tomorrow," Rob says, gathering his jacket and backpack from the stool next to him.

"See you tomorrow," I echo and give a quick wave as he heads toward the door.

I know that I should also go home, but I feel worse than I did when I came in. I check my texts to see if by any chance Hailey has responded to me, but unfortunately she still has not replied, so I try one more time.

Jack: It's me again. Please give me another chance. I know it's too soon and too complicated to say this, but I love you.

Chapter Thirty
Ellie

Some people say everything happens for a reason, and ordinarily I think those people are full of shit. But this morning I'm starting to question if there isn't something behind that wisdom.

When I left the house this morning, I planned to be out for almost the whole day. Maureen and Darcy were covering my classes so I could go to the doctor, and then I had a day full of annoying errands. But after dropping the kids off at school, I realized I left my phone at home, so I had to swing back and get it. As soon as I walked in, the phone was ringing on the counter, so I picked it up, but it wasn't until I answered that I realized it was Jack's phone – what are the odds that we both forgot our phones at home on the same day?!

"Ellie? Is that you?" Jack asked.

"Yes, it's me. Why are you calling your phone?" I asked him.

"I couldn't find it, so I was trying to call it and I hoped it was just somewhere in my office, but it looks like I left it at home," Jack said, sounding deflated.

"It was right here on the kitchen counter," I told him.

"Okay, I have classes all day, so I'll get it tonight when I get home," he said.

"Okay," I replied and hung up.

Had it not been for my conversation with Sydney, I would have put his phone down, gone to find my phone and gone on with my day. But as much as I didn't want to believe her, I also wanted to find out for myself, and standing alone in the house with Jack's phone seemed like the perfect opportunity. I wasn't sure where to start looking for clues. Did I need to look through his emails, or scour his calendar for secret meetings? But it turned out, all I had to do was look at his most recent text message to a skank named Hailey to see the black and white evidence of his affair.

Jack: It's me again. Please give me another chance. I know it's too soon and too complicated to say this, but I love you.

***

My rollercoaster of emotions through the day from outrage to indignation to devastation has ended in exhaustion and I am under the covers at eight forty-five in the evening. I told Sydney that I wasn't feeling well (which is entirely true) and asked if she could make sure Izzy and Max got to bed on time. It was hard to manage the look of pity she gave me, but she hasn't said anything since she broke the news, so at least we don't have to *talk* about my imploding marriage.

"Why are you in bed?" Jack asks. I heard his footsteps in the hallway, so it's not a total surprise, but I'm still rattled when I hear his voice. "Are you sick?"

I went through dozens of speeches in my head today, and even practiced a few of them out loud, but now I can't bring myself to say any of them. I don't know if it's because I can still pretend this isn't happening if I don't say anything, or if I just can't bear to hear his lame excuses, but either way, I can't do it.

"I'm just tired," I tell him, reaching over to turn off the lamp on my bedside table.

"How was the doctor's appointment?" Jack asks, sitting down on his side of the bed and facing the opposite wall to take off his shoes and socks.

I'm shocked that he actually remembered I was supposed to go to the doctor today, considering that topic has been essentially off-limits, not to mention his attempt to completely avoid me.

"Actually, I had to reschedule the appointment, I couldn't make it today," I tell him. This is more-or-less the truth. The doctor's office called me when I was forty-five minutes late and I was still sitting in the kitchen staring at the text on Jack's phone; at that point we mutually determined that I needed to reschedule.

"Oh. So when is the appointment now?" Jack asks.

"The day after tomorrow," I mumble into my pillow.

"Should I come with you?" Jack asks.

I can't help but laugh at his offer. This morning I would have been fooled by his attempt at a turn-around, but now I know what's really going on. "Don't worry about it," I say. "It's right in the middle of the day, I know you have other things going on." I try to keep the sarcasm out of my voice, since I don't want this to turn into an argument, even though I'm desperate to have one, but I'm not ready to do it yet.

"If you're sure," Jack says.

"Oh, I'm sure," I tell him, attempting to sound sincere.

"I'm going to go downstairs to get something to eat. I promise to clean everything up when I'm done – I saw that you already cleaned up for the night," Jack says.

"Alright, thanks," I say through tight lips, wondering what else will result from Jack's guilty conscience.

Chapter Thirty-One
Sydney

"What are you doing in here?" my mom asks, when she stumbles into the kitchen, wearing a gray fleece robe I've only seen her wear twice before. Once when she had the flu and the other time was during a power outage a few years ago when the house was about the same temperature inside and outside.

"You said you weren't feeling well last night, so I figured maybe you were still sick. I thought I could make breakfast for Max and Izzy, so you could sleep in," I tell her, as I smother an extra-crispy piece of toast with too much jam in hopes that Izzy doesn't complain about the crunchiness.

I thought she would be happy, but her face falls and it looks like she's about to cry. "Syd, you didn't have to do that," she tells me. "Here, let me finish doing it," she says, easing the knife out of my hand.

"Did you already have breakfast?" my mom asks, as she heads to the fridge to get fruit and yogurt to supplement the meager breakfast I've made so far.

"Yeah, I already ate," I lie.

"Let me get this ready and I'll throw something on so I can drive you to school," she offers, sounding frazzled. It always pissed me off that my mom was so perky and pulled-together in the morning in her tiny yoga outfits, but it's actually far more distressing to see her looking like a sad slob. I know I should probably ask how she's doing or ask if she's confronted Dad, but she doesn't seem to want to talk about it, and honestly, I have no idea what to say.

"Don't worry about it. Jenna is going to give me a ride to school – I already texted her," I tell her.

"Great," she says, sounding relieved.

"And remember, I have that soccer clinic today after school with the pro coaches. I think it goes until six. But Jenna can give me a ride home," I assure her.

"Right. I remembered. But that would be great if she could give you a ride home. I'm glad you girls are hanging out again," she says, taking a break from slicing mango to look up at me.

"When were we *not* hanging out?" I ask her, finding it easy to slip back into my usual state of frustration.

"Never mind. It doesn't matter," she says, busying herself with the fruit.

"Jenna is here," I say, feeling irrationally annoyed, as my phone chimes.

"Have a good day," she says, trying her best to be cheery and act like she isn't wearing her sad bathrobe and in desperate need of a shower.

"Thanks, you too," I say, happy to be leaving for the day, even if it means I'm heading to school.

***

"Isn't it kind of weird that they are bringing in special trainers for practice today?" Jenna asks from her spot next to me on the

243

locker room bench, as she's stretching her purple sock up over her perfectly toned calf.

"I don't think it's *that* weird," I reply. "Maybe it will make practice more interesting," I offer, while trying to persuade my own navy blue sock to make its way over my shin guard and past my slightly larger calf, after too many times in the dryer.

"Girls, get onto the field!" our coach yells into the locker room. "You need to warm up before they get here – five laps around the field and then we'll do sprints while we wait," she adds.

There is a collection of moans and sighs, as we gather our backpacks and soccer bags and slowly make our way out of the locker room, sixteen pairs of cleats clicking along the floor as we go. Someone watching us right now would think we were here for detention, rather than the lucky few who made it onto the Varsity soccer team.

By the second lap, the endorphins start to kick in, or something like that, and everyone finds their pace. Jenna falls into place next to me, and although we are both breathing more heavily than normal, it doesn't keep us from talking. "I think I just saw one of the trainers for today," Jenna squeals.

"Where?" I ask, looking around the field.

"He just went back to his car. But he is so hot, and he's young, like in his twenties! I assumed Coach would bring in someone old, because you know, she's old; but this is going to be So. Much. Fun!" Jenna exclaims, as she sprints ahead of me laughing.

We all finish our laps and are greeted with the fabulous news that there won't be time for sprints because the guest trainers are already here, so they are going to get started with the clinic. Coach tells us all to grab a ball and dribble to the center of the field and find a partner to pass with while we wait for further instructions.

As I'm jogging and dribbling, I see the guy that Jenna was talking about and he is definitely worth staring at. He has spiky blonde hair and a square jaw, and his fitted gray t-shirt shows off his muscular chest; he looks oddly familiar, but it's probably because he looks like he should be in a deodorant commercial.

I'm focusing on my passing and footwork, when I hear Coach yell for us to "huddle up" and meet our trainers. I turn around just in time to hear her say, "We are very fortunate today to have these five players from Fairfield's Varsity soccer team. I expect all of you to give one hundred and ten percent and..." but I don't hear anything she says after that point once I lock eyes with Brandon. The look on his face as he recognizes me is utter bewilderment. There is absolutely no option at this point - I turn and run back toward the exit as fast as I possibly can (it looks like I am getting my sprints in after all).

I hear Coach calling my name, but there is no chance in hell I am turning around.

I want to run directly out of the field and never look back, but I have to grab my bags. Stopping at the massive pile of bags on the track to dig for my stuff is not the quick exit I was hoping for, but at the very least I need my phone, and there is no way I'm ever coming back here to get it.

"What are you doing here?" Brandon asks, tapping me on the shoulder from behind. He is slightly winded from sprinting across the field after me, but he's in such great shape that he'll be back to his normal heart rate by his next sentence.

I finally locate my bag, mocking me at the bottom of the pile, pull it out with a hefty tug and turn around to face Brandon.

"Why are you here?" he asks again, begging me to provide him with an answer that is anything other than what it appears to be.

"I'm so sorry!" I cry, tears streaming down my cheeks. "This isn't what I meant to happen," I try to say, although through my sobs, I'm not sure if my words are understandable.

"Oh my God, how old are you?" Brandon asks, his face turning a scary shade of white.

"I'm sixteen," I admit, still sobbing. "But I'll be seventeen in two months," I offer meekly.

"I have to go," Brandon says, his green eyes flashing with anger and what I think is pain, but maybe I'm only projecting my feelings onto him. He turns and runs back toward the group in the middle of the field, leaving me all alone.

Chapter Thirty-Two
Ellie

Sitting in Tarantino waiting for Erica, I'm reconsidering my decision to meet in a restaurant rather than in my living room. When I texted her this morning to see if she could meet, I was shocked that she could actually do it. Even more so when she said that she wasn't working today, had a sitter and could come to Westport. I am in desperate need of a trip to the grocery store, so going out to lunch seemed like the best idea, but two vaguely familiar women just walked in and it's only a matter of time until someone I really know comes through the door. I asked for this table in the back corner for privacy, but I'm not sure it's going to matter if a twist of bad luck decides to send Lara here for lunch today.

Fortunately, I don't have any longer to sit here and stress about it, because I see Erica walk past the window and then open the front door. All the diners turn to stare as she strides back to my table; her stunning red hair and red-carpet worthy wardrobe grab attention wherever she goes.

"So sorry, the train was running late," Erica says, as she slides into the chair across from me.

"Don't worry about it! Thanks for coming all the way up here. And especially on your day off," I emphasize.

"Oh stop. I'm so happy I could do it," she says. "And you seemed a little upset," she adds, taking a sip of the sparkling water that I ordered for her.

"I've had better days," I say and smile half-heartedly.

"Have you and Jack talked any more about a decision?" Erica asks, getting right to the point.

"I'm not sure Jack is part of the decision making process any longer," I tell her, not trying to keep the bitterness out of my voice.

"What does that mean?" Erica asks, looking concerned.

Even though we are at the table in the corner, and my back is against the wall, I scan the dining room one more time before I speak, just to ensure there is no one here I know. "Jack's having an affair," I tell her.

"That's impossible!" Erica answers. "Jack would never do that to you!" she says. It's a funny response considering Erica's history, but I suppose she feels she knows the kind of guy who would cheat and she doesn't think Jack is that guy; which is exactly what I thought until a few days ago.

"It's true. I didn't mean to find it, but I found it in his text messages. Her name is Hailey," I tell her and cringe as I say her name.

"Have you talked to him about it?" Erica asks.

"Not yet. But I don't know how much there is to say," I shrug.

"You *have* to talk to him," Erica presses. "You've been married for almost twenty years! You have three children and you're pregnant! You don't just throw that all away!" Erica admonishes.

"I never said I was throwing it all away. I don't know what I'm doing right now," I admit.

"I know I'm not the best person to offer guidance on this," Erica admits. "And I promise I'm not trying to defend him. But you need to talk to him," she pleads.

"I will. I'm just not ready yet," I tell her.

"So what does that mean about your conclusion?" she asks, pointing at my stomach underneath the unnecessarily baggy, navy cashmere sweater I chose for today.

"I don't know," I whimper. "I just keep thinking about what it would be like to actually have a baby right now, and aside from the few, precious moments of cuddling with a sleeping infant, I can't think of anything except how much harder everything is going to be if I have a fourth child. But then I think back to twenty years ago, and it's enough to make me wonder if I can really go through it again. So I had almost gotten myself to the point where I was going to have the baby and figure it out, even if Jack wasn't thrilled, he would come around. But now this happens, and I'm just not sure I can have the baby if Jack isn't even in the picture anymore!" I explode.

"Oh Ellie, I'm so sorry," Erica says.

"It sucks," I agree.

"When do you have to decide?" she asks.

By the look on my face, she must realize she hit a nerve. "I'm so sorry. I didn't mean it to come out that way," she apologizes.

"It's okay," I tell her. "I'm right past eight weeks now, so technically I still have a little while to make a decision, but if I'm going to have a D&C, I would want to do it as soon as possible," I affirm.

"I know you think that I don't support this, but I will support whatever you decide to do," Erica tells me. "I can come to the doctor with you if you want." she says.

I'm taking a sip of iced tea as she says this and I start to laugh so hard that some of the tea actually comes out of my nose.

"What? What's so funny?" Erica asks, looking baffled.

"Nothing, sorry! It's *definitely* not funny," I say, trying to compose myself while wiping the tea from my mouth. "It's ironic, and somewhat terrible, and I laughed because I just can't believe how I keep fucking this up. I just remembered that I rescheduled my doctor's appointment the other day when I found Jack's text and my new appointment is right now," I tell her.

"Should you go?" she asks, looking concerned.

"No, I'll never make it on time," I explain, and my phone rings as soon as the words are out of my mouth. "That's the doctor's office asking where I am," I say to Erica.

"Aren't you going to answer it?" she asks, as I put my phone back in my purse.

"I can't handle it now. I'll call them back this afternoon and I'll find a new time when she can see me," I say.

"Do you want me to come with you?" Erica asks.

"No. This will just be a regular appointment. I promise I'll let you know what I decide and if I want you to come up for that appointment," I tell her, reaching out to squeeze her hand to attempt to convey how grateful I am for her support and our rekindled friendship.

***

Jack: I think I forgot to tell you that I'm giving a lecture tonight at the business school - I'll be home around 10 – they'll have snacks here, so don't worry about me for dinner

I stare at Jack's text as I'm sitting in the middle school parking lot waiting for Max to finish after-school tutoring. There are so many potential responses; I don't know where to begin. Should I tell him that I didn't plan on worrying about him for dinner anyway? Should I ask if he's actually at a lecture, or if he's really at a cheap hotel with Hailey? Should I tell him not to bother coming home? Instead, I settle for the lamest response of all.

Ellie: Okay

As annoyed as I am about Jack's flippant text and his assumption of normalcy, I am somewhat relieved to delay the conversation for at least another day. I'm not sure that I was going to confront him tonight anyway, but it's getting harder to be around him and act like I don't know that he is a cheating slime ball. I think he's attributing it to pregnancy hormones or the tremendous stress of the decision we're facing, so he hasn't called me on my attitude, but some point soon that's going to end.

My phone chimes again and I assume it's Jack, but this time it's from Sydney.

Sydney: can you pick me up now????

Ellie: was soccer cancelled? The weather is beautiful?

Sydney: can you come or not???!?!?!??!?

Ellie: I'm at school waiting for Max. I'll be there as soon as I'm done here

Sydney: thx

I'd love more information about why soccer was cancelled or why she can't get a ride with Jenna, since she would always prefer to ride with Jenna or her other friends than with me, but it doesn't look like I'm going to get that kind of report.

Sydney is standing by the curb dressed in her soccer clothes, far away from the actual entrance to the high school where I would normally pick her up. When I pull up next to her, she opens the door, slams it and slinks down low in her seat with out even saying "hi."

"Is everything okay?" I venture, although based solely on her body language, I'm sure I'll regret the question.

"Can we just go home?" she asks, sounding incredibly angry.

Having a teenage daughter should have taught me that the question and answer period is officially over, but I'm already pissed at Jack and I really want to know what happened with soccer and why Sydney's suddenly so mad when she has been in a great mood recently, so I push. "Did something happen at soccer?"

"What do you think?!" Sydney screams at me, her face turning a purplish shade of red as she yells.

I would normally scold her for speaking to me like this, but I say nothing. And Max would never miss an opportunity to tell her that she's going to get in trouble, but from his seat in the back, he must sense that this is different and he keeps his mouth shut.

When we arrive home, Sydney races from the car, runs to her bedroom and slams the door so hard that I fear for the hinges.

Max, Izzy and I have pancakes and fruit salad for dinner, which is becoming a new staple, and we are all in bed by nine o'clock and fast asleep long before Jack comes home. Sydney and Jack are both gone in the morning by the time I get up.

I'm not sure if there are specific criteria that need to be met for your life to officially fall apart, but if so, I'm pretty sure I tick all the right boxes.

Chapter Thirty-Three
Sydney

"Are you going to eat *anything*?" Mary asks, as I push the salad around on my plate before giving up and covering the whole tray with a pile of napkins.

"I'm not hungry," I tell her, which is entirely true. I haven't eaten since I saw Brandon on the field two days ago and I can't imagine ever eating again.

"It's better to do a cleanse, then to not eat *anything*," Katie adds from across the lunch table.

"My mom does those every week," Stephan chimes in.

"I'm not doing a cleanse, I'm seriously not hungry," I tell them, wishing everyone would stop staring at me and my tray full of salad and go back to their own conversations.

"This food is so gross, you can't blame her," Jenna says, smiling at me. Jenna is the only one who knows what's going on since she recognized Brandon on the soccer field. Even though we haven't been as close lately, she's been surprisingly supportive. Well, supportive may be an overstatement, but she called to check in that night, and she hasn't told any of the other girls; so that's pretty cool. But she also keeps telling me that I need to sleep with someone else to get over him, and the only reason I think I like him so much is because he's my "first fuck" and a hot college guy – so that part is totally wrong and unhelpful.

"My parents are out tomorrow night. You guys want to come over?" Jenna says, addressing the table.

"I love your negligent parents," Stephan laughs.

"I'm there," Katie says.

"I'm in," Mary says.

There is a cheer from the boys at the end of the table, which I assume means they will also be joining.

"Sydney?" Jenna says, looking at me accusingly.

I was supposed to go to Fairfield tomorrow night to see Brandon, but now that won't be happening; my heart aches as I think about the prospect of never seeing him again.

"I'll be there," I say sadly.

"I'm doing this for you," Jenna says earnestly. "You'll get drunk. You'll hook up. And you'll get over him," she says, nodding wisely.

"That's never going to happen," I tell her. "And not that I would even think about it. But who are you suggesting I hook up with? One of *these* guys?" I whisper, pointing to the crew at the end of our table.

"They're not *that* bad. And I'm not suggesting you date any of them, I'm just saying for one night," Jenna explains.

On that note, Stephan yells out, "My dick is totally bigger than Mr. Moore's, want me to whip it out right here and show you?" and then explodes in a fit of laughter, followed by cheers and howls from his friends.

I sip my rum and Diet Coke and try to smile when someone says something that I know is supposed to be funny, but the effort is enormous.

Stephan suggests a game of strip poker, and although I'm not sure that Katie or Jenna even know how to play regular poker, they both laugh and eagerly agree.

"I'll sit out the first round," I tell them.

Jenna shoots me a look that says she doesn't approve, but she's already voluntarily taken off her jean jacket to get the game started, and is now sitting at the card table in her tight, short black bandage dress, so I don't think she's too concerned about me.

I take out my phone to see if by some chance I missed a text from Brandon. I've checked it every fifteen minutes for the last three days, so it's virtually impossible, but still possible. Of course there is no response. I feel like I've restrained myself. I sent one text the night of the soccer debacle, asking if I could explain. And then I sent one yesterday, apologizing again and asking if we could talk. I know that I shouldn't text him again until I hear from him, but I can't take the silent treatment.

Everyone at the table is getting drunker by the minute and losing clothing at a rapid pace, so not surprisingly, no one notices when I escape to the kitchen. I planned to send him one more text, but my fingers have other ideas and before I know it, they are dialing his number. I hold my breath as the phone rings. I'm sure he won't actually pick up, if he won't return my texts, but then a miracle happens and Brandon answers on the fourth ring.

"Hi," Brandon says. His voice sounds nothing like the warm, friendly, adoring one I've grown accustomed to.

"Can we talk?" I ask, hopefully.

"I'm leaving for a party in a minute," his voice is cold as ice.

I know it isn't welcoming, but he didn't hang up on me either, so I take this as my chance. "Brandon, I know that I lied and I'm so sorry about that, but I never meant for it to happen like this. Jenna and I said we were older when we went to that first party and I never thought that I would meet you and it would turn into something, and then after that I thought if I told you I was really in high school that you wouldn't want to keep seeing me," I dump out the explanation, while attempting not to cry.

"I *wouldn't* have kept dating you, because you're sixteen and I'm twenty!" Brandon yells. "Sydney, don't you realize how that makes me feel?" he asks.

"But, we're so good together. And I'm *almost* seventeen," I plead.

"It can't work," Brandon says emphatically.

"Can we still talk? I only have one more year of high school," I beg, starting to feel him slip away.

"Sydney, you lied to me about everything! I really don't think we have anything else to talk about," he says. "I gotta go," Brandon adds, and then ends the call.

I stare at my home screen in disbelief; I can't believe it's over – I was dating the most perfect guy in the world and he actually liked me back, and now he hates me and I'll never see him again.

"Looks like you need a refill," Stephan says. I hadn't even heard him come into the kitchen, but from the familiar dopey look on his face, it doesn't appear that he overheard anything, or else he's a pretty good actor. I begin to object that I haven't

257

even finished my drink, when I notice my cup is surprisingly empty; I guess I didn't realize I finished it while I was talking to Brandon.

"Sure, I'll have another one," I tell him.

"What do you want?" he asks, taking the cup out of my hand.

"Rum and diet," I answer.

He takes my cup to the makeshift bar we've created on the center island and fills it up with an alarming amount of rum and a splash of Diet Coke, adding a couple of ice cubes as an afterthought. "Here you go," he says, handing it back to me, and taking a sip from his own beverage.

"Holy shit, this is strong," I say, after I try it.

"Have a little bit more and you won't even notice it," he advises. "You could use it," he says.

"What's that supposed to mean?" I ask.

"Nothing," he says, rolling his eyes, and turning his UVM baseball cap around backwards, to give me a better look at his obnoxious, but symmetrical and unfortunately attractive face.

"No, seriously, what did you mean by that?" I press, taking an extra large swallow of my drink; Stephan is right, it really does get better.

"You're always so uptight, and sometimes you can be a bit of a bitch, but I think you'd be fun if you'd just loosen up a little bit," he adds.

I think about what he says for a minute and my initial reaction is to be offended and tell him that he's an asshole, but then I realize that's exactly what he's expecting me to do.

258

"So I just need to drink more, and I'll be more fun?" I ask, but I smile after I say it, trying to let him know that I'm not going to jump down his throat.

"You don't have to drink more, but it helps," he laughs. "I'm just saying that you're smart and beautiful and funny, in a mean way, but still funny, and if you stopped worrying so much, or whatever it is that keeps you from hanging out, then you'd have a lot more fun," he concludes.

"Wow," I say, feeling a little blurry from the booze, but also from what Stephan just said. "I don't know what to say," I respond.

"My work is done here. I'm needed back at strip poker," Stephan says, topping off his drink with an absurd amount of vodka, "You coming?" he asks.

"Sure," I reply, following him out of the kitchen. "And thanks," I tell him.

"Whatever," he says, shaking his head. "But don't tell anyone. I don't want it to get out that I'm not always a total ass," he says.

"Your secret is safe with me," I laugh. "Besides, I may not even remember in the morning," I add, taking another large gulp of my drink to match Stephan. My head is already feeling pleasantly fuzzy, and I'm one step closer to forgetting about Brandon for the next few hours.

Chapter Thirty-Four
Jack

The house is eerily quiet and I am the first one downstairs, as is the case on every Saturday morning, but the tension running through the walls destroys the tranquility, even though Ellie is still asleep. I make a full pot of coffee before I remember that she won't be having any, and then I worry that it's going to start another argument because I'm too insensitive to remember that she can't drink regular coffee.

I hear footsteps on the stairs and check the time; it's only eight fifteen, which is far too early for Ellie or Sydney to be awake, and I'm sure Max is up, but he'll stay in his room until hunger forces him out. Izzy would be the obvious choice, but she had a sleepover last night and won't be home until this afternoon.

"Hey Syd, what are you doing up so early?" I ask, as Sydney appears in the kitchen.

"Why do you care?" Sydney sneers.

"Hey, what's with the attitude?" I ask, trying not to sound too annoyed, even though I have no tolerance for her teenage moodiness.

Sydney doesn't answer me, and proceeds to grab a mug from the cabinet and pour herself a cup of coffee from the carafe on the counter, adding milk and sugar like a pro.

"What do you think you're doing?" I ask her, caught off guard.

"Having a cup of coffee," she replies. "What does it look like?" she questions, her voice dripping with sarcasm.

"Since when do you drink coffee?" I ask. I'm quite certain that she shouldn't be drinking it, but I momentarily wonder if it's something Ellie allows and I just missed it.

"Since forever," she adds, taking a gulp from her mug, and she winces slightly as she swallows, but attempts to hide it – I'm not sure if it's because it's too hot or because she doesn't actually like coffee.

"What's with you this morning?" I ask, tired of her arrogance.

"Nothing," she says emphatically. "I'm going back to bed," she says, turning on her heel and exiting the kitchen, leaving me alone once more to wonder what the hell just happened. Sydney is known for her uneven temperament, but unfair as it may be, it's always been directed at Ellie. At times, she's been a little grumpy around me, but never outright bitchy like this! I have no idea what's going on, but I can't imagine it's good.

***

Thirty minutes later, I hear footsteps on the stairs and part of me hopes it's Sydney returning to apologize, or at least continue the argument, so we can resolve it; but the other part of me doesn't have the energy for it. However, I won't have to worry about it, because it's Ellie, dressed in a black and yellow yoga outfit – she kind of looks like a bumblebee, but I wouldn't dare say that out loud.

"Shouldn't you still be asleep?" I ask her, a feeling of déjà vu washing over me from my earlier conversation with Sydney.

"I'm teaching the ten o'clock class," she says nonchalantly, grabbing a water bottle from the cabinet and filling it from the door of the refrigerator.

"But you never teach on Saturdays," I remind her, as if she didn't already know this.

"I'm teaching today," she replies. "And I'm having lunch with Jillian after class, so you'll need to pick Izzy up from her sleepover and take Max to rock climbing," she adds coolly.

"Were you going to tell me?" I ask her.

"I'm telling you now," she says casually. She looks at her watch and then adds, "I need to go," and then picks up her bag and keys from the counter and disappears.

For the second time this morning, I'm left sitting in my favorite chair on my favorite morning in my favorite pajamas, feeling bulldozed and like a total shmuck. On the assumption that it can't get any worse, I decide to send Hailey one more text message.

Jack: Hey Hailey – I'm really sorry. I'd like to talk if you'll give me another chance

I don't expect to hear back although a piece of me is hopeful that eventually she will give me another shot. But I certainly don't anticipate getting a reply five minutes later, so it's quite a shock when my phone buzzes.

Unknown Number: Hi Jack, this is Hailey's aunt. I think we need to talk. She doesn't know I'm reaching out to you, so please don't tell her.

Chapter Thirty-Five
Ellie

My phone rings as I'm pulling out of the parking lot after class, and my stomach clenches the way it always does when my phone rings during school hours. Even though the display reads "unknown number" I'm still convinced there will be a school nurse on the other end of the line telling me I need drive directly to school to collect my vomiting child. I take a deep breath and answer the phone, "Hello?" I say, expecting the worst.

"Is this Ellie Miller," an unfamiliar voice asks.

"This is she," I reply.

"My name is Gladys. I'm Dorothy Kreamer's housekeeper. She asked that I give you a call," she tells me.

"Is everything okay?" I ask, feeling panicked.

"Everything's okay, but she is feeling a little under the weather and if it isn't too much trouble, she was wondering if you might be able to stop by," she explains.

"I would love to stop by," I reply. "When would be convenient?"

"Her schedule is wide open, so whatever works best for you. She rests more in the afternoon, but it isn't always at a certain time," Gladys clarifies.

"Could I come by now?" I ask. "I'm just leaving work, but I could be there in twenty minutes. Is that too soon?"

"That would be wonderful," Gladys says.

When I pull up to Dorothy's estate, it's slightly less overwhelming than last time, but only slightly. Some of the autumn leaves have fallen since my last visit, providing an even more spectacular view of the sun sparkling off the Sound as I drive toward the house.

There is no one standing outside to greet me today, so I ring the doorbell and wait. Gladys quickly arrives in the foyer and appears delighted to see me.

"Thank you so much for coming over. *And* for coming so quickly," she praises. "Dorothy was thrilled when she heard you were on your way," she says.

I peer behind Gladys, expecting to see Dorothy on the sofa where we sat last week for tea, but all I see is a vase of orchids.

"She's in her room," Gladys says, noting the confusion on my face.

I follow Gladys up the grand staircase and down a long hallway past six closed doors before we reach Dorothy's room. Gladys raps her knuckles softly on the door before slowly pushing it open.

I assess the scene and hope that my face doesn't reveal my dismay. It's evident that the massive bedroom was majestic in its day, but the king-size canopy bed, along with the matching furniture is quite dated. However, the decorating is not my cause for concern. The lights are dimmed and the heavy curtains drawn. Dorothy looks tiny lying in the oversize bed in a blue nightgown, her white hair fanned out behind her on a pillow. The glass night table is covered with prescription bottles, a crystal water glass and an inhaler.

"Hi Dorothy!" I say, with as much enthusiasm as I can mange.

"Oh Ellie, you're a doll. I'm sorry you have to see me like this," she apologizes.

"Don't say another word. I'm so happy I could come over," I tell her.

"Gladys, could you get a chair for Ellie?" Dorothy asks.

"Of course," Gladys says, as she quickly disappears into an adjoining room and reappears with a metal folding chair.

"Isn't there another chair?" Dorothy asks, seemingly appalled.

"This is perfect!" I say, grabbing the chair from Gladys, unfolding it and taking a seat next to the head of the bed before Dorothy can object.

"If you're sure," Dorothy says.

"I am," I insist. And then to Gladys I say, "Thank you so much."

"I'm sorry you aren't feeling well," I tell Dorothy.

"Don't get old," Dorothy says, sounding more candid than I've ever heard her before. "I shouldn't complain," she corrects.

"Feel free to complain to me. I feel like that's all I do lately." I say.

"I find that hard to believe," Dorothy scoffs.

"It's true," I say, nodding my head.

"I don't think I've ever heard you make the slightest grumble," Dorothy states.

"Believe me, I grumble plenty," I protest.

"What have you been complaining about recently?" Dorothy asks, looking intrigued.

"I'm not here to bother you with my problems," I tell her, laughing.

"But I want to hear about them. I haven't left the house in over a week, and all I do is think about my own concerns. I would love to hear about yours," Dorothy says.

For a split second I actually consider telling her about the baby, or about Jack's infidelity, but I can't do it. Instead, I settle for another problem that's been bothering me, but I've been too busy with my other worries to think about it.

"I think I'm having a mid-life crisis," I blurt out.

"You wouldn't guess it from looking at you," Dorothy says. "But I know there's more under the surface," she adds wisely.

"I don't know what I want to do with my life. I feel like I'm stuck. Do you know what I mean?" I ask.

"Is this about your husband?" Dorothy guesses.

Although Jack is part of it, he's not the only piece of the puzzle, so I don't feel like I'm leaving anything out when I answer. "Not really. It's about me. Do you know what I did before I taught yoga?" I ask her.

"No," Dorothy replies, looking at me expectantly.

"I was a social worker. I helped people," I tell her. "And now all I do is help rich skinny ladies get even skinnier," I moan, even though I know that isn't true, and it isn't fair.

"Is that what you really think?" Dorothy asks.

"Yes. No. I don't know," I answer. "I loved it when I started. It was the perfect answer for me at the time when Izzy was a baby and I couldn't work full time anymore and this felt like I could have it all."

"And now?" Dorothy asks, readjusting her position on the slippery beige pillowcase.

"It doesn't feel like that anymore. It's not that I don't *like* yoga, but it's not my passion," I tell her.

"What is your passion?" Dorothy asks.

"I don't know," I reply, sounding like a sullen teenager.

"I think you do," Dorothy says.

"I want to feel like I'm helping people. I loved that part of the job. It wasn't always fun, and it wasn't easy, but I was good at it," I tell her.

"You know that I took a class with Darcy once?" Dorothy asks.

"Oh, I didn't know that," I reply.

"I think she's a better yoga teacher than you are," Dorothy says.

I feel like I've been punched in the stomach and the look on my face must convey just that.

"Let me finish," Dorothy says with a smile, although I can't figure out what gem she's going to come up with next.

"I never wanted to take another class with Darcy, because it's *just* yoga. Your classes are so much more. When I said that you saved me these past few years, I meant it. You may not have realized what you did for me, but it was priceless. You *do* help people Ellie. And I'm sure you are a wonderful social worker. If you want to give up yoga and go back to social work, then you should do it," Dorothy recommends.

I let her advice sink in and bask in the glow of her kind words before I remember why this plan doesn't work. "I can't afford to be a social worker," I tell her.

Dorothy is quiet for a full minute. I actually wonder if she even heard me, but then she responds. "Forgive me for saying this, but I can't imagine running the yoga studio provides a lot of money either. I'm sorry, I know it isn't polite to talk about things like this," Dorothy adds.

"Please don't apologize," I say to her. "You're right," I laugh. "It's not that I'm making millions, but after five years, Body & Soul is actually turning a fairly good profit. I can work around the kids' schedules and I almost never need a babysitter. If I go back to social work, I'm going to have to start from scratch finding patients and the hours aren't always as flexible, and my friend Erica was telling me that insurance has become such a nightmare that she barely makes any money," I babble on, unable to stop myself from this rant that I'm sure is of no interest to Dorothy.

"I'm sorry to hear that," Dorothy says, shifting in the bed as if trying to find a more comfortable position. I had momentarily forgotten that she was even sick as I was so caught up in my own petulance.

"It's okay. I'm sorry to bother you with my problems," I apologize.

"It's not a bother at all," Dorothy promises. "My children don't come to me with their concerns, so I'm happy to lend an ear for you. And it's a good distraction," she says, using her hand to indicate her surroundings

"Happy to help," I say.

"Why couldn't you keep the yoga studio *and* be a social worker?" Dorothy suggests. "You don't have to teach yoga anymore, but then you would still make money from owning it, right?" she asks, demonstrating yet again that she is so much more than the un-assuming older lady I initially thought she was.

This thought has crossed my mind before, and I'm attempting to think of the response that sounds least pessimistic for my reply to Dorothy. "That is an option. But when I really think about it, I just don't think it would work. The only reason the studio works is because I'm there to manage it most of the time. I would have to hire a full-time manager if I wasn't there and that would cost a lot of money. I feel like I would end up doing both jobs and of course I already don't spend enough time with the kids," I add.

"I understand. It's all so complicated," she says thoughtfully.

"Who knew life was going to be this hard?" I say, trying to make a joke.

Dorothy offers a pained smile, but I can't tell if it's a reaction to my poor joke or if she's uncomfortable.

"Are you feeling okay? Is there anything I can get you?" I ask her.

"I'm fine. I'm just getting a little tired. I may need to take a little rest," Dorothy says.

"Of course. Do you need me to get Gladys? Can I do something?" I inquire.

"No, no. I'm just going to doze off after you leave. Thank you so much for coming to visit me today. You really are so kind," she says, reaching out with one hand from under her blanket to squeeze my arm, the enlarged blue veins in her hand more pronounced than they were even a week ago.

"Of course," I reply. "I'm so happy I could come over. I'll try to stop by later this week," I tell her, mentally reviewing my calendar to see when I might have time.

"Ellie, I know you have a lot on your mind, but I have a feeling it will all work out," Dorothy says knowingly, not responding to my comment about coming over later in the week.

I just smile and nod, because it doesn't seem appropriate to do anything else. Dorothy only knows a fraction of my troubles, and those seem unlikely to be resolved. If she had any idea how messed up my life was, I'm sure she wouldn't be saying that.

Chapter Thirty-Six
Jack

Although I looked up April's gallery online, it still didn't quite prepare me for the real thing. To be honest, I'm not much of an art person, but standing in front of the plate glass windows on Bowery, even *I* could tell that the artwork inside was impressive. From the write-up on the website it seems that April's sculptures and paintings have become very popular over the past ten years and now go for ten to twenty thousand dollars a piece. When I open the door and walk inside, I try to keep those prices in mind so I don't inadvertently knock over something that costs the price of my first car.

"Hello?" I call out, my voice echoing throughout the warehouse, bare except for a couple of benches, iron sculptures and the paintings hanging on the exposed brick walls – none of which are good at absorbing sound.

"Jack, is that you?" says a voice, although I can't see who it belongs to.

"It's me," I reply, feeling slightly foolish, unsure where to stand or sit.

"I'll be out in a minute," she calls out.

Seconds later, a woman appears from the back of the gallery and although it was only one night and it was twenty years ago, I have no doubt that this is Nikki's sister. From what Hailey told me, April must be in her late forties, but she could easily pass for thirty-five or younger - she is stunning. April shares the same long dark hair as Nikki and Hailey; only hers is pulled back in a braid that falls halfway down her back. Her eyes are a lighter shade of blue, almost aqua, and her skin is slightly darker than Hailey's, either from more time in the sun, or just a naturally darker complexion, either way, it makes her eyes even more striking. She's wearing a gigantic white smock, covered in paint splatters, but even under the shapeless garment, I can tell that she shares the same body type as her sister and niece.

"Thanks so much for coming all the way down here," April says, reaching out to shake my hand with a surprisingly firm handshake.

"No problem," I reply. "I was very interested in meeting you, but Hailey didn't seem ready," I tell her.

"That's what I wanted to talk to you about," she says.

"Here, let's have a seat," she says, pointing to one of the backless benches in the middle of the room.

It's slightly awkward to sit on the bench and find a good position to face April, but after a few minor shifts, I land on something that isn't too uncomfortable. "I know that it's taking me a little while to figure out the best way to make this work with Hailey and..."

April cuts me off before I can go any further. "Look, Jack, that's not the problem," she says bluntly.

"Oh?" I ask, confused and relieved at the same time.

"I didn't even realize that Hailey had contacted you until a few days ago. In fact, I didn't even know that she had your name or information," April says.

I'm not sure where this is going, but this does explain why Hailey didn't want me to meet April and it clarifies her strange behavior regarding her aunt.

"She said that her grandfather didn't tell her about me until she turned eighteen, and then when he died, she decided to come find me," I explain.

"Jack, I don't think there is an easy way to tell you this, but you aren't Hailey's father," April says, shaking her head slowly as the words tumble out of her mouth.

"What do you mean?" I ask, "Is this some kind of joke?"

"No, it's definitely not a joke. And I'm very sorry that you've gotten mixed up in all of this," April says sadly.

"Mixed up in what? What's going on?" I plead, my voice rising as I start to get angry.

"It's complicated. Hailey was never supposed to find out about you," April says.

"Can you please explain what's going on here?" I demand, my tolerance for April's vague allusions having reached its limit.

"Hailey thinks you're her dad, but you're not," April begins.

"And why is that?" I nearly spit.

"Nikki was already pregnant the night you met her," April reveals with a sigh.

"Bullshit!" I yell out, before I can stop myself.

"It's true, Jack. Nikki was dating this total loser, Kenny. They'd been together on and off since high school, and my parents hated him; well, we all hated him. And then she got pregnant. I still don't know if she planned it when she met you, or if the one-night stand was just a happy coincidence, but a couple months later when she told my parents that she was pregnant, the only reason they didn't totally flip out was because she told them that Kenny wasn't the father," April says, pausing in her story to give me a minute to take it all in.

"This is crazy. How do you know that I'm not Hailey's dad? How do you really know that she was already pregnant and she wasn't lying about that too?" I ask.

"I know this is a lot to absorb, but I promise she wasn't lying. I knew she was pregnant before she met you that night on Sixth Street. And we also have a DNA test, but anyway, let me finish. So my parents helped her raise Hailey because they thought she belonged to some fancy PhD student in New York. She made them swear they would never contact you, and honestly I don't think they wanted to because they were worried you might try to take her away," April explains.

"So that's it?" I question. "What happened to Kenny?" I ask with disdain.

"Kenny disappeared after it became clear that she was pregnant. She told him it wasn't his, and even if he thought the baby was his, he wasn't the type of guy who would want anything to do with a kid. But then after Nikki died, Kenny resurfaced. He was in his thirties and had matured a little bit, but mostly he was looking for money. He claimed that he knew Hailey was really his kid and he wanted full custody. Somehow, my mom was able to keep my dad and Hailey from finding out the truth, but there was a DNA test and she learned that Kenny was Hailey's real father. She paid him a lot of money to go away, and no one's heard from him since then," April says, wrapping up her story.

"So how did I come into the picture?" I ask, my curiosity winning out over my anger at this point.

"As I told you, I only found out a couple days ago. It seems that my dad never ended up learning the truth, and he held on to the business card that Nikki took from your hotel room all this time. He gave that to Hailey on her eighteenth birthday and told her that it was time she knew who her dad was and that when the time was right, she could find you if she wanted," April says.

"And then when he passed away, she came looking for me," I say, finishing the story on my own.

"Seems like it. She told me that she wanted to defer her acceptance to school and come work with me in the gallery, but she never mentioned anything about you. I promise," April swears.

"So now what happens?" I ask, feeling utterly deflated.

"When she finally told me about you, I had to tell her the truth," April admits.

"Oh no," I say, my feelings instantly switching from anger and self-pity to concern for Hailey.

"Yeah, she's having a hard time taking it all in," April tells me.

"Has she tried looking for Kenny?" I ask.

"She found him pretty quickly," April says, staring down at the floor.

"And?" I ask.

"He's in prison in Kansas," she replies.

"Holy shit," I say.

"Honestly, it's not much of a surprise, knowing Kenny. But it sucks for Hailey," April says sadly.

"I don't know where that leaves me."

"I'm really sorry you got dragged into this," April says. "But I guess there's nothing more you need to do," she tells me, shrugging her shoulders, and essentially dismissing me.

I look away from April and gaze at the paintings covering the exposed brick walls. I don't have an eye for modern art, or whatever genre this falls into, but looking at the blurred lines and crazy designs makes me think of Hailey and triggers something. "What if I don't want to be done?" I ask.

"I don't understand?" April questions, raising her perfectly arched eyebrow. "You aren't her dad. Other than one really drunken night with Nikki twenty years ago, you have no connection to Hailey or our family," she clarifies, like I've missed something.

"I know. I get it. But Hailey just keeps losing people. First her mom, then her grandparents, and now her real dad is a deadbeat and stuck in jail. I don't want to do the same thing," I justify.

"But you barely know her," April argues.

"I'm *getting* to know her," I maintain.

"And Hailey says you haven't even told your family about her," she gloats, playing her trump card. "If you weren't willing to tell them when you thought she was actually your daughter, why would you go out on a limb to have a relationship with her now, when she's just a stranger?" April accuses.

"That's fair. And I know I screwed that up," I admit. "I know it doesn't make sense, but I feel like we have a connection," I tell April, glancing around once more at the eccentric shapes on the wall in search of a better way to explain my feelings.

"Do you like that one?" April asks, referencing the piece I landed on. It's almost entirely orange, with swirls of blue and what looks like an eye in the bottom left corner.

"I'm not sure I get it. I think I'm more of a facts and figures kind of guy," I tell her. "I hope that doesn't offend you," I quickly add.

"It's perfectly fine," she laughs. "It's a bit out there," she admits. "Hailey isn't really into it either, but she's starting to get into it a bit, or at least she's trying," April says.

"She told me she was enjoying it so far," I offer.

"I think she's more like you honestly, she's great at math and science, did she tell you that?" April probes.

"She didn't," I admit sheepishly.

"She didn't get it from Nikki, and she definitely didn't get it from Kenny, but it's true. I think my parents struggled with her sometimes because she's so different from me and Nikki. I did okay in school, but was always more passionate about art, and Nikki was a bit of a wild child. But Hailey's great in school, and really smart. My parents did the best they could, given the circumstances, but I feel like she missed out on the gifted stuff or challenging academics that she should have gotten," April muses.

"That's a shame," I say. "But she seems to be doing okay."

"She's a trooper, that's for sure. And don't get me wrong, The University of Texas is a great school, but I don't think my parents even considered letting her apply anywhere else. They went there, and Nikki went there, and they live, well *lived*, in Austin, so Hailey had to go to UT," April says.

"You don't think that's where she wants to go?" I ask April.

"I don't think she knows what she wants, because this is the first time she's been given the chance to make a decision for herself. I'm shocked, and really proud of her, for deferring for a year and coming to New York. But I'm worried about sending her back to Texas," April finishes.

I'm not sure why April has decided to open up to me about Hailey if we're done with the discussion about our relationship, but it's probably best not to push it. "It's only November. It's not too late for her to apply to other schools now," I offer, hoping I'm not overstepping.

"Hmmm," April replies.

"It's just a thought," I tell her.

"I'll think about it," she says, tabling the discussion.

"I should probably go," I say, standing up and awkwardly stretching out my left foot, which was trapped underneath my leg the entire time so I could twist at just the right angle to face April without being intrusive.

"Thanks for coming Jack. I know this hasn't been easy for you," April says kindly, but still with a tone of dismissal.

"I'd still like to reach out to Hailey. If that's okay with you," I add, although I don't think I should have to.

"Let me think about it," April says. "Jack, what would you be to her?" she asks.

"What do you mean?" I ask.

"You aren't her dad. You aren't related to her. You aren't a friend of her mom's, I mean, let's be honest. You're a guy in his forties and she's nineteen. What kind of relationship is that?" April questions.

Hearing April put it this way, I have to admit that it does sound pretty strange, but against rational judgment, I'm not willing to let it go. "A positive male influence?" I suggest.

The look on April's face tells me that this description isn't a winner and I need to try again.

"A pseudo step-father?" I offer.

"Are you going to tell your family?" she asks.

"Yes," I reply firmly.

"Let me talk to Hailey, and I'll let you know," she says.

I walk back out onto Bowery and the chilly air takes me by surprise. It's pitch black outside now, which is quite symbolic of the day and night change that just occurred in my life in the past hour since I entered the gallery. Most men would probably be filled with relief after today. Rejoicing in their good fortune that they hadn't told their wives yet, and now they would never have to. So maybe this makes me the dumbest man alive, but it doesn't feel that way.

Chapter Thirty-Seven
Sydney

There's a buzz in the junior hallway on Wednesday morning and I can't figure out what's going on, but I honestly don't care. I was so hung-over all weekend that I didn't feel quite as bad about Brandon, but mostly because I couldn't get my head to stop pounding long enough to be sad. But now that the alcohol is out of my system, I can be miserable again. I don't know what I expected to happen. I knew he was mad, and I knew he wouldn't like the age difference; but somehow I thought when he finally talked to me, he would remember how much he liked me and just be okay with it.

"Did you get yours?" Chelsea asks, popping up beside me right after I slam my locker shut, with far more force than necessary.

"Get my what?" I ask.

"Your SAT scores," she says, with an implied "duh." "They were posted last night."

"Oh," I reply, letting this news sink in. "I took mine at New Canaan, remember? So mine won't be back yet," I say, feeling temporarily relieved, but scared for the inevitable.

"Actually, I know someone who took them at New Canaan on the same day as you did, and he got his last night," Chelsea says excitedly. "That means yours are probably up too!"

"Hmmm," I reply, stalling for time.

"Do you have your code?" she asks.

"It's at home," I lie, knowing full well that I also have it typed into my phone.

"I guess you'll have to wait until you get home," she relents.

"Wait, how did you do?" I remember to ask.

"Pretty well," she answers, running her hand through her short purple hair, but the glint in her hazel eyes and the smirk on her face make it hard to conceal her delight.

"How well?" I ask, giving her a playful shove.

"Fifteen twenty," she answers, trying to hide her joy, but with that score, it's almost impossible.

"Holy shit!" I yell out, causing a couple kids nearby to turn their heads and look over at me. "That's amazing Chelsea!" I exclaim.

"Thanks," she shrugs. "I'm sure you'll get the same," she nods.

"I'm not so sure," I reply.

"Text me after school when you get your score," she says. "I have to get to class."

"Okay," I agree, although I have a feeling I'm not going to want to share my score with anyone, least of all someone who got above a fifteen hundred!

***

Thankfully, no one's home when I get back from school. I took the bus home for the first time since freshman year, but it meant I could skip soccer practice and didn't have to deal with my mom. Jenna almost convinced me to go to practice with her rationale that there's only a week left in the season, and I would feel better if I got some exercise, blah, blah, blah, but then I got the text that my mom had to take Max and Izzy to the doctor. The appeal of an empty house for two hours was far greater than running laps, especially if I'm going to contemplate a peek at my SAT scores.

There's a half-empty box of Entenmann's chocolate chip cookies on the kitchen counter when I walk inside. This might be a new low in my mom's rebellion on a lifetime of health food. I grab one from the box on the way upstairs, but similar to all food since Brandon dumped me, it has no flavor and I have no appetite. I was finally hungry last night, but I was over it three bites into dinner. I never used to believe people who said they were heartbroken; it sounded fake, but now I know it's the worst kind of illness.

In my room, I stare at the blanket tacked to my wall and decide yet again to leave it there because it reminds me of my calls with Brandon, even though it looks stupid and I clearly don't need it anymore.

Before I can change my mind, I log on to the testing site and pray that my results aren't up yet, or that miraculously the scores are amazing and I pulled it off even without enough studying and preparation. The hourglass on the screen lets me know that the website wants to torture me even more. Finally the page loads and my name appears at the top with a math score of six hundred and ten and an evidence based reading and writing score of five hundred and fifty, for a total score of eleven hundred and sixty. My heart sinks. I know that this isn't the worst score ever, but for me it's pretty bad, and it's definitely not a score that will get me into Yale. This will seem bitchy, but I overheard Jenna in art class today, and she said she got eleven ninety! Jenna's parents will probably donate a building to get her into school somewhere anyway, and I think she wants to go to a party school so it doesn't really matter; but

I can't believe she scored higher than I did! I was supposed to get a fifteen twenty like Chelsea. But instead, I fucked around all fall with Brandon, and now I don't even have anything to show for it!

A chime on my phone interrupts my pity party, and on reflex I wonder if it's Brandon, but then I remember that I'll never hear from him again.

Chelsea: Did you get your scores? I bet you beat me!

Syndey: Nope – they weren't up yet, must be something weird with the system ☹

Chelsea: Oh well – they'll be up soon!

I couldn't possibly tell her what I got. She would never look at me the same way again. Being a smart, somewhat-popular girl, is a unique position in the social landscape, and if I lose the brains, then my whole identity is gone. My phone chimes again and I almost don't look at it, because I can't go on and talk about Oxford and Yale and pretend like everything's okay, but luckily I do.

Jenna: Practice finished early. Want me to come get you?

Sydney: Sure! Where are we going?

Jenna: Stephan's house

Sydney: On a Wednesday?

Jenna: His parents are away this week, he's just having a few people over

I wouldn't normally go anywhere on a Wednesday night; honestly, until the past two months, I've been so busy studying that I didn't even know people went out during the week. But it beats sitting around here and waiting for my mom to get home and answer annoying questions about school and pretend everything is okay. And it certainly beats watching her try to avoid my dad without having the backbone to confront him, or throw him out of the house, which is what I want to do.

Sydney: Come get me

Jenna: I'll be there in 10

Chapter Thirty-Eight
Ellie

The receptionist doesn't say anything when she checks me in for my appointment. She seems to treat me in the same friendly manner in which she treated the heavily pregnant woman in front of me, but I wonder if there's a note on the inside cover of my file that says I missed two appointments and I'm irresponsible and inconsiderate.

"Dr. Vasquez is running about ten to fifteen minutes behind," the receptionist calls to me as I leave the window.

"Okay, thanks," I reply. It's not like I'm in a position to complain when I've missed and rescheduled two appointments at the last minute. I take a seat next to the pregnant woman who checked in before me. I leave a buffer chair between us, the standard office protocol, and grab a magazine from the end table to thumb through while I wait.

"I keep thinking it will be my last time coming here for an exam, but this guy doesn't seem to want to come out," the pregnant lady says to me, rubbing the pink t-shirt that looks like it is about to burst Incredible Hulk style over her enormous belly.

"When are you due?" I ask, folding the magazine and placing it in my lap.

"I was due six days ago," she says, looking fairly distraught.

"I'm so sorry," I tell her, sympathetically.

"Everyone tells me that I shouldn't be in a hurry because once he comes I won't get any sleep and I should enjoy my last days of freedom, but I can't take it anymore," she complains, shifting in the chair and moving her left hand to her lower back to get comfortable, although it appears to be an impossible task.

"You aren't going to get a lot of sleep once the baby comes, but I'm sure you aren't getting much sleep now," I say, trying to remember what it was like to be that pregnant, although I never went past my due date.

"Thanks," she says, pushing her long black hair behind her ear. "Sorry to complain to a perfect stranger. My husband would die if he heard me talking to you. He thinks I share everything with everyone, which I guess is true," she laughs, her dark eyes shining.

"It's okay," I assure her. "Men don't quite understand," I tell her, realizing just how true that statement has proved to be recently.

"Do you have kids?" she asks.

"I have three," I reply. I don't know why, but I always assume everyone knows that I'm a mom, which is a ridiculous assumption. And sitting in this office, I also tend to assume that everyone is pregnant and not here for an annual visit or another medical issue, but it seems that this young woman, who is likely not even thirty, is better educated, or at least more open-minded in her assumptions than I am.

"Wow! How old are they?" she asks, appearing daunted by the idea of my brood, I wonder what she would possibly think if she knew I was also pregnant!

"Sydney is sixteen, Max is twelve, and Izzy is nine," I tell her, watching the awe or possibly panic in her eyes as she tries to imagine that scenario.

"Wow," she says again.

"Sometimes I find it pretty hard to believe too," I confess.

"Carol?" the nurse calls out.

"That's me," she says, scooting to the edge of her seat and using the arms of the chair to hoist herself up.

"Good luck!" I say, as she walks back toward the exam rooms.

"Thanks," she replies.

I open my magazine again, but find that I no longer have any interest in the top ten kitchen styles in Architectural Digest. I know I won't see Carol again, unless coincidentally someday in the future we both end up here for a checkup; but I'm oddly jealous of the road ahead of her. I don't want to and can't go back in time, but the early days of the first pregnancy and the first baby are so magical. Unfortunately, I didn't appreciate it at the time, because I was too busy worrying about anything and everything that could go wrong; but if only I knew what it would be like to have a second baby or a third, or a fourth... I wish I could tell Carol to appreciate every moment of her first baby, when it's just her and her husband and the baby. But she doesn't want the advice of a stranger from the waiting room, and even if she heard me, she will worry and obsess like every new mother, and the cycle continues.

"Ellie?" a different nurse calls out, holding a tablet in her hands, and possibly the same note that speaks of my negligence.

I stand up slowly from my chair and follow her back to the exam rooms, wishing that I was twenty-eight years old and six days overdue, or here for my annual pap-smear, or honestly that I was anywhere other than my current reality.

"Take everything off, put on the gown open to the front, you know the drill," the nurse tells me, handing over the soft pink gown and matching belt. "Dr. Vasquez will be here in a few minutes," she says, closing the door gently behind her.

If possible, the room looks even more sterile and less welcoming than last time I was here. I quickly strip down, slip on the gown and hang my clothes on the back of the door. To avoid looking at the multitude of photos of the female reproductive system on the walls, I keep my phone with me to scroll through Instagram as I wait for the doctor. I haven't been on the app in a few days, and if it were up to me, I would never go on the site. But for the studio, I need to "stay relevant" as Maureen reminds me, and as every parent with a teenager, I need to be on here to follow Sydney and her friends and make sure they aren't ruining their futures. Although now that kids know how closely their parents follow their social media behavior, I find it hard to believe they would do anything too crazy on there; although I do wonder about some of Sydney's friends' judgment - at least I don't have to worry about Sydney's.

"Knock, knock," Dr. Vasquez says, as she slowly opens the door.

"Hi Dr. Vasquez," I say to her, trying to muster a cheerful greeting.

She opens my file that is sitting on the desk, and then quickly logs in to the computer. "Sorry, I still like to take handwritten notes, but everything else is in the computer or on those little tablets. I'm trying to switch over, but I'm having a hard time," she explains. "It's driving everyone here crazy that I can't make the jump," she expounds.

"That's okay," I reply, because it sounds like the right thing to say.

"All right, so it looks like you are here for an ultrasound today, is that right?" she asks.

"Yes."

"It looks like you had to change your last two appointments. Was everything okay? How are you feeling?" she questions, looking at her notes.

"Sorry, something came up and I couldn't make it," I say weakly, ignoring her other questions.

"You're almost nine weeks now, so I'll do a quick scan and check to make sure everything looks good," she says, putting down the folder and pulling the portable ultrasound machine over toward the exam table.

I'm expecting her to look in her notes and see the comments from our last visit and ask what happened with the D&C appointment, or why I changed my mind, or if I want to talk about anything, but she doesn't do any of that. I don't know if she assumes that since I cancelled the D&C from twelve days ago that I feel confident about my decision, or that my mere presence here today for a check-up means there's nothing to talk about, but either way, she's all business today.

"Hmmm, let's try and find the right spot, you know everything's tiny right now," Dr. Vasquez says, once she's inserted the massively uncomfortable wand, and I've lost the remainder of my dignity. I stare at the ceiling and try to locate the same slightly discolored area I found at the last visit to occupy my time.

"Okay, there's the fetus," she says, moving the cursor around on the screen. "Hmmm," she says, moving the wand more than I would like. Then she sighs, followed by another, "hmmm," and some more wand movement, and then she removes the wand completely.

"Ellie, why don't you get dressed and meet me in my office," Dr. Vasquez says in a much softer tone than before, pushing the ultrasound cart back to the other side of the room.

"Is there a problem?" I ask. Although after three pregnancies, nothing like this has ever happened, so I already know the answer.

"Let's talk in my office," she says uncharacteristically, taking my file with her and excusing herself.

I slowly pull on my black leggings, cozy gray cashmere hoodie and black ankle boots. It's difficult to describe my feelings as I'm getting dressed, but I almost feel like I'm in a room of syrup, or some other viscous substance, that is preventing my arms and legs from moving at my command. I know the doctor is expecting me in her office, and I hate making people wait, but I just can't make myself go any faster.

The door to her office is wide open and Dr. Vasquez is sitting behind her oversized mahogany desk typing on the computer when I slink into the room and settle into one of the tan leather club chairs on the visitor side of her desk.

"Why don't you pull the door closed?" she suggests, so I get back up and do as she advises.

"Ellie, this is never easy news to deliver, but you have three beautiful, healthy children at home, so hopefully that will make this a little easier to bear," she begins.

I nod my head, but don't say anything.

"There was no heartbeat on the ultrasound today," Dr. Vasquez says. "I can't tell from the image, but it looks like there hasn't been any growth in at least a week, if not longer," she says solemnly.

I knew from the moment she stopped the ultrasound that this was what she was going to tell me, but hearing it out loud still comes as a surprise and I feel the hot tears begin to roll down my cheeks.

"As you know, almost one in five pregnancies end in miscarriage in the first trimester. I know it doesn't make it any easier, but that pregnancy wasn't going to make it and this is your body's way of handling that," she says, with a mix of compassion and experience.

I know that I'm supposed to respond, or at least make eye contact, but I can't seem to pull my gaze up from my lap where my eyes are trained on the beginning of the loose thread on the hem of my sweater. We sit in silence for several minutes, until I have to ask the question before I burst. "What if I had come in last week?" I ask, through the sobs.

"What do you mean?" she asks, looking puzzled.

"I was supposed to come in two different times last week and I missed the appointments. What would have happened if I came in then?" I ask, finally able to look her in the eye.

"Ellie, I don't know if we would have seen a heartbeat last week, but I can tell you that you couldn't have prevented this outcome by seeing me last week," she emphasizes.

"Are you sure?" I ask.

"At this point in the first trimester it's too early to do anything. We wouldn't have put you on bed-rest or given you medication. There's nothing I would have done differently if I saw you last week," she says adamantly. "Even with all the technology we have today, there are still almost twenty percent of pregnancies that are not viable in the early stages," she explains.

"Okay," I reply.

"Unfortunately, your body will now need to go through the steps to get rid of the pregnancy, so you will either start to experience the miscarriage in a few days, or you will need to have a D&C," she explains. "We can talk more about that, or you can take a little while to absorb this and call me later today or tomorrow if you want?" she offers.

"I'd like that, if that's okay," I say, relieved at the opportunity to put it off, even for only a few hours.

"No problem. You can stay in here as long as you like," she tells me. "Give me a call tonight when you are ready to talk," she says. "And Ellie, I know you weren't sure about keeping the baby in the first place, but either way, this is still hard," she says, the first indication that she even remembers our previous conversation; but of course she does.

I only stay in her office for another ten minutes, and then I feel capable of making it through the waiting room and back to my car without drawing attention. My emotions are all over the place, and it's difficult to accept that an hour ago when I walked into the office I was pregnant, but now I'm not. Although, I guess I've been walking around thinking I've been pregnant, when I really haven't been for over a week. I feel empty and sad, mixed with a sense of loss and confusion. But as much as I try to fight it, the overwhelming emotion I have right now is relief. I'm trying to ignore it, but it's washing over me like a wave. Thankfully, all of the positive feelings of relief are quickly squashed as the guilt comes crashing in and I chastise myself for daring to feel relieved.

My first instinct, before I start the engine to make the twenty-five minute trip home to Westport, is to call Jack. I have to tell him what's happened. But when I pull up his name in my favorites, my finger hovers over his mobile number, but I can't pull the trigger. It's childish to say that he doesn't deserve to know; because of course one thing doesn't have anything to do with the other, but I'm so angry with him that I simply don't want to talk to him about anything. I don't want to share my sadness, or my relief, or my guilt. In fact, now that I know we won't be having another baby, maybe it's finally time to confront him and figure out the next chapter of life on my own.

Chapter Thirty-Nine
Jack

"Why are you still here?" Ellie asks, sounding annoyed as she pushes past me to get a juice glass from the cabinet.

"I moved my office hours so I could help out at home this morning," I reply, taking my newspaper and moving to the kitchen table to get out of her way. "I dropped Max and Izzy at school," I add, to make conversation, although she clearly already knows this.

"Thanks," she mumbles, reading something on her phone and barely paying attention to me.

Last night I laid in bed for hours trying to figure out the exact words to use to tell Ellie about Hailey. I'm sure as I was drifting off I landed on something that sounded halfway decent, but now that I'm sitting ten feet away from her, I can't think of anything that isn't going to make her hate me. I went back and forth on the argument that she had an abortion and didn't tell me, so my one night-stand makes us even; but I don't see that coming out in my favor.

"I'm going to get dressed for work," Ellie says through tight lips, as she takes her glass of cold-pressed orange juice and turns to leave the kitchen. It was strange that she wasn't already in her yoga clothes, since she never stays in her pajamas, except on Saturdays.

"Wait a second," I call out, before I can stop myself. I may not have the perfect script, but I have to take the bull by the horns, to use one of Rob's favorite expressions. "Can we talk for a minute?"

"What *is* it?" Ellis spits, turning on her heel. "*I* don't want to be late," she says angrily.

"Why are you so mad at me?" I ask her. This certainly isn't part of my strategy, but I'm getting tired of her tone over the past week. I know we didn't agree on what to do about the baby, but it's time to put it behind us. And I'm the one trying to move past her betrayal, so I don't know what she has to be angry about – at least not yet...

"Seriously?" she says, in a tone that rivals Sydney's sarcasm on her best day. She marches back into the middle of the kitchen and slams her glass down so hard on the marble island that I'm shocked it doesn't shatter. "You want to know why I'm mad?" she sneers.

"I want to know why you've been giving me the silent treatment, and when you do talk to me, you practically spit in my face. Yes, I think I have a right to know," I reply, raising my voice. I have to take off my suit jacket and place it on the chair next to me, because I'm already getting so worked up that I can feel myself starting to sweat in the chilly kitchen.

"*You* have a right to know?" Ellie says, and gives a little laugh, her blonde hair bouncing off her shoulders as she chuckles. I can't imagine what she possibly finds funny about this scenario, but her demeanor is making me even angrier. I was supposed to be calm and collected when I confessed, but this is turning into a disaster.

"What's so funny?" I ask, tapping my wingtip against the wooden floor as I try to rein in my temper.

"It's definitely not funny. It's just somewhat ironic," she says.

"What is?" I ask, my patience growing thin.

"I *know* Jack. Okay? I know all about Hailey," she fumes. "You can stop sneaking around and lying about it," she says, shooting daggers at me with her shining hazel eyes.

"How did you find out?" I ask, which I'm not sure is the right reply in this situation.

"Is that the best you can do?" Ellie asks. "You want to know how you got caught? That's all you can say for yourself?" she jeers.

"No, that's not it. I just want to explain," I say, struggling to find the words that I practiced for hours last night.

"I don't think there's much to explain," she says, drumming her fingers on the shiny white marble.

"I'm sorry that I didn't tell you sooner," I begin.

"You're just sorry you got caught," she huffs.

"No really, I was actually going to tell you about it this morning. That's why I stayed home from work," I tell her.

"That's so *big* of you," she mocks, wrapping her threadbare cream robe tightly around herself and crossing her arms protectively in front of her body. "I don't know if there's anything else that can be said here. I don't need to be late to the studio for this," she argues.

"So that's it?" I ask, throwing up my hands in outrage. "Look, I know this must be a lot to digest. And I feel terrible about how it happened. But I've been able to come to terms with the abortion you kept from me all those years ago, I think you can at least stay here and have a discussion." I flinch as the final words leave my mouth, because I swore I wasn't going to make this about keeping score.

"Did you really just say that?" Ellie asks, but I know it's a rhetorical question. "You are honestly comparing having an affair and falling in love with another woman to my decision not to keep a pregnancy with some guy from my third date when I was twenty-three?" she asks, her tone implying that I couldn't possibly be that moronic.

"I think affair is a quite a ridiculous stretch - and falling in love? I think it takes more than a few hours to fall in love," I jeer, wishing I could rephrase that comment as soon as I say it.

Ellie purses her bare lips and squints her eyes like she's trying to figure out what's going on. "Don't bother lying about it, Jack, it's too late," she says.

"I'm not lying. I know I fucked up back then, and I know I fucked up now by not telling you sooner, but it certainly wasn't an affair, and I was never in love with anyone else," I maintain.

"So why did you tell her that you loved her?" Ellie challenges, gesturing at me wildly with both hands.

"What are you talking about?" I ask, looking at her like she's officially lost it.

"I saw your text to her. That's how I found out," she says triumphantly.

"My text to who?" I ask, still confused, but slowly starting to put the pieces together.

"Oh my God, stop playing dumb, Jack, it doesn't suit you. I saw your text to Hailey where you said you loved her, okay? Can we stop this charade now?" she asks.

"Do you know who Hailey is?" I ask Ellie, feeling on solid ground for the first time all morning, although unfortunately nowhere near in the clear.

"She's the home wrecker you're having an affair with," Ellie announces.

"Hailey is the eighteen-year old girl who turned up in my office a couple of months ago and told me she was my daughter," I say, sitting back down in my chair for support.

"What?" Ellie says, stunned, and nearly speechless for the first time all day.

"I had sex with someone in Austin at Richie's bachelor party," I admit, hanging my head so I don't have to face Ellie. "It's no excuse, but I was trashed, and I barely knew what was going on until the next morning," I acknowledge.

"Richie's bachelor party?" Ellie asks, appearing to try to remember when that was.

"It was in the end of 1999, a few months before we got engaged," I reply, providing the timing that I know she is searching for.

Ellie takes a seat on the stool at the counter, as if she needs to sit down to digest this information. I know I shouldn't take this as a good sign, but the fact that she's still in the kitchen is positive.

I should probably wait for her to say something, but I can't handle the silence. "It was stupid and wrong and I'm really sorry. It didn't mean anything," I promise her. "I don't know if you'll believe me, but I thought about telling you when I got back from Austin, but I figured it would just hurt you more. It sounds dumb now, but it's what I thought at the time," I tell her.

298

"So nineteen years later you have a mystery daughter? Your stupid, drunken, one-night stand got some girl pregnant?" she asks, resting her head in her hands, unwilling to look at me.

"That's what I thought until yesterday," I say, trying to find the right words.

"Huh?" Ellie says, looking confused, and rightfully so.

"There are more details, but it turns out Hailey isn't actually my daughter. She thought that I was her dad because of some weird family drama with her grandparents before they died, but I'm not," I tell her, exhaling and slinking back in my chair.

"But you *did* have sex with her mom?" Ellie points out.

"I did. And I know that was a terrible thing to do," I acknowledge, "but I'm definitely not her father," I explain.

"So, Hailey and her mom have tracked you down and they want money or something? What are they looking for?" she asks, with a heavy dose of skepticism and irritation.

"Hailey's mom died when she was eleven, she was only thirty-one," I say.

"Oh God, that's horrible," Ellie says, recoiling.

"And Hailey's grandparents had a lot of money, and left it all to her, so she isn't looking for any money. Her grandfather gave her my name a few months ago on her eighteenth birthday, and it doesn't really matter why, but he was led to believe that I was the father because her actual father is a total douchebag. In fact he's in prison right now," I say, with an air of superiority.

"Oh," Ellie says, leaning back against the counter, no longer looking ready for battle.

299

"I get that this is far from ideal, but it's been a lot for me to absorb too," I say.

"And you found out yesterday that she wasn't actually your daughter?" Ellie questions.

"Yes. Last night I met her aunt and she told me the whole story," I explain.

"Kind of ironic," Ellie says, her eyes starting to water like she is going to cry; it must be the hormones.

"What is?" I ask.

"Yesterday I found out that I'm not pregnant anymore," she says, bursting into tears, her head collapsing onto her arms, so all I can see is blonde hair heaving up and down.

I'm in shock by her revelation and not sure how to react or comfort her. I get up to move closer to her and rub her back while making shushing noises, until her weeping slows. "What happened?" I ask quietly.

With her face still in her arms she snuffles, "I went in for my check-up and they did an ultrasound. There was no heartbeat."

"Oh honey, I'm so sorry," I say, continuing to rub her back, and trying to get a handle on the whirlwind of emotions whipping through my own body.

"I was having such a hard time figuring out how we were going to manage with a fourth kid, and I still wasn't sure, but..." she trails off.

"I know," I say, tracing small circles on her back the way she likes me to do to help her fall asleep.

"I'm sad and confused," she says, picking up her head slightly to look at me.

"I can imagine," I tell her. "Well, I'm trying," I admit.

"And I feel relieved, even though I didn't want it to happen this way, and that's the worst part," she cries, putting her head down again, her body racked with sobs.

"You have nothing to feel guilty about," I tell her. "Hey, look at me," I say, lifting up her chin and staring at her beautiful, blotchy face and bloodshot eyes. "You can be sad, but you can't feel bad about this," I tell her.

She doesn't say anything, but the look on her face says it's okay for me to continue.

"We have a great family. We have three great kids. We still have some things to figure out and work through, but we can do it," I say hopefully, feeling confident that we're strong enough to find a way to get past the issues with Nikki and Hailey.

"Oh crap! What are you guys still doing here?" Sydney says shattering our moment as she staggers into the kitchen.

"What are *we* doing here?" Ellie says, using the back of her hand to wipe her eyes and nose, her mood flipping from devastated to incredulous.

"I thought you went to school early?" I chime in.

"I thought *you* took her to school?" Ellie asks, glancing at me.

"Sorry, I peeked in her room and I thought it looked empty, so I assumed she was gone," I admit, sheepishly.

"So, why are you still home?" Ellie asks, directing her aggravation at Sydney.

"I'm not going to school today," Sydney announces, heading toward the coffee pot.

"What do you think you're doing?" Ellie asks, as Sydney begins to pour coffee into one of my Yale mugs.

"What? Dad lets me," Sydney says glibly.

"That's not true! It was one time," I try to defend myself, but Ellie isn't even paying attention to me.

"Pour that out, you're not having any coffee," she demands.

"Isn't that what you drink when *you're* hung-over?" she challenges.

"Huh? What did you just say?" Ellie asks.

"I'm going to take this and some Advil and I'm going back to bed," Sydney declares, and leaves us both speechless.

Chapter Forty
Ellie

"Did she just say she was hung-over?" I ask Jack, trying to get a grip on the situation. Before Sydney's revelation, this morning was already more drama than most people could handle in a lifetime; I don't know how I can possibly add a teenage daughter with a drinking problem to the mix.

"I'm pretty sure that's what she said," Jack says, shaking his head in disbelief. "Oh my God, I wonder if she was hung-over last weekend when she had coffee too? Clearly she thinks that's what you do to treat it. She was acting tired and weird on Saturday morning. *And* she was being completely awful to me," Jack adds.

"Oh, well that part might not have been from drinking," I divulge.

"What do you mean?" Jack questions.

"I really don't want to get into this now, but Sydney saw you and Hailey together," I tell him. "On campus."

"She did?" Jack says, perplexed.

"Yes, she's the one who told me about it initially and then I saw the text. So she's been really mad at you too," I confess.

"That explains a lot," Jack says. "Wait, I remember that. I saw her that day too, but I didn't think she saw me," Jack adds.

"So she saw you with an eighteen-year old girl and immediately thought you were having an affair?" I ask. "That leaves me with a lot of questions I don't want to ask," I say.

"Oh God, no, that's disgusting. I don't know what she thinks she saw, but now I remember it. I was walking with Hailey and I saw Sydney, so I grabbed her arm, to try and pull her out of the way, so Sydney wouldn't see us. But Sydney was with a guy that day. He looked older, and they looked really close. I was so worried about being seen with Sydney, that I totally forgot about the guy until now," Jack discloses.

"So our daughter was walking around at Yale with an older man and you're just remembering it now?" I say, completely exasperated. "Anything *else* you forgot?" I say, trying to hide my frustration.

"They may have been holding hands," Jack says, his face and ears reddening as he shares the news.

"How old was this guy? Twenty? Thirty? Forty?" I interrogate.

"Probably closer to twenty," Jack says, wincing.

"I wonder what else we've missed?" I question out loud, running my hands through my disheveled hair.

"What do you mean by that?" Jack asks.

"Sydney missed her SAT's, she's drinking, she's dating some older man. I mean this couldn't be more of a cliché! We're so busy with our own crap, that our honor student has become an after-school special," I vent.

"I'm sure it's not that bad," Jack soothes.

"There's only one way to find out," I say, standing up to march upstairs and discover what's been going on under our roof while I've been preoccupied with my own issues.

***

Jack and I don't waste any time getting to the second floor, and there's no way Sydney missed the sound of our feet thundering up the stairs, even with the plush Oriental runner to cushion our steps. I don't even bother with a courtesy knock as I push open her door and Jack follows me into her room. The curtains are drawn, and there's a mildly unpleasant smell of sweat mixed with something I can't quite pinpoint. For a moment I'm reminded of Dorothy's sick room, but Sydney's current pain is self inflicted and doesn't deserve my sympathy (or does it? I wonder briefly).

"We need to talk," I say to Sydney, pulling down the duvet, removing the pillow that is currently covering her head, and making myself comfortable near the foot of her bed. Jack shrugs and looks at me as if to say "what should I do?" Or "where should I sit?" and I point to the floor. He nods and slides down to the floor in his navy suit pants and crisp button down and leans back against the wall; I try to stifle a smile, because this isn't the time for that even though he looks ridiculous.

Sydney grunts as the pillow is removed and buries her face further into her blue floral sheets, but without the extra bedding, there's nowhere for her to hide. "I don't want to talk," Sydney mumbles.

"Have you been drinking?" I ask her, keeping my voice level, although it's a difficult task.

"I had a few drinks last night," Sydney says, like it's not a big deal.

"Since when do you drink?" Jack asks her.

"C'mon Dad, *everyone* drinks, it's not a big deal," Sydney replies, as if she can barely tolerate this conversation.

"I don't care what everyone else does. I care what *you* do," Jack says, repeating the famous line of parents everywhere, but I have to hand it to him for keeping his cool. "And since when do you do what everyone else does?" he asks.

"It was just a few beers," Sydney says, rolling over on the bed and pressing her fingers to her temples.

"Either it was more than a few beers, or you can't handle a few beers," I tell her.

"Huh?" she says.

"You're lying in bed too hung-over to get up," I point out.

"You're too young to be drinking any night of the week, but we'll get to that in a minute. Seriously, what are you thinking? Drinking on a school night?" Jack asks.

"School doesn't matter," Sydney says flippantly.

"What do you mean by that?" I inquire, shocked by her remark.

"It's not like I'm getting into college, so why bother with high school," Sydney says, rolling back over, so she's facing the wall.

Jack and I exchange confused looks and I point to him, letting him know that he should tackle it.

"Syd, why would you say that?" Jack asks calmly. "Of course you're going to get into college. You're so smart and you're a great student. Is this about Yale?" he asks, worriedly. "You know you don't have to go there, you can go wherever you want," he assures her.

"I got a D on my chemistry test and I failed the SAT's!" Sydney yells. "What do you think now?"

I'm proud to say that I'm faster to respond than Jack, even though I think we're equally surprised. "What do you mean you *failed* the SAT's?" I ask her. "And you know you can take them again," I assure her. "You're so hard on yourself, I'm sure it's not that bad," I say.

"I scored eleven hundred sixty," she announces. "Do you think Yale will like that score," she says sarcastically.

"Probably not," Jack admits, smiling in spite of himself. "But like your mom said, you can take it again. It's one test, and the grade in chemistry is one grade. It happens," Jack says, calmly, in his wise professor voice.

"Like I'm going to listen to *you*," Sydney snaps at Jack.

"Right," I say, trying to catch Jack's eye, while Syd wraps her long hair over her eyes to conceal her face in the absence of any legitimate hiding place. "She's still mad at you," I try to mouth to Jack, but it comes out with some sound.

"Wait," Sydney says, bolting upright. "*You* aren't mad at him anymore?" she says accusingly.

"It was a misunderstanding," I say to her. "We still need to work through some things, but Dad isn't cheating on me," I tell her.

"I'm not sure this is going to be less complicated for you, but the girl you saw me with at Yale thought I was her dad, from a woman I knew a long time ago," Jack says, brushing over a host of details. "But it turns out she isn't."

"Huh?" Sydney says, looking at both of us like we've lost our minds, which is entirely appropriate.

"I know it sounds outrageous, and we'll give you more information when the time is right," Jack says smoothly, "but the important thing is that no one is having an affair. I understand why you were upset with me, but you don't have to be mad anymore," Jack says, as if he can shut it all off in two sentences.

"Can I be alone now?" Sydney asks, kicking her feet around at the end of the bed like she used to do when she was a toddler.

"Not quite yet," I say. "We'll get back to the drinking another time," I say, although it's killing me a little bit to let it go. "But Dad mentioned that when you saw him at Yale, you were there with someone. We want to know more about him?" I say, shifting slightly on the bed, while trying to keep my composure.

"It doesn't matter," Sydney says defiantly.

"I think it does," Jack pipes in. "That guy looked way too old for you and you looked way too close to him," Jack adds. "And what were you doing with him on campus? Is he a student there?" Jack says, starting to lose his poise.

"I don't want to talk about it, okay?" Sydney yells.

"No! We're going to talk about this," I say, raising my voice. "It's not okay to sneak around with older men when you're sixteen years old. I want to know what's going on," I demand.

"He dumped me, okay! Are you happy?" Sydney wails.

"Of course we're not happy you got hurt," Jack jumps in, trying to control the situation. "We just want what's best for you."

"Right," I nod and agree, although it's taking a lot of willpower not to read her the riot act. "So what happened?" I nudge, anxious to find out if there's some pedophile roaming free, or what else Sydney has been subjected to.

"I met him at Fairfield, that's where he goes to school. I lied about my age and told him I was a freshman at Yale. When he found out the truth, he dumped me and now he won't talk to me," Sydney sobs.

"Oh," Jack says, sounding pleasantly surprised and daring to wink at me without Sydney seeing; I know Sydney is devastated, but I think this is far better news than we were expecting.

Sydney is completely tangled in her sheets and has now shifted her position so she is lying face-down diagonally across the bed. I try to slowly inch up the bed so I can rub her back and provide a small amount of comfort, like Jack did for me only a short time ago.

"I'm sorry we haven't been here for you these past few months," I say to her, while lightly tickling her back.

She doesn't respond, but I can feel the tension ease ever so slightly from her shoulders, so I keep scratching and talking. "Your dad and I have had a lot going on, but it's not okay that we've been ignoring you," I say to her.

I know she's listening, so I decide to keep going. "It's no excuse for drinking or lying or sneaking around with college boys, and that can't continue; but I'm sorry," I tell her, feeling a small bit of guilt float away as the words come out.

"*We're* sorry," Jack corrects.

"Are *you* apologizing to *me*?" Sydney asks, raising her head slightly, her chestnut hair framing her heart shaped face as it falls.

"This doesn't completely absolve you," I promise her, "but I think we've all had a really rough fall and could use a bit of a reset," I say, thinking how true this is for all three of us.

"Why don't you get some more rest," Jack suggests. "Seems like today is a good recovery day. Let's talk more tomorrow morning," he says, using Sydney's dresser to pull himself up from the floor.

"Okay," she says skeptically, but there is visible relief on her face, and she looks more at ease than she did when we came in.

***

Back in the kitchen I check my phone and see five text messages from Darcy and a voicemail from an unknown number.

"I don't think I'm going to make it to class on time," I joke, reading through Darcy's panicked texts from an hour ago. I shoot off an apologetic text and promise that I'll make it up to her.

"I missed office hours again, my students are going to riot. But I have to leave soon to get to my lecture," Jack says. "Is that okay?" he asks.

"That's totally fine," I tell him, without a trace of anger or irritation for the first time in weeks.

"This is probably Darcy's last attempt to get me – poor Darcy," I say, playing the voicemail on speakerphone.

"Hi Ellie, this is Gladys, Dorothy's housekeeper. I'm so sorry to have to call you with this news, but Dorothy passed away in her sleep last night. Please call me when you get this."

"Oh my God. Oh my God!" I repeat, staring at my phone in disbelief.

"I'm so sorry," Jack says, having heard the message. He didn't know that I'd grown closer to Dorothy recently, but he heard me talk about her over the last few years and knew how much I liked her.

"I just saw her a couple days ago," I tell him, shaking my head. "She wasn't feeling well, but she didn't seem that sick."

"But she *is* older, right?" Jack asks, trying to put it nicely.

"She's eighty, but that's not that old anymore. And until recently she hasn't even seemed that old," I tell him.

"I just can't believe she's dead," I say, tears filling my eyes yet again and my chest growing tight as it hits me that I'll never see her again. It feels like a lifetime since I woke up this morning, but it's only ten-thirty. How could so much have happened in only a few hours?

"Are you going to call her back?" Jack prods.

"I'll call her soon. I just need a minute. You can go ahead and go to work," I say, giving him the go ahead I think he's looking for.

"Are you sure?" he says, but he's already reaching for his suit jacket.

"Yes, I'm sure," I promise him.

"Call me if you need anything," he offers, stepping toward me and kissing me lightly on the lips. I return his kiss and let my lips linger on his soft lips – they feel reassuringly familiar even though it's been too long since I've felt them. This certainly doesn't solve all of our problems, but when we pull away, I feel hopeful.

"Thank you so much for coming," Gladys says, wrapping me in a warm embrace as soon as she opens the door. Her eyes are red rimmed and her face shows evidence of the tears she's shed.

"Of course," I say, returning her embrace, and letting her head fall on my shoulder as fresh tears begin to fall.

"I'm sorry," Gladys apologizes; wiping her eyes with a lace handkerchief from her pocket and pulling herself back into the foyer. "It's just so hard to accept that she's really gone, even though I knew this was coming," she says.

"You mentioned something like that on the phone, but I had no idea she'd been sick. Until the other day," I add.

"She didn't want you to know," Gladys tells me. "Come on in, I made us some tea," she says, and leads us into the living room where I first sat with Dorothy just a few weeks ago. The room looks exactly the same with the overstuffed linen sofas, the antique end tables and the enormous Turkish rug in shades of burgundy and gold; but somehow it all seems empty without Dorothy here.

"She was diagnosed with late stage pancreatic cancer five months ago," Gladys says, pouring me a cup of tea and placing it in front of me.

"Oh no," I sigh, trying to think back and remember if there were any signs. "Couldn't they do anything? Chemotherapy or any treatment?" I ask.

"She was so strong at the beginning. But the doctors said it wasn't treatable, and anyhow, I don't think Dorothy would have accepted it, even if it was an option," Gladys adds.

"Was she in pain?" I ask, not wanting to hear the answer.

"The doctors did a great job of managing her medications, so she wasn't in much pain," Gladys assures me.

"Do her children know? Where are they?" I ask, the thought just occurring to me.

"She didn't want them to know either," Gladys says sadly. "She called them yesterday when she was certain that it was close to the end," Gladys said, wincing.

"That's terrible," I respond, stirring my tea, although I don't think I can drink it.

"It's what she wanted. The children and grandchildren will be arriving over the next few days," Gladys tells me.

"How long did you work for Dorothy?" I ask Gladys.

"Twenty-five years," Gladys replies proudly. I started working for her when I was thirty," Gladys says, her dark eyes shining with tears again.

"That's a long time," I reply. I would never ask what she's going to do now, but that's all I can think.

"Dorothy had a letter she wanted me to give you," Gladys says, handing me a thick cream envelope, with my name in loopy script on the outside. "I'll leave you alone for a bit," Gladys says, excusing herself.

I hesitate for a moment before opening it, unsure what to expect. The past twenty-four hours has been an emotional roller coaster that will take months, if not longer, from which to recover; I'm honestly not sure I can handle one more thing at this point.

Dearest Ellie,

If you are reading this, it means that I am gone. I'm sorry that I didn't tell you I was sick, but I didn't want it to influence how you thought of me. I want you to know how special you are and how much you've meant to me. You've made such a difference in my life since Norman passed away; please don't ever forget that.

There will be a lawyer in touch with all the details of the will, but I wanted you to hear this from me. I would like you and your family to have my house, its contents and the property. My children don't want it, and I know that it will be as special to you as it was to Norman and me. I don't want the house to be a burden, so I have also set up a fund to take care of the taxes and the maintenance.

I also want you to be able to do what is important to you, and I think you have a gift for helping people. I am leaving you five million dollars to start a social work practice, so you don't have to worry about making money and you don't need to charge your patients. I know that you will make a difference in people's lives.

I'm sure you are wondering about my family, but please don't worry about them. They will be getting the majority of the estate and they won't miss the house or the money I'm giving you. I've also made sure Gladys is well taken care of. She has no interest in staying in Westport, and she plans to retire in Arizona where we've already bought her a house.

You have such a special place in my heart. Please take care of yourself and your family and don't take any of it for granted.

Love, Dorothy

I read the letter a second time, before placing it in my lap, still in complete bewilderment at its contents. I glance out the floor-to-ceiling windows at the early afternoon sun reflecting off the water, and try to wrap my head around the idea of actually living in this house. It seems impossibly out of character for Dorothy, but I can't stop myself from looking at the ceilings to see if I'm on some hidden-camera reality show.

"She was an amazing woman," Gladys says, re-entering the room and claiming her seat on the sofa.

"You knew?" I ask, with surprise, waving the letter in the air.

"Of course. I didn't read the letter," Gladys clarifies. "But Dorothy told me what she was planning to do," she says, tidying up the untouched tea cups and putting them back on the tray, a habit that must be difficult to break after all this time.

"I'm not sure I can accept it," I tell her, looking around again at the marble foyer and grand staircase.

"You have to!" Gladys insists. "It's what Dorothy wanted. She loved this house and she wants you and your family to inherit it," she maintains.

"But what about her family? She said they would be okay with it, but I'm not so sure," I tell her, refolding the letter and placing the heavy paper back in its envelope.

"It's no secret that Dorothy and her children did not have a great relationship. Although I wasn't here when they were growing up, I've certainly been here for long enough to see that and I think it's fair to say that I've become very close to Dorothy and she has told me a lot over the years. But I do know enough about this family to know that they have somewhat come to terms with their dysfunctional relationship, and that no one in the family wants this house and Dorothy certainly would not want them to have it," Gladys says.

"But," I begin to challenge.

"And they each have plenty of their own money and will be getting plenty more, so they won't have any issues," Gladys says.

"Did Dorothy tell you to say that?" I ask, my lips starting to curl into a small grin.

"She might not have been at her best yesterday, but she did give me a few talking points in case you put up a fight," Gladys tells me, smiling for the first time since I walked in the door.

"I can't believe I'm saying this, but it feels like I'm home," I say, and I swear for a split second I can feel Dorothy there with me.

Epilogue
Westport, CT – June 2021
Ellie

"Mom, where are you?" Sydney calls out.

"I'm in here," I reply, from the depths of my closet.

"Where's *here*?" Sydney yells back, her voice getting closer. "Give me a little bit of help, or I could spend the next fifteen minutes looking for you," she adds.

"I'm in my closet," I tell her. "I can't decide on the right shoes. Come and help me!" I plead.

"I still get lost here," Sydney jokes, poking her head into my colossal walk-in closet.

"We've been here over a year, you don't get lost," I tease, pretending to roll my eyes, but it's all in good fun. And I won't admit this to her, but there are still several rooms at the end of the hall that we haven't decided what to do with, and every time I come out of one of them, I turn the wrong way.

"You look beautiful," I gush to Sydney, noticing her properly. At eighteen, Sydney is the most beautiful girl in the entire senior class, actually the entire town, or perhaps all of Connecticut, and I'm only a tiny bit biased. She is wearing a short olive green dress, that certainly isn't inappropriate, but shows off her curves perfectly and is the perfect shade for her light summer tan and envy-worthy mane of chestnut hair. But the most notable difference in her appearance is the smile on her face and the look of confidence that she's finally able to wear. After the past year and a half at The Hopkins School with some new friends and supportive teachers, she has blossomed.

"You have to hurry up," Sydney reminds me.

"I know! What shoes should I wear?" I ask, holding up a pair of nude three-inch heels in one hand and a pair of flat, silver, strappy sandals in the other.

"Definitely the heels," Sydney says.

"But I'm going to be on my feet the whole time," I argue.

"Then why did you ask my opinion," Sydney counters, looking slightly impatient.

"Okay, fine, I'll wear the heels," I concede. "Are your brother and sister ready?" I ask, steadying myself on the oak dresser in the middle of the closet, so I can put on my shoes.

"They have been waiting with Dad by the front door for the past ten minutes," she says. "He sent me up here to find you," she informs me.

"Oh, so it's just me?" I confirm.

"Yes, Mom, everyone else is ready. Let's go, they can't start without *you*," Sydney emphasizes and walks out of the closet.

"I'm right behind you," I call back. Before I go, I turn and take one more look in the mirror. My blonde hair is swept back off my face in a simple French twist and secured with a zillion bobby pins and half a can of hair spray, so it won't come loose, even if the wind knocks me over when I walk outside. I've learned that this close to the water, it's like an entirely different climate some days from the other side of Westport. My makeup is relatively low key, but I did use a little more than usual because they said it wouldn't photograph well if I wasn't wearing enough, though I opted for heavier on the eye and light on the lips. The dress is my favorite part. It's a rainbow striped halter dress from a local boutique in town. Now that I'm not doing yoga every day, or multiple times a day, I no longer have quite the sculpted physique that I did for the past six or seven years, but the added curves have made me look softer and, if I believe Jack, much sexier.

"Seriously Ellie," Jack's voice yells up the stairs, "We have to go now!"

"I'm coming, I promise," I say, as I exit my closet and pass through the enormous master bedroom, which is slightly less imposing now that it has our old furniture in it, but it's still more space than two people need to sleep. Before I turn off the light, I pick up the framed picture that I keep of Dorothy on the dresser – Jack thought it was a little weird at first, but he got over it. "Wish me luck!" I say to my friend and benefactor.

***

After eleven months of demolition, construction and renovation, my vision is a reality. Jack had trouble picturing it when I first told him the idea, as well as most of the other people I told, but once the work was underway he started to get it, and now that it's complete, it's difficult to believe it hasn't always been this way.

"You did it," Darcy says, wrapping her arm around my shoulder. We both take a step back to admire the buildings side by side with the attractive silver and white "Grand Opening" sign in front of the brand new "Mind Matters" Clinic on the right.

"I couldn't have done it without you," I tell Darcy, giving her shoulder a squeeze through the gauzy material.

"Oh please. You handed me a well-oiled machine. I just had to keep it that way," she laughs. "You're the one who thought to snap up the dry cleaner next door when it went on the market and then turn it into a clinic," Darcy says, pointing to the gray-shingled building with a red ribbon over the doors.

Jack saunters over in his navy sport coat, khaki pants and yellow button-down shirt open at the collar, the picture of the handsome economics professor trying to look laid back. He may have a little more gray in his thick dark hair than he did a couple years ago and there are new crinkles at the corners of his cornflower blue eyes; but when I look at him, I see a good man, not without flaws, but then again, I certainly have my share. However, I think we've come back stronger as individuals and as a couple.

"You ladies admiring your handiwork?" Jack asks, planting a kiss firmly on my lips and a quick peck on Darcy's cheek.

"Maybe just a little," Darcy laughs.

"You should!" Jack says to us. To me he says, "Hailey just texted, she's here but she can't find a place to park because of the great turnout," he jests. "I'm going to go give her a hand."

"Okay. Don't take too long, I think I'm supposed to give my speech soon," I tell him.

"Got it," he says, flashing me the thumbs up sign as he walks away.

"Congratulations!" Erica says, appearing by my side. There is only a small parking lot, and not a ton of green space in front of the buildings, so every time I turn around I keep bumping into a familiar face – although I guess that's what today is all about. "I'm so happy for you," Erica praises.

"Thanks so much! And thank you for coming," I tell her.

"I wouldn't miss it!" Erica replies.

"I think I'm going to get started with my little speech soon," I tell her. "I just need Jack to get back, he went to help Hailey find a parking space," I say.

"There they are," Erica says, spotting them walking across the street. "I know you've explained this to me, so I understand it's not possible, but don't you think they look alike?" Erica says with a smirk.

Darcy, Erica and I all turn to look as Hailey and Jack cross the street, and although there is definitely no blood relation, it's hard to deny some similarities. Hailey is certainly a striking young woman, which is something I wasn't quite prepared for when she first came into our lives. Jack and Hailey both have dark hair and similar complexions, although her skin tone is a darker olive, but it's something about the way they carry themselves, and the easy banter back and forth that we are witnessing right now.

"Maybe it's a Yale thing?" Darcy suggests, playfully.

"I don't think all the students at Yale look the same," I reply. "Though on second thought, there might be something about hunching over those economics textbooks in those old libraries that does something to them," I joke.

"How was the end of her freshman year?" Erica asks.

"It was great," I tell her. "She loves Yale and she declared that she wants to major in economics. She's even planning to help Jack work on his research this summer. They are doing something with economics and outcomes and single mothers. They've explained it to me several times, but I still don't quite get it," I laugh.

"Amazing how that turned out," Darcy comments.

"We're here," Jack announces as he and Hailey join our little circle.

"Hi Ellie, congratulations! This is so exciting," Hailey says, stepping toward me so we can hug.

"Thanks for coming," I say to Hailey. I feel like a broken record, having said this so many times already this afternoon, but it doesn't lose it's meaning. I'm eternally grateful for everyone's support. "Sydney is over there," I tell her, pointing in the direction of the door to the yoga studio where Sydney is handing out pamphlets.

"Great, thanks!" Hailey says, making a beeline for Sydney where they embrace like long-lost friends.

"Do they still get to see each other much?" Erica asks.

Jack answers the question before I have a chance. "All the time. With Sydney at private school in New Haven and Hailey at Yale, they see each other for lunch and coffee whenever they can, it's a little out of control, but I'm not going to be the one to put a stop to it."

"We never would have predicted this friendship, but sometimes those are the best ones," I say, repeating what Jack and I say to each other all the time.

"What happens next year?" Darcy says.

"Obviously they won't see each other quite as much with Sydney down at UT in Austin. But Hailey still has friends down there, so she said she wants to go visit, and of course, Sydney will come back up here for her breaks," I say, rehearsing what I've told myself when I start to get nervous about Sydney being so far away.

"Quite a funny twist of events," Jack says, looking at the two girls standing side-by-side handing out pamphlets to the crowd. "I think you're up. Jillian's waving," Jack says, pointing to Jillian at the front of the crowd, motioning to me with her bangle bracelets clinking wildly against each other with each wave of her arm.

I take a deep breath as I walk up to the mock podium at the front of the crowd and try to remember the short speech I wrote out last night. I opted not to bring a written copy, but that might not have been a wise choice.

"Let's hear it for the woman of the hour," Jillian says, as I reach the podium and Jillian hands me the microphone. "I'm so proud of you," she whispers in my ear, as she steps to the side.

I look out at the crowd of eighty or ninety people here today and feel proud of what I've accomplished and what I will be able to accomplish after the clinic opens today; I think Dorothy would be proud too.

"Thank you all so much for coming today," I begin. "A wise woman once told me not to take what I have for granted, and I try very hard not to do that anymore. I think there are times in our lives when everyone needs help. Some of us need more help than others and we don't all need the same kind of help. But I want to do my part to offer counseling to anyone that needs it, because I feel that's an important part of overall wellness, and I don't think that finances should get in the way of good mental health.

Additionally, as most of you know, I've spent the past seven years of my life helping people in one way or another through yoga, so when I moved into this new chapter, I didn't want to leave that behind completely. Many of you may know Darcy Klein, the new owner of "Body & Soul." Well, we have come together to create a complete complementary wellness offering that merges mental and physical health for our patients, since we strongly believe that helping people isn't one size fits all.

We look forward to serving the community, helping people in whatever ways they need help, and hopefully making sure you don't want to take anything for granted, because after all, isn't that what it's all about?"

Jack is there to wrap his arms around me as soon as I step away from the mic, and I can hear the applause in the background. "I messed it up a little bit at the end," I say into his shoulder.

"It was great," he says, squeezing me tightly.

"You think?" I ask, looking for confirmation.

"I know it," he says. "Dorothy would be so proud of you," he says, using one of the lines we have come to rely on.

"I think she would be very proud," I agree, looking up at the wispy clouds in the sky, secure in the knowledge that this next chapter in my life is the right one.

THE END

Acknowledgements

Dear reader, thank you!! Thank you for buying and reading my books; the paperbacks, the e-books, the kindle unlimited downloads – I'm eternally grateful for every single copy.

I also want to thank my sister, Sarah Nelson for continuing to be my first reader and providing endless support throughout the writing process. It's wonderful to have someone who loves what I write, even when it needs a lot more work.

A huge thank you to Aimee Kaplan, Erin Ginsburg, Tade Reen and Kathy Soderberg for reviewing and editing my writing and providing incredible feedback to make sure this book reached its full potential!

I am incredibly fortunate to be surrounded by a great group of friends and an amazing community in Pelham, NY. I wouldn't be able to raise my family and write if I didn't have the amazing support network that I do.

Almost last, but certainly not least, I want to thank my family for continuing to support me and encourage me and try their best to understand this path that I'm taking that has strayed quite a bit from my marketing and consulting career.

Finally, a huge thank you and all of my love to my three amazing daughters and my husband for cheering me on and inspiring me on a daily basis. You are my whole world.

Rachel Cullen is a graduate of Northwestern University and NYU Stern School of Business. She worked in consulting and marketing in San Francisco, London and New York and currently lives in Westchester, NY with her husband, three children and her two large dogs. *First Came Us* is her fourth novel; she is also the author of *The Way I've Heard It Should Be*, *Second Chances* and *Only Summer*.

www.rachelcullenwriter.com

www.facebook.com/RachelCullenAuthor

www.instagram.com/rachelcullenauthor